Those Women of the Coromandel

Other Books by Ranga Rao

Novels
Fowl-Filcher
The Drunk Tantra
The River is Three-Quarters Full

Short Stories
An Indian Idyll and Other Stories

Translations
Classic Telugu Short Stories
That Man on the Road

Literary Criticism
R. K. Narayan (a monograph)
R. K. Narayan: The Novelist and His Art

Monograph
Bal Vikas for Lok Vikas

Edited Volumes
Full Flame: Infinite Scenarios
Full Flame: Volume II: Unconditional Love

Those Women of the Coromandel

a novel

RANGA RAO

ALEPH

ALEPH BOOK COMPANY
An independent publishing firm
promoted by *Rupa Publications India*

First published in India in 2022
by Aleph Book Company
7/16 Ansari Road, Daryaganj
New Delhi 110 002

Copyright © Vijaylakshmi Vadrewu 2022

All rights reserved.

This is a work of fiction. Names, characters, places, and incidents are either the product of the author's imagination or are used fictitiously and any resemblance to any actual persons, living or dead, events or locales is entirely coincidental.

No part of this publication may be reproduced, transmitted, or stored in a retrieval system, in any form or by any means, without permission in writing from Aleph Book Company.

ISBN:978-93-93852-15-1

1 3 5 7 9 10 8 6 4 2

Printed in India.

This book is sold subject to the condition that it shall not, by way of trade or otherwise, be lent, resold, hired out, or otherwise circulated without the publisher's prior consent in any form of binding or cover other than that in which it is published.

Contents

Part I: Miss Beston / 1

Part II: Monsoon Maiden / 19

Part III: BA Garu / 63

Part IV: Nephew / 117

Part V: Worker Aunt / 159

Part VI: Podumburra / 207

Acknowledgements / 263

Part I

Miss Beston

Miss Beston spotted them through her window. She rushed out with her rifle.

In the heart of the Coromandel jungle, a spectacle greeted her: two pubescent girls stood before her, decked in the most charming style of jewellery south of the Vindhyas, as though they were on a formal visit. And alone, all alone.

'Thank God I shot that leopard this morning,' she said to her shikari.

'Absolutely,' said her tufted gomastha from behind the shikari.

Little Worker Aunt widened her large kohl-lined eyes and stared at Granny Appachchi on her hip, as though she was a mango discovered days after the harvest, hiding under a leaf—a dagudukayi.

'I am glad we have left the hounds behind on the boat,' Miss Beston said to him.

'Absolutely,' said the gomastha.

Little Worker Aunt widened her eyes again and slowly turned to look at her vadina's, sister-in-law's, face. Perched on her hip like a water-pot or an outsized terracotta doll, lovingly enclosed by an arm, she had proved the trusted pilot even in the jungle. Worker Aunt only worried now about the thorn wedged in her sister-in-law's foot.

'Who are you looking for?' asked the white woman.

The famous Boat Woman's Telugu sounded just a bit odd, but it made sense, almost as much as that of a local speaker. She towered over them, a good six-feet tall. As though the very forest goddess had materialized before them, suddenly, in the hoof-path, and in a white man's clothes.

Granny Appachchi slid down…but in a second Worker Aunt recovered and lifted Appachchi and placed her back on her hip.

'For you,' said Granny Appachchi, from her cosy vantage.

The white woman widened her deep-set, blue eyes.

'For me?'

She smiled sweetly. She turned to her shikari and said, 'I am honoured.'

'Absolutely,' said the gomastha from behind the shikari. 'These little girls are from Karanam Mangayya's family, madam.'

'I know. Brahmins. All the more shocking.'

The girls now turned their heads and stared at the two guns the shikari was carrying.

'White hibiscus,' said Granny Appachchi.

'What did she say?'

Before her gomastha could open his mouth and say 'Absolutely' once again, Granny Appachchi repeated, 'White hibiscus.' The gomastha's face fell.

The gomastha did open his mouth again but Worker Aunt anticipated him. 'You look like a white hibiscus,' she explained.

Miss Beston smiled. The gomastha was fidgeting with his pigtail; it looked like a malfunctioning lightning conductor laid low by an uncommon bolt.

When the gomastha began explaining the compliment, Miss Beston looked around, as though for a white hibiscus. Worker Aunt put her charge down on her feet and formed the lotus mudra, trying to conjure up the flower for the white woman.

Miss Beston got it, or some idea of it.

'Of course!' she said and laughed.

But she wasn't certain she was being admired.

'You are a red hibiscus!' she returned the compliment. 'You too! No less!'

She was charmed by Granny Appachchi's complexion.

Later, Miss Beston gathered enough from her munshi and her

own personal library on Indian flora and fauna, especially on the fascinating lotus, to deliver a discourse to her European visitors, who spread it all over the Raj, calling the information the Lotus Sutra.

The colourful party reached the boat on the canal. The dogs had started barking from far away.

The little girls did not worry about the hounds; they forgot all about their encounter with the wild as Miss Beston's boat home appeared before them on the Blotton Canal. What a home to live in! A home which floated, rocking gently, in the canal. It was anchored firmly, tethered with a python rope to a huge jamun on the bank.

'You are welcome,' the Boat Woman said with a sweet smile, 'to my cottage....' Then, taking a quick look at a framed mirror in front of her, she said, 'White hibiscus!', smiling to herself.

The Boat Woman attended to Appachchi's foot. She bent down, cleaned the little foot with alcohol—'Spirit,' she told the girls as their nostrils dilated—carefully extracted the thorn from it, and swabbed the spot with a white lotion. 'Red hibiscus!' she said, lifting Appachchi to the mirror, and then Worker Aunt, 'Creamy hibiscus!'

'Punditji,' she told her munshi, who had appeared, 'I need to work on my Telugu. Just to win the approval of these young ladies. And learn all about the lotus.'

'You will, no doubt,' he said, smiling. 'Can anything in the world stop you?' He turned to the little girls and acknowledged their greetings.

'How are you, little girls?' he said to them with a cheerful smile. 'As mischievous as ever?'

The girls nodded vigorously. They felt completely at ease.

'These are brainy girls, Miss Beston, I have taught them the alphabet.' He patted Worker Aunt on the head and said, 'This girl is the best brain in my experience.'

'Better than mine?'

'That, I cannot be sure,' he said.

Both of them laughed. The little girls joined in, simply because the adults were laughing.

Worker Aunt told the munshi how her little sister-in-law had guided her through the jungle. Appachchi had said to her, 'She is not far, vadina. After finishing off a leopard in the morning she has gone back for the day and tied up her dogs.' And Appachchi had added something that had worried Worker Aunt then: 'The Guru of the Stream told me this, he was standing next to us a moment ago, didn't you notice? Without the command of Lord Siva, even an ant will not bite you.'

Granny Appachchi confirmed: 'He lifted a foot. Two thorns were stuck there!'

'Yes, Meenakshi,' said the munshi and put his right hand on her head, 'you have already received His grace.'

'Is this the same holy man you were talking about, Punditji?' asked the white woman.

'Yes, the same.'

'Can I also join your school?' Miss Beston asked the girls.

'No need for you to go to the school,' said little Granny Appachchi, 'our teacher comes here to teach you.'

'You know everything about me!'

The girls nodded.

Miss Beston turned to the munshi.

'True,' he said, softly.

'Let's see,' the white woman said with a smile, 'how much you know about me. What time do I get up in the morning?'

'In Brahma Kalam,' said Granny Appachchi.

'In the small hours,' the munshi translated.

'True!' Miss Beston almost shouted, delighted.

Appachchi followed up with a brisk account of a typical day in the life of the Boat Woman. It was graphic and complete.

'No, I haven't told her,' said the munshi to the white woman's unasked question.

During the years and decades that followed, Granny Appachchi's words and actions would cease to surprise members of her family, as well as the villagers. She would also gradually stop mentioning the Guru's presence.

Miss Beston tended to avoid body contact. After the impulsive act of lifting the girls to the mirror, she kept a practical distance between them and herself. The one question she had left unasked because it was too personal, the munshi answered later: they both were married, each to the other's brother.

Miss Beston received at least one appeal a week for bride money. These girls were different; they had married within the family. 'Marrying and giving in marriage in this country is,' Mr Blotton, a veteran engineer, had observed, 'sharp, short, and decisive.'

She had been charmed by the girls' mangalasutrams but she did not touch them. The girls became self-conscious when they caught her staring at them and tucked the gold discs into their tiny blouses.

Miss Beston now remembered the dogs; they had torn a leopard to shreds. She did not want any accidents.

'Have you told your people at home you're here?'

Worker Aunt glanced at Granny Appachchi.

'If I know them, they have not,' said the munshi.

Worker Aunt looked at Appachchi again.

'They will be missed back home,' Miss Beston said. 'Take the girls home in the bandy.'

And the young woman herself walked a distance behind the cart, gun in hand, jodhpurs tucked into gum boots, engaging the girls in small talk until they put the jungle behind them. Her shirt kept heaving and bouncing, it took all of Granny Appachchi's strength to keep herself from giggling.

The Boat Woman waved goodbye to them.

'Thank you for Brahma Kalam.'

'Thank you,' the girls shouted back.

During their next visit to the boat house, a visitor was present, who described to Miss Beston how soap was made. It was quite an exposition; the girls listened open-mouthed, getting little of it. They were quite impressed all the same.

'Our nalugupindi powder is healthier and less bothersome,' Worker Aunt had said, 'and what is more, aromatic as well.'

Years later, during those few happy years of family life with BA Garu, Appachchi recalled the visit to the Boat Woman. BA Garu gave a complementary presentation himself. As Granny Appachchi realized later, Miss Beston was an apt pupil of all kinds of knowledge, like BA Garu. And, on occasion, she showed it, like BA Garu. BA Garu had gone back to Babylonia and Rome in his explanation.

'Saponification,' he said, 'is the reaction that made soap. The word is derived from the Roman Mount Sapo.'

He described how the people of India used to wash themselves with various herbal and vegetable powders; the Greeks and then the Romans too had rubbed the body, not with soap, but with olive oil and sand! 'A scraper, called a strigil, was then used to scrape off the sand and olive oil, also removing dirt, grease, and dead cells from the skin, leaving it clean. Afterwards, the skin was rubbed down with salves prepared from herbs.' Appachchi was delighted.

The white woman's gifts that day included a large piece of soap, soft as beehive wax. The Boat Woman washed her face to demonstrate its magic; instead of any vegetable or herbal powders, she told them, use this to wash your face.

The two little girls returned home, stealing into the house through the back door.

There was no risk of anyone spotting them; it was the quiet afternoon hour, when the diligent housewife sought a few moments of sleep, and the elders were either snoozing or engaged in reading or listening to the scriptures. The smell of butter boiling in the kitchen floated in the air. The flame in the puja nook flickered, fluttered its golden wings like a restive butterfly.

Safe behind the well's parapet, the girls raced each other. Inspired by the Western vision of feminine beauty they had just encountered,

Granny Appachchi started soaping her face and by the time she washed it and was ready to soap it again, her pal had done it too. They went on a binge, almost reducing the bar of soap to nothing. It was sheer exhaustion that stopped them. Groggy, heads spinning, they pulled a wiping cloth each from the clothesline in the backyard, next to the byre from where the cows watched the girls with fascination and not a little envy, and the bulls with some amusement—the milch buffaloes couldn't, of course, be bothered. The girls dabbed their faces the way their white friend had done.

They looked at each other, and their mouths fell wide open. They burst out laughing.

'What have you done to your face?' they shrieked.

'I'll show you!' said the practical Worker Aunt. She strode up to the veranda of the western wing and took down the hand mirror. She took one look at her own face, which was coated with a thick layer of white, and she grew rigid with shock; slowly, she turned the mirror to her vadina.

They had been turned into spectres. Appachchi exclaimed, 'And look at our hands!'

'The white woman is a sorceress, I have no doubt,' said Worker Aunt. 'Oh Ramarama, save us please, wherever you are!' Worker Aunt cried.

They hugged each other and burst into sobs.

The lady of the house arrived. The moment they saw her they raised the volume of their cries; the cows were more concerned now, the bulls overly, shamelessly amused.

When Worker Aunt's mother managed to get the full story out of them, she moralized: 'You silly fools, you have been using the soap! This is what comes of talking to strangers. You are getting to be adults soon, you silly girls, though anyone who takes one look at you will believe you both have already had your first menses, especially you—' she looked sternly at Worker Aunt, 'it's time you covered yourself with a paita. You do not know who to talk to and who to avoid. I can understand the little girl getting into scrapes such as these. But you are a sensible girl. What has gone wrong with you? Now don't do anything, just wrap yourselves in my saris and sit there—no, on second thought…both of you, go, get some gingelly oil, get into the bathroom shed, and take off your clothes, I will be there in a minute. I shall be back after giving the afternoon tiffin to your grandfather.'

The lady came back, applied a thick coat of gingelly oil to their faces and then wiped it off. She showed them their faces in the mirror. The girls' energy revived, though their faces now looked like wheat dough waiting to be dropped into the frying pan.

The visits did not end; for though he did not like little Indian girls seeking a white woman's company, and that too a clever businesswoman's, Karanam Mangayya allowed his granddaughters to go. It raised his reputation in the Brahmin quarter. Besides, Seshacharyulu was there. He'd be a chaperon for the girls.

∞

Miss Beston introduced them to Brahma Kalam, a concept she relished and which she'd included in her repertoire only recently. Like so many Indian traditions, she said, this was congenial to the climate.

Miss Beston's wise eyes observed the two faces in front of her, both first-timers, one still looking startled, and the other, haunted. She picked the second. He didn't wait to be addressed.

'Miss Beston! This is a savage land you have opted for! I was on my way here in my dholie and a terrible racket greeted me on the road—drums, pipes, tambourines, cymbals, whatnot, shouts and screams, fireworks, a sea of people, men, women, even urchins! I peeped out and what do I find? A man in a trance seated in that lotus posture inside a crude shrine-like structure erected on two stout bamboos carried by six or seven palanquin bearers. It was a merry procession, I thought they were heading for revelry, for a heathen mimicry of a Roman orgy. I looked at the enshrined creature, he was in a trance, and they had tied him securely to the walls of the shrine...' His voice fell to a whisper as he continued, 'He looked deadly pale, his head slumped. I asked my coolies what was happening. They told me. What a way of carrying a corpse to his burial! Macabre!' His voice rose, 'This is a savage land! As brutish as the ones encountered by the great conquistadores!'

Miss Beston agreed with him: 'Like the one Cortes and the conquistadores faced!' she added, patting down her bun, which was professionally gathered in a purple silk net at the back of her head. 'Besides, imagine carrying our dead in an open upright coffin.'

She seemed satisfied with the universal groan that followed.

'Not so fast, though,' she resumed. 'Patience is the only virtue you can practise in this land. The dead man belongs to the Saivite sect,' Miss Beston clarified. 'They bury their dead in the lotus pose for easy access to heaven. You have had an excellent introduction to this land and its people.'

She did not wait to savour her mirth. She pointed to the other young man.

This bespectacled youth confessed to a different kind of revelation: this India was turning out to be rather different from what he had been prepared to believe. Miss Beston glanced at him, as she carried a vase full of white and red hibiscuses with a purple lotus at the centre to the dining table, encouraging him to continue.

'The moment I set foot on the jetty at Calcutta,' recalled the young visitor, 'I was besieged by young Indian boys. Overgrown urchins, I thought. Though they were all clothed decently in those flowing white garments! I had almost taken out a few farthings in my fist. "No," one of them said. I was surprised he was speaking English! "Books, please," he said, "can you spare any books, recently published books, for us?"'

'Books published in England? Recently published! Believe me, they mentioned several authors—Wollstonecraft, Wordsworth, Keats, and Shelley—the one they were really and eagerly looking for was Shelley.... Imagine, Miss Beston, Shelley on the banks of the humid Hooghly! If only he were alive, I am sure he would have been tickled no end.'

Miss Beston agreed.

She gave them the case history of Seshacharyulu, her munshi, the man who knew eleven languages, all learned on his own with the help of dictionaries. The idea had come to him from Sir Thomas Munro: good old Munro had learned Spanish with the help of a Spanish–English dictionary 'just to read *Don Quixote*.'

The pundit had said wistfully, 'Nahi sarvasarvam janaathi.' No one knows everything. The two of them had read up the English greats: Chaucer, Spenser, Shakespeare, and Milton.

'And going back,' she continued, 'to the savage country…the wild—this morning there was a commotion near the market, a leopard had carried off a dog. So, be careful.'

Her munshi admired her from a distance.

∽

The sisters-in-law generally took these fearless decisions in Brahma Kalam.

Brahma Kalam: the dark, realizing its time has come, relents, yielding quietly to diffused starlight. The room lightens a bit, now you can find your way around without stumbling against a teapoy or a stool. That morning, little Worker Aunt, already bathed and dressed in her pattu half-sari, hair oiled and combed smooth, shining like armour, had arranged her class books in a neat pile, yesterday's timetable to the left and today's to her right. Dutifully, carrying a load of jewellery, and the mangalasutram with its huge gold discs, she offered a prayer to Goddess Saraswati and read aloud from her storybook:

'Blessed, glorious, rich with quality produce of field and dairy, endowed with the sacred, the holy, the beneficent, providing fulfilment of life-giving rivers like Ganga, Godavari, Krishna, Yamuna, Sindhu, Tungabhadra, Kaveri, Brahmaputra, and their holy riparian lands, in whose sacred territories were born munis, rishis, yogis, tapodhanas—embodiments of sacrifice, holy men, great devotees, avatars—is this glorious land known as Bharatabhoomi. In this land are many towns and villages and hamlets. Among them is the great agraharam known as Pasupugollu in the region of Nellooru. In this agraharam lived five hundred Brahmin families, engaged in yagnams and yagams, also engaged in charitable acts and donations, ever occupied in contemplation of God. The other five hundred families were those of farmers, traders, and other castes. Even these were ever engaged in principled living and righteous conduct and devout lifestyles.'

Granny Appachchi rushed in with a load of books.

'You are late again,' observed Worker Aunt. Granny Appachchi, bathed and dressed in another glowing half-sari, smiled. Her attention wavered: outside the casement window, a rain tree was in bloom, promising a fragrant dawn.

'Brahma Kalam is God-Present time,' said Worker Aunt, 'very sacred.'

Said Granny Appachchi, 'Show me a time when He is not present.'

On this question they did not agree throughout their lives.

Granny Appachchi's birth had been greeted with jubilation. The grandparents on either side promptly declared that she would be the bride of BA Garu, a pot-bellied four-year-old with a propensity for getting into scrapes. Worker Aunt, hardly two years old, had been thrilled for her brother because everyone else was. And she exercised the prerogative of the sister-in-law; she teased Granny Appachchi ever since she could remember, even before their betrothals. Worker Aunt would take Granny Appachchi aside and disclose to her how the entire family knew that Appachchi had come rolling in a flood after a great cyclone and that her parents had picked her up right on their doorstep.

'Did I come floating on a peepul leaf like Krishna?' Appachchi asked eagerly.

'Certainly not,' said Worker Aunt, 'you came floating like a piece of firewood.'

It took great effort on everyone's part to convince Appachchi that her sister-in-law was just joking. And, of course, once Appachchi realized what her vadina was up to, she gave it back to her. In the decades that followed, Worker Aunt received from Granny Appachchi much more than what she had given—at least that's the impression Worker Aunt carried around. They built up over the decades a formidable pile of such irresolvable matters, and relegated them, out of consideration for each other, to their mental lumber rooms. Finally, a couple of years before Worker Aunt's death, they would take the debate to another level. Worker Aunt would conclude: 'We understand ourselves better than we understand others. And Granny would retort, recalling the Guru of the Stream: 'We understand others better than we understand ourselves: the end of all education is self-realization; achieved in a single birth, a series of births, in a hundred years, ten thousand years…. Be free, be divine!'

For now, the sisters-in-law recited their lessons together and planned another daring visit to the Boat Woman of Sakhinetipalli.

℘

Miss Beston's boat perched on level ground in the wide-backed, deep-bosomed canal. She was continually on the move, shifting camp almost every fortnight. Though business took her away from time to time—she operated in an eighty-kilometre stretch, the most luxuriant of the Coromandel—she always returned to Sakhinetipalli and anchored herself there. This was her 'home'. 'My native place,' she told her Indian visitors. They loved it. Later, she turned it into a joke with her visitors.

And one item invariably found mention in Miss Beston's discourse to her visitors and in every letter home. Everyone came to call it Miss Beston's window.

Miss Beston loved that window of her boat: in fact, it was two windows facing each other. As the canal ran from north to south, she had a shuttered window opening on the east in the morning, and another looking out west in the evening. Europeans shunned the sun; she welcomed him, and, after a hectic day in the jungle or the diamond mines, sitting next to the window, she would manage to get for herself, over the next four decades, a deep tan. The white hibiscus evolved into a rare species: 'Copper hibiscus,' Mr Blotton teased her.

Through the window she loved to survey the green thickets and watch the newly redone Grand Trunk Road and its bustle. She worked near the window, taking in all the attractions and distractions outside the window. And, of course, all her spare time was devoted to observing the highway. Like an astronomer in her attic, waiting patiently for a new planet to swing into view, a new earth!

Miss Beston never seemed to miss anything. Something told her to move to her window and pick up her spyglass in time.

'Come here, and quickly,' she told her guests now. 'Watch that spot.' They crowded around her worktable, looking east. A wayfarer came into view. He was a Brahmin in dhoti, an angavastram draped over his bare shoulders, tonsured except for an expansive pigtail. He held the hand of a little boy, who was already tonsured and wearing the sacred thread.

'Do you know where they are headed?'

After a brief silence, one chipped in, 'Masula.'

'That's right, Masulipatnam. And where in Masula?'

No one knew.

'To Mr Black's English school. C. P. Black Esquire was the Assistant Collector of Guntur. Black had been posted in Masula in 1852. He starts free schools wherever he goes. I am thinking of recommending a transfer for him every two years!'

They laughed.

'Most of you may not know this,' said Miss Beston. 'In the Coromandel, as is generally the case in southern or northern India today, a Brahmin's livelihood has some well-established sources— some from patients, because he is the village medic practising age-old Ayurveda. He also acts as corpse bearer; it is not easy to get people to act as corpse bearers in this country—it includes presiding over appeasement rites for planets, annual rites, and accepting food as one of the seven Brahmins as laid down in their shastras, as well as accepting a pacification fee during eclipses, and reciting the panchangam—the date, day, auspicious and inauspicious hours of the current day—at every door. He also asks for weekly meals at every Brahmin home. Knotting up the grain donations in various parts of his dhoti, he can engage in outright begging; finally, then, the high point of the creature's career is lending out the moneys at exorbitant interest rates.'

Her munshi followed every word with joy.

Miss Beston looked through the spyglass again for a minute or two. When her audience seemed ready, she resumed.

'Now, this Brahmin is teaching his child a radical new lesson. They will have walked around twenty-five kilometres before evening…. But why is a little Brahmin boy being led by his priest father to an English school?'

She looked at her munshi.

'A Muslim tahsildar has told the Brahmin,' the pundit said, 'to put his bundles of palmyra texts away. "If you teach your son the Vedas, he will only be good for mendicancy. Send him to the English school. That's where the future is."'

'Impressive,' responded Miss Beston, 'the Brahmin had now set out to implement the sage counsel.'

Later, on Christmas Eve, 1870, Miss Beston recorded in her diary: 'English has become very popular; even the children of Bhotlu (Brahmins), who read the panchangam instead of reciting to learn Sanskrit, are studying English.'

The little boy grew up to become one of the most admired judges of the Madras province. Miss Beston was in touch with him throughout.

Miss Beston called for her dholies and her personal palanquin—an exquisite affair, painted in primary colours to withstand the Coromandel sun. She advised her visitors to get dholies of their own: a dholie could be made by a native carpenter in one day.

As the visitors came out, they savoured the sight of the canal.

The canal was a wonder to Miss Beston's English visitors. As wide as the Thames, it was a gift to the Indians from Major Blotton. Only the Indians called it by his name, to the whites it was the Coromandel. The canal was full to the brim here, brisk, purposeful, self-effacing. The clear stream was comprehensive, carrying all sorts of things, from broken golden paddy stalks to abandoned chappals and carcasses. From time to time a fish flew up, cavorted mid-air like a trapeze artiste, and plopped back and disappeared into the water.

'Cleopatra's barge,' the Scholar of Oxenford mumbled.... 'She is great.'

The boat defiantly faced upstream. Though Miss Beston had not banned fishing, there were no anglers anywhere in sight. 'Watch out, she is no plebeian. Not a woman to trifle with.'

The scholar took off his glasses, blew on them, pulled out his magenta silk handkerchief, wiped the glasses, and put them on again.

'I must try Brahma Kalam.'

Part II

Monsoon Maiden

Father was fascinated by fire. If he had been allowed to, he would have nursed the kitchen fire but that area was out of bounds for the head of the family. At the time of sacred rites, he would zealously aid the purohit in building up the homam. He reconciled himself to the option no one could deny him: he stoked the bath fire, the bath fire which began its career in a niche enclosed by three chunks of rock, but over the years, especially after Appachchi got involved, became a neat oven, cemented with clay and washed every day with water mixed with cow dung.

Other people of his age, for example his friends in the taluk, would go for walks, but he enjoyed sitting there, cheroot between his lips, building up a blaze through a dextrous arrangement and re-arrangement of the pieces of firewood, a central log resting on the floor hosting several slender sticks on it. In no time, golden pennants reached up to the bathwater cauldron, the largest anyone could use, black with generations of soot. He had specially chosen the driest of firewood the tribals brought from the jungle and hawked in the lanes of the hamlet—though the lumber thieves had made this difficult to do by now.

All the commotion in building the bath fire would rouse Appachchi from her slumber before sunrise. She kept rubbing her eyes, yawning and grumbling softly so Father did not hear—but Father was settled near the bath fire and had already built up a blaze. Now Father gazed at the raging hearth with unconcealed satisfaction. The fine luminous vibhuti-like ash that had settled on the sides of the rocks inside radiated white heat. Father's cheroot burned bright in his mouth. He expressed his approval as Appachchi's mother led her to the paved circle in a corner of the veranda, decorously enclosed by old bed sheets behind the bath fire, and had her soaked, scrubbed to a shine by one or more of the maids. When there happened to be visitors, a whole host of cousins coming down for the summer vacation, for example, Father kept careful count; he would invariably notice the absentee idler or professional bath-hater among Appachchi's cousins—'monkey brigade', he would call them with affection, and, taking the cheroot out of his mouth so that his voice could reach any part of the sprawling mud bungalow, roared out the child's name. He had an exceptional memory for names and faces.

In a cheery mood, he would offer inspiration: 'The English people rise early.' The white people had impressed him. Especially Mr Blotton, the Brahma of the Godavari anicut, with whom he had worked a month on deputation and who he had helped sort out his accounts and administration, until he was sent by the Kumpini Bahadur to give the benefit of his experience to the Raja.

All Indians were in dire need of role models, Father declared, for him Mr Blotton fit the bill. Thus, it was on every occasion: 'The English people this' and 'The English people that.'

Worker Aunt's teasing should have put Appachchi off the rains; it didn't. Like any child, she also loved the summer for the mangoes, not necessarily ripe—in fact, the greener and sourer the better! The blazing Rohini season had only attractions for the children of the hamlet.

However, the monsoon was her favourite time of the year.

'You are an elemental girl,' her father said.

Appachchi inherited something of his pyrotechnic talent. 'I am a born fire-maker,' she would boast to her guests, 'though not a cheroot-chewer.'

'Don't ask her for a few live coals to fire your kitchen oven,' Worker Aunt would caution them, 'she will rub her palms and burn down the whole village!'

Appachchi's father took as much interest in getting his cheroots made as he did in making the bath fire. Lanka tobacco—the best in the country—was fetched from a town over twenty-five kilometres away. For this important mission, Appachchi's maternal uncle—they all called him Nephew—was always chosen, and he brought back that horrible weed rolled in a gunny and put it all in the front room at one end of the veranda.

In the veranda school were around two dozen boys and girls picked from almost every home, hut, and shack of the hamlet. It was run by Nephew for the duration of the summer, when the courts were closed, the arrival of the Lanka tobacco was announced to the children by the pervasive pungency. For a couple of the pupils, though, Appachchi's classmates in school, the stench was a treat; these boys' lips proclaimed to the world they had been enjoying their fathers' stocks. All of them, smokers and non-smokers alike, looked forward to the next stage. Father sent word through his Revenue Department connections to the master craftsman from the town, who arrived with his apprentice. The apprentice, a little boy, carefully creased out, stalk by stalk, the leaves, large as the wings of a fruit bat. Then the master cut each leaf with a round knife like an expert cobbler and trimmed it with a large pair of scissors, and then rolled it into a ruler. Just one leaf was enough to make a sizeable cheroot. The trimmings went into the next cheroot. The assistant then piled them into a dozen cheroots each and bundled them in brown paper with a single withe of jute bark. When the cheroots had all been counted, they were put into a huge clay pot which was big enough to accommodate comfortably the burliest of the Forty Thieves.

When it was all over and done with, it was Appachchi's privilege to respond to Father's call and run and get him a cheroot. Removing the reed mat, she lifted the mud tray covering the cheroot pot. The stench of the weed hit her like uncorked steam. After a while, though, she began to like the smell and toyed with the idea of trying one—she even consulted her seasoned colleagues of the veranda school—but that had to wait until she came to know the toddy tapper decades later.

Now she put her hand in, grabbed a pack, and rushed back to her father.

Appachchi discovered the weed won friends for Father. He rewarded a sincere workman with a cheroot; or a toddy tapper driving his cart to Junction, the toddy barrel spilling its potent brew all along the way; or a Chenchu tribal hawking genuine jungle honey; and, not so often, to an honest subordinate revenue official or a karanam who pleased him with hard work, Father gifted a whole bundle of one dozen cheroots. The fortunate man received the prize with both hands as though it were a casket of jewels.

One of the last sights for Appachchi every night was the glow of the cheroot as Father sat and relaxed on the dark veranda, chatting with a villager or just by himself, alone, sitting silently in the open, communing with the stars. 'So thick and bright,' the Boat Woman remarked to Mr Blotton later, 'I have not seen the sky so luminous in any other part of the world. India is star-rich.'

Mr Blotton corrected his compatriot quietly: 'Soil-rich, water-rich, people-rich.'

Appachchi dozed off.

A few days before their alliances were formally settled, the two girls, now nicknamed Davanam and Maruvam (aromatic leaves used in garlands), had vied with each other in a mango competition inspired by Nephew. He was a great lover of the forbidden fruit. And he would pay a heavy price for it later in life.

Naked except for their silver and gold fig leaf waist strings, they made such a mess with the thick juice that their fathers laughed heartily. Their mothers had smiled too, equally charmed, muffling laughter with the ends of their saris.

At the end of it all, when the girls had been washed and dressed, Nephew told them a story. Though the context or the provocation was not clear, he began with the moral of the story: 'Dandam dasagunam bhaveth'—the rod teaches plenty of virtues. He was probably speaking from his own legal experience because he had already been set up as a vakil in Rajahmundry. Or he was probably inspired by the presence of some of the betrothal guests sitting behind the veranda pupils:

'Anaga anaga (once upon a time), there was a rich landlord. He owned vast fields irrigated by a huge tank; he commanded endless orchards of mango, custard apple, guava, amla.... He was only bothered about the produce, not the well-being of the trees. And like a Kumpini tax collector, he was ruthless. No tax payment, no mercy.'

The guests knew what he was talking about. Appachchi's father had already saved several of them from these devils.

'His field hand came and reported to him that a particular mango tree—the third from the northern boundary—had not fruited the year before and hadn't blossomed this year when all others in the orchard had.

'The landlord knew what to do, he had received the remedy from his father. So, he collected all his field hands and a couple of carpenter's assistants. Armed to the teeth, they made a dreadful vision, a nightmare at noon. The landlord spearheaded the group, his best friend whom he had rehearsed with followed the procession at a distance, head slumped theatrically like a mourner in a funeral procession. If you were a mango tree gone barren for the second year running and expecting execution any day, this would be enough to burst your heart.

'They entered the orchard, talking loudly, almost shouting to each other, as though they did not possess normal hearing. In fact, all of them had suddenly gone deaf—stone deaf, to be precise. The crows and the mynahs and the rock pigeons in the orchard shrieked in terror and rose as one and hovered far above. They pitied the victim: a great abode, support, neighbour, companion, about to bite the dust that day, that fateful day.

'The landlord went up to the much-maligned tree and stood menacingly close. He looked the accused up and down, eyeball to eyeball, and spoke, delivering his lines in the great histrionic style of wandering street players:

'"So, this is the tree which will not bear fruit but still expects its landlord, poor me, to support it with precious water and expensive manure? Oomn, oomn," he moaned magisterially, ominously. "Orey, are you all ready?"

'"Yes, sir!" they responded.

'"Or are you all also so many good-for-nothings sticking to your poor master like leeches and bleeding him white?"

'"No, sir!" all of them shouted as one. "We are no parasites, we have what is known as gratitude. Our landlord gives us rice and we repay him. We are self-respecting workers. No greater virtue in the universe than gratitude, sir!"

'The landlord swung violently around, a veritable rakshasa in fury, and the crowd fell back in terror.

'"Good, good," he smiled wryly, "but this fellow is not. My father had brought this creature as a sapling—one among many orphans—from the uplands. With his own hands he raised this orchard, an orphanage, cleaned up the wilderness, dug a well specially for their drinking water, made the place hospitable for mango trees, dug aprons around the saplings for water, brought cow dung and other manure and fed the roots. And hardly has my father passed away, this ingrate shows its character. I don't like this but—the law is the law—it has to be done. Now give me that axe."'

'Three in one—magistrate, jury, and executioner,' growled Father.

'Hardly had the irate landlord raised the deadly weapon over his head,' Nephew continued, 'when his friend, a picture of mute melancholy so far, rushed in.'

'"Please, please, please, don't do this, it is awful for a man like me to see the execution of this great tree, spreading its branches and sitting here like a huge eagle in contemplation, verily Lord Vishnu's vehicle, Garuda himself."

'"Then what do you want me to do? Add one more parasite to my household?" The landlord looked around, as though to identify and count their number. He swung the axe over his head and brought it down on the roots of the mango tree, though cunningly reversing the sharp edge, and bringing down the blunt side.

'"No, no, please," cried the friend and held his hand, "I don't want you to do this, my friend. I am sure this wise mango tree understands your predicament, your feelings, better than any human here. Oh you, great tree! Please help my friend, he is a man with a large family, a huge establishment—his monthly rice bill alone comes to a hundred rupees. Remember a single rupee fetches us a bag of rice today. If you don't give him understanding, who will? Please show your gratitude."

'"All right, I shall take your word that the creature will learn responsibility," the landlord conceded.

'Everyone nodded their heads and sighed solemnly with relief at the accused being released on bail, though conditionally and with one sterling surety. Until the defaulting tree went out of sight, everyone dutifully carried long faces.

'In just a week, the tree blossomed; it bore so much fruit that summer that the whole village rejoiced.

'The tale has left for Kanchi and we for home,' Nephew concluded.

Father grunted and, taking the cheroot out of his mouth for a moment, said, 'How is their 'Rithmetic?'

Decades later, Worker Aunt remembered the tale and her vadina didn't when Granny Appachchi was brought to tackle another difficult case.

At the time, Granny Appachchi wasn't content with just one, though, moving up and down the scale before the Guru of the

Stream finally blessed her, though he himself said that he was just an instrument, so to say, a lever.

As Appachchi entered her teens her preference for the monsoon grew. She loved especially the onset. When she closed her eyes, it felt like a god's wedding procession approaching from a distance, with firecrackers and a party of musicians blowing long curved trumpets, blaring away, cymbals clanging, drums booming. The Lord and His Consort relaxed royally in the palanquin as the procession moved out of the village on its way to the next, receding, softening. When Appachchi opened her eyes, against the overcast sky, a bonus appeared: a surprise of egrets.

Unless the orchestra played to her total satisfaction, for at least a couple of hours, it did not qualify for the title.

As Appachchi grew up, she observed sometimes a slight change in the musical score, a change of raga. The thick black clouds gathered on the horizon, now like the elephant brigade of Lord Indra leading his battle formations, now like slate serrations crawling up the sky, quietly rolling on the heavens with an occasional grunt or two, as though clearing their throats preliminary to the assault. And Lord Indra gave them full support from above: he brandished his diamond weapon in a silvery war dance.

When Appachchi was fourteen, still waiting for her nuptials, and BA Garu hadn't joined her, too busy with his studies at Madras University to begin family life, she made it a memorable monsoon for the entire family and beyond. Appachchi climbed up to the terrace of the granary, the only terraced building in the entire village, on a weather-weary ladder. She was not alone; a chubby baby was in her arms, the infant boy of a visiting aunt. She'd brought him with her without letting anyone know, not even the mother, and when they made a fuss about it later, she said with impressive realism, 'Who would've allowed me to take the little fellow up?'

That year the monsoon had arrived in the village without much fanfare, the lightning less and thunder muted, as though some special instructions had been issued from above to not make a show. And then the first sprinkle, large crystal pellets—as though the god was testing his reach—a few here and there, spattered the dust of the summer. The summer didn't object or feel offended, for its reign had already climaxed with the scorching of the dreaded Rohini and it knew, as with all things, its time too had come. Now the first scouts swiftly rolled up little globules of dust greedy for the moisture. Though Appachchi's parents kept the granary itself clean, leaving no temptation to rats and bandicoots, no one seemed to have remembered the open terrace—and at first the parched dust grabbed the droplets and swallowed them up like a frog on the sandbank of the river, but then Lord Varuna began throwing energetically, more of them until it was no longer tentative. The globules linked arms and formed a surge, and the dust knew its time had come. It retreated, melted, and merged in the sacred element. No more dust...just rills of a fluent crystal.

Meanwhile, the baby in Appachchi's arms shuddered and gurgled. Shutting his long eyelashes tight, he giggled. When his front was soaked, Appachchi turned him around, getting her own dripping hair away from her face, kissing the baby and singing at the top of her voice.

Meanwhile, at the house they had discovered the baby was missing and Appachchi's celebratory off-pitch concert attracted them. 'She just cannot come down the ladder now!' the baby's mother shrieked continuously, as though she wished to match the monsoon's deafening outpour. Appachchi had forgotten the ladder, now drenched and slippery. Hearing the commotion below, she stopped singing, leaned over—almost giving a heart attack to everyone below—and shouted at the top of her voice, 'Go back, go back! What is the fuss all about?' She continued, 'It is good for the baby. He will never have a cold in his life. Am I not right, Father? And I can climb down and up again with him in my arms, don't you worry.'

But Father tucked up his dhoti, put the nearest scrubbing cloth on his head and, carefully testing every rung—water not being his element—went up the ladder and stretched out his hands for the baby.

'No, Father, I can come down with him in my arms, let the rain stop,' she shouted.

'I know, child!' he shouted back. 'You can do that. But the rain won't stop now and'—the Anglophile that he was went on—'the mother of the baby is rather upset, can't you see? Give the baby to me, and you yourself should come down carefully. Wait, let me take this baby down, and I shall carry you down myself.'

The fond father carried two kids down, the first one in his arms, then the second on his shoulders, balancing his luggage each time like a circus artiste.

'Takes up the infant in her arms and dances in the rain! Appachchi has been foolish!' This was the unanimous consensus, sponsored by the neurotic mother.

'You will kill the fellow with a cold,' shouted Granny Appachchi's granny. The baby was twice smothered—by the monsoon, and now by the mother.

'But, Father, you yourself told me it is a divine bath.'

'No, child, recall what exactly I told you: when one becomes wet in the rain during the Uttharayana period, when there is both rain and sun, it is called divya snanam, divine bath.'

'Now,' continued Father after a fit of sneezing, 'where is the sun?'

'Behind the clouds!'

Father laughed and laughed and sneezed and laughed, almost choking. Pleased with her own wit and forgetting she herself was drenched, Granny Appachchi helped her father dry himself using several of his freshly washed dhotis from the wooden chest of drawers—yet another breach of discipline.

'That's enough foolishness for one day,' said her mother, 'now run to the bath shed and take off your clothes. I shall give you a hot head bath.'

Appachchi dropped her langa, pulled off her choli and flew to the bath shed.

'What am I going to do with this girl!' said her mother. She turned to the girl's father and whispered fiercely, 'You should be ashamed.'

When she heard of the incident, Worker Aunt was not amused either. Now her brother would have to discipline Appachchi. Fortunately, she reminded herself, he was equally hare-brained. Dondu dondey (made for each other)!

Since that day, Granny Appachchi came to be called Monsoon Ammayi, Monsoon Maiden.

Not long after this her mother took the two girls on a pilgrimage to the Guru of the Stream. During the earlier visits, the Guru had not said a word to her. He'd just put his callused palm on her head and smiled. Now he whispered to her, 'I shall be with you always.' And, leading her by the hand to the stream, he sat on a jutting granite boulder and seated Appachchi and Worker Aunt next to him while the devotees settled around and listened to his discourse.

> After all, Krishna Himself served as a charioteer.
>
> Not only this. After His work as charioteer was over for the day, He used to take the tired horses to the river and wash them.
>
> When the rajasuya yaga was being performed, Krishna came and asked Dharmaja to allot some work to Him. Dharmaja did not know what work to allocate, so he asked Him to indicate what work was suitable for Him. Krishna went close to him and confided: 'I have a special qualification.'
>
> Dharmaja, who knew Krishna better than anyone else, was very curious. 'I am fit for removing the leaf-plates after people have eaten and left.' He did it.
>
> The Lord sets the example for the devotees to follow. He teaches that service done to any living being is offered only

to Him and is accepted by Him most joyfully.

Happiness is other people, of other people. Help ever, hurt never! Be free, be Divine!

This was the first discourse Granny Appachchi could really follow and she thought, as she listened to more and more of the Guru's discourses, that the central theme was service to mankind: 'Hands that serve are holier than lips that pray.' Years later, Granny Appachchi shared this discourse with Podumburra, her neighbour Lakshmamma's son, and his friends at the veranda school. It made a profound impression on Podumburra.

⁂

A storm had spoilt all the outdoor tamasha Miss Beston had planned, especially the fireworks show which she arranged regularly for her European customers.

'You are truly a gooroo to us,' said the scholar of Oxenford, the expert on Sapon and sundry other things. Most of Miss Beston's visitors blended business with scholarship and a dash of spirituality.

Miss Beston smiled self-deprecatingly and fingered her gold and diamond chains. 'You mean that I should discard all these, and all that I need in their place are those mandrasi beads?'

Miss Beston concluded the day's meeting: 'Thomas Macaulay's Minute just confirmed what is already a fact. These Indians are learning English on their own, without any official aid from the Kumpini Bahadur, even before Macaulay. Now let us celebrate, let us raise a toast to Her Majesty, the Empress of India!'

Miss Beston urged every group of India probationers to visit Mr Black's school in Masula.

Masula itself, she said, was next only to Madras. Sir Thomas Munro called it the capital of the Telugu country. The first English factory on the east coast had been set up there in 1611. The British valued the Coromandel commercial connection; in 1632, they obtained what to them was the 'golden farman' from the Golconda Nawab, put it in a palanquin, and took out a grand procession.

When her visitors complained of the land and the people, Miss Beston moved briskly to another discourse on India.

It was of course, for most of them, Miss Beston agreed, 'a difficult, alien country'. As for her, she did not try either to civilize her physical surroundings or set the style of the new colonial society; she did not try to impose the conventions and niceties of European civilization on this frontier life. Life was not a battle against unfamiliar climates, hostile natives, physical hardships, loneliness, poverty, and isolation; her Indian career was of very real and lasting significance. She added that she did not live the life of the sahib people as most others did, but fashioned a unique business style of her own.

As a reward for her guests' patience, she gave them a few practical tips. She alerted them about the pests of the Coromandel.

'The plagues of Egypt are nothing in comparison, especially the ones in Cis-Tumbudra and Godavari provinces.'

And she also warned them against crude conduct.

'Don't offend the upper castes of India: for all the show of deference, they have seen over the centuries all kinds of foreigners come and go, though Southern India has had a relatively restful history. Besides, they consider us as no better than their outcastes; I am sure our own munshi's wife keeps a pot of Ganga water ready at home to purify him after each visit to me.'

She said she concerned herself only with the non-spiritual needs of her visitors. She told them to furnish their coolies with lathis. She had only recently come face to face with a cobra de capello.

She mused for a while. Her mind went back to the natives and their curious ways. 'The holy waters are convenient for washing away a man's sins, and as efficacious as a pope's bull for this purpose. So, the government imposes a levy of one rupee and even the poorest have to pay!'

On another day, she cautioned them against going native.

'Ethos undertow!' the Boat Woman of Sakhinetipalli warned the more thoughtful among her visitors, 'watch out for the deadly ethos undertow!'

She took a pull at her hookah, a most exquisite work in brass and bronze from Moradabad.

'Watch out for the ethos undertow,' she said. 'Be warned against the lotus-petal air of India.'

She offered a smoke to her visitors; the hookah did a round and came back to her. She nodded towards her gomastha, who hastily excused himself and tied his tuft up nervously. They all smiled.

'Forewarned!' said a guest happily. 'Forewarned is forearmed!'

'Unfortunately not,' said Miss Beston. 'The saddest truth in the world is people never learn, people are human....'

Her guests opened their eyes wide; there must be something profound there. A prosperous entrepreneur is a sage subject, as sagacious as Her Majesty, the Empress of India. Her Majesty's government was now in effective control of the Indian territories. To celebrate the royal proclamation, a dinner would have been preferred by her friends and business contacts, but with a banquet on board a luxury boat anchored in a canal almost as wide as a river back home, in the thick of the Coromandel jungle, and at night, 'You could expect a whole lot of uninvited guests coming in.' A grand luncheon was a more practical option for a get-together. She offered the three great luxuries of Anglo–India: wine, cheese, and ham. And, what's more, her punkah puller was a Muslim, proud and poor, a scion of the Mughals.

On Miss Beston's request, Seshacharyulu recited the Rules for Food, as given by the lawmaker and sage Manu: 'A Brahmin should take food once in the morning and once in the evening according to the Vedams. He should not eat at other times. This rule is as important as agnihothram, ritual fire.'

Seshacharyulu recited: 'A known person is a visitor. Only a

previously unknown person is a guest.' He quoted Apastamba: 'The guest, children, elders, sick people, and pregnant women should be fed first.

'Bhiksha should be given three times to brahmacharis and sanyasis. If possible, and if accepted, food can be given more number of times.'

'Hindus pray to their gods regularly,' Miss Beston informed her guests.

On popular request, Miss Beston talked to her guests on 'Kreeshna' and 'Arjoon' from 'Sanskreet', and episodes from the life of the warrior god Rama.

Then she asked for the dancers to be brought in.

As the nut-brown troupe were shown in, she received their salaams with a gracious smile. She called for her ayah and enquired, 'Has Mr K— anchored his boats under a bank?'

The native dancers performed for her guests.

Occasionally Miss Beston shook her arms to adjust armlets, bracelets, and rings, and took a pull at her hookah.

She sighed in bliss. 'I hope I am not too acclimated.'

As the time came for her visitors to leave, Miss Beston gave them a further list of dos and don'ts on hunting in the Coromandel: 'It is not correct, strictly speaking, to shoot a hog in India under any circumstances. And, ha, imported candles are brittle—Bengal candles are better.'

'But you are a native yourself. Look at this extraordinary boat, or sequence of boats, and look at your table!' they retorted.

Miss Beston's boat was custom-made. The vessel's interior architecture, unusually high ceiling, plain walls, and French doors draped in muslin, the thick thatch and spreading eaves over the sides that insulated and shaded the main cabin; the plants in pots, the hunting trophies and the servants clad in white, the walls outside wrapped in khus grass: all of this branded the boat unmistakably Indian.

And the hookah.

'That's commercial sense,' Miss Beston dismissed them. 'To prosper in India, you need fitness—physical, mental, spiritual. In minor but critical ways, adapt to the climate, the land, and its people. Model yourself on the water drop on a lotus leaf.'

Miss Beston's guests couldn't really make out at any time whether she was joking or being serious. It was her style to keep her company in doubt regarding whether she was for or against whatever she took up for discussion at the parties she threw after a hectic morning in the field.

Now, she had turned poetic: 'water drop on a lotus leaf!'

They knew it was a serious matter; they better pay attention.

Appachchi particularly enjoyed feeding the cows and the buffaloes: it was another enjoyable part of the day's routine. As soon as Worker Aunt took away her hot water to the bathroom shack, Appachchi cooked horse gram.

Cooking horse gram was a rite bordering on the sacred.

The job was performed in the cattle shed, on an open fire, which was always a big risk. The thatch of the shed had actually caught fire once, and it had been rebuilt with Mangalore tiles. Appachchi went about it methodically, with great relish. She first cleaned up the hearth, which was just a few stones arranged to keep the bundle of dry sticks under the cauldron. On festival days she even applied turmeric and kumkum to the stones. Once she finished cleaning the hearth of the previous day's ashes, the field hand wished it were larger, so he could place a gunny sack in it and sleep there—it was the neatest place in the whole house. She selected the best and driest coconut fronds from a corner of the byre, occasionally shooing off a rat snake, and arranged them, making a mattress for the live coals she brought on a dry cow dung cake from the kitchen. She fanned them to a flame, and then once the fire caught on, selected dry coconut shells and delicately placed them on the frond bed, taking care that the flames were not choked for lack of air but were curling their tongues around the dried shells. In no time the fire rose to lick the cauldron. Once the water came to a boil, she measured out the horse gram, poured it into the cauldron, and covered the cauldron with a large lid. The scent of boiling horse gram escaped from underneath the battered lid. From time to time, Appachchi lifted the lid with her bare hands—it was hot, one of the visiting grandchildren tried to lift it and scalded his fingers—and stirred it with a large wooden ladle. After a while she lifted the lid, scooped out a little of the gram and pressed it between her thumb and forefinger before putting it into her mouth. She nodded approvingly, and, as though seeking the sanction of a higher authority, took a little more of the boiling gram, blew on it, and went to Lakshmi, her favourite cow, who eagerly lolled her tongue and lapped it up, while the other cattle, the cows, the bulls, and the bullocks grew restless and salivated freely. Everyone was amazed at the way Appachchi cooked horse gram—just the right degree of softness to give creatures—human and animal—the satisfaction of having eaten the best gram in the world. As she stirred the gram in the pot, its steam and scent spread throughout the backyard. The cattle in the byre rent the air with their clamour for breakfast. She called out to them, 'Yes, coming, coming, I have to cool the gram, otherwise you will burn your snouts and tongues and will starve for a week.' She put out the fire, and with the help of a field hand, lifted the cauldron. While the horse gram cooled, she supervised the cleaning of the byre. Occasionally, she called the field hand and together they drained off the surplus water into a bucket for a later feed and carried the cauldron out into the open air to cool faster.

 She went about her other chores now. When necessary, she mixed more of the husk and brawn in the trough. Finally, the call all her wards had been waiting for came. Granny Appachchi instructed the field hands to feed the cattle. She rang a bell hung from the eaves of the byre, sending everyone into a frenzy. She took care of the calves and the cows; the field hands then led the big bulls and finally the bullocks to the trough. Each got a bucket of the horse gram, and a second round of the bran and husk feed.

She loved watching the cattle, loved the way they rushed to the trough like schoolchildren bursting out at noon to rush home to eat the midday meal, she loved the way they dipped their snouts deep into the food, she loved watching them gulp and guzzle. And with brush and cloth she scrubbed them herself.

'Granny Appachchi,' Podumburra, their neighbour's son, told her decades later, 'you would have made an excellent matron in a school hostel.'

For years, Miss Beston had been a greatly admired figure in the entire South of India. Now, she took another brilliant step. After a proper though distant courtship, she went back for a short vacation to England and married a member of the titled gentry. She returned to India with her husband in tow.

She hadn't told anyone except her munshi before she'd left for England and returned with Sir Edward. Her compatriots organized a wedding reception and wondered how she had managed to land such a high-ranking member of society. She smiled and changed the topic; only Munshi Seshacharyulu knew. It had been an arranged alliance. Now she printed her name embellished with a coat of arms on her visiting cards and left them judiciously at the collection boxes of the civilians that mattered and also handed them out to her business contacts. The card carried her maiden name.

Sir Edward was a busy politician; he spent a few weeks in India and then went back, promising to return. And he did, periodically. Miss Beston also began visiting England not once a year, as earlier, but twice. When she received a letter of felicitations from the Empress, the whole province rejoiced. Her friends came from long distances just to take a look at the Queen's handwriting.

She had now made a name for herself in the British Empire. Her daughter Jane came a year later, when Miss Ann Beston was just thirty-one.

⁂

Young Appachchi's daily routine was fixed, fixed by herself. Even in the winter, when the weather was cold as the inside of a well, she brushed her teeth and washed her face, drank milk even as it was sizzing softly in the milk bucket which the cowherd had handed to her, right after milking. Then she went out with a basket and collected cow dung from the lanes and alleys, following the herds as they mooed their way to the jungle pastures. She returned home, threw the dung on the dung heap, washed herself, and plucked malli buds, just enough to string garlands for herself and Worker Aunt. They both loved garlands tucked in their thick plaits. They also vied with each other in drawing muggulu with coloured powders in the backyard and right on the street in the front of the house.

Granny Appachchi watered the plants, put some manure in their beds, and made cow-dung cakes. When the cattle had left for the pastures, she had a quick bath behind the byre. Then she wrapped herself in a sari. She held her long and luxuriant hair in her hands, whipping the water out of it, and wrapped it in a cloth.

Appachchi heated the water for Worker Aunt to bathe and sat down for a hearty meal of cold rice and congee, or taruvanee, with a piece or two of avakkai or some other pickle from the numerous jars lined up like well-fed soldiers on a heavy elevated shelf in the kitchen. Worker Aunt, ever correct and proper, wouldn't eat until she had bathed and performed the puja.

And then Granny Appachchi sat out on the parapet of the well and opened a book. She always read aloud, as though unless her ears caught the matter, her head wouldn't.

Like she loved cattle and the monsoon, she loved trees and plants too. When she was little, the first thing she used to do at dawn was to go round her father's garden and assess the growth of her favourite plants. She would note how many buds of malli and parijatham had blossomed that day. If she suspected anyone had plucked a single flower, she would scream at them, and her father would join in. She would treat everyone as a potential or actual enemy: casual visitors were warned in unmistakable terms to desist, the village cattle were kept outside the thorn-bush fence on pain of being handed over to the cattle pound, the family's own byre was turned into a strictly watched prison camp. She would allow birds in, but she spared no effort to destroy rodents. She was particularly busy during the caterpillar season.

Later, at her in-laws, she would squat before each plant, tenderly taking a leaf in her own hands and carefully examining it for any evidence of depredations by pests. She tipped the culprit on to a smooth slab of Kadapa slate stone, and with a potsherd, beheaded it. This would grow into such a passion that she'd offer her services in the season of pests to the villagers, who welcomed her in their own fields. While the coolie women or the field hands could eliminate a dozen or so pests, Appachchi could end the careers of a hundred or more. Appachchi joined the rows of coolies picking their way through the fields, hand-picking inch by inch, yard by yard, acre by acre, occasionally standing up to straighten her back. A battalion of birds followed her to pick up the decapitated and still writhing creatures she left on her path. No one would believe that this was a Brahmin woman, the daily-wage labourers would say. Appachchi would become the champion exterminator.

Worker Aunt was revolted by Appachchi's behaviour and she'd attempt to dissuade her sister-in-law from going on frenzied murder sprees. One night, Worker Aunt got up, disturbed by the light of a hurricane lantern in the backyard. Picking up a lathi she quietly came out to discover Appachchi's bed vacant. She walked into the backyard to find her sister-in-law hunting caterpillars. Worker Aunt threw up her hands, shrugged her shoulders, and returned to her bed. Dondu dondey!

⁂

Appachchi's fascination with the Boat Woman ended suddenly. The Boat Woman had introduced him as a visitor from England. 'The clerk of Oxenford,' she had laughed and glanced conspiratorially at her munshi. He was the scholar who had lectured on various topics of import, such as saponification.

'This fellow touched me,' Appachchi said. She shivered as though the poison fever was upon her, she made a face as if she was about to throw up.

'Where?' asked Worker Aunt, very concerned.

'Here,' she whispered.

When they returned home, the girls didn't disclose the humiliation to anyone.

The following day, they arrived at the boat with a basket wrapped in a thick cloth after the Boat Woman had left with all her entourage on one of her numerous missions—felling timber, hunting, or prospecting for diamonds.

'It is a gift,' they gestured to the white visitor.

Appachchi signed to him to come and take it. The moment he opened it, out fell a cobra. The two girls pushed the terrified man off the boat, the swirling post-monsoon waters hugged the scholar. A rat snake was negotiating the stream at the same time.

Appachchi flung the cobra after him: 'Naga, go after him.'

And he did, or seemed to.

'What have you done, you lout?' the Boat Woman hit him hard with the butt of her hunting crop when she returned. The fellow started blubbering. 'Is this all that Eton has given you? And Oxford! You must be a fake, a fraud!' She turned around restlessly and came back and hit him again. He screamed again in pain. Her husband,

Those Women of the Coromandel

wintering in India, came and gently turned her away, pushing him out of the boat on to the canal bank.

'I have been carefully building up the trust of these people...' roared Miss Beston, 'They are from the leading Brahmin family of the Circar districts. The whole Coromandel will now rise against us.' She jumped out of the boat. 'Venkanna, get the gun, quick,' she thundered and went after the culprit, who was still dripping. Her husband rushed after her and restrained her again.

'I don't want to see him again, tell him to make himself scarce. Or I shall flay him alive and throw his flesh to crows and kites!'

'Blame Tindh,' she whispered to herself.

This English scholar was in the service of the Maharaja of Tindh and had journeyed via Hyderabad and Thallapalle en route to Sakhinetipalli. He was looking for ancient Indian manuscripts and artefacts.

BA Garu threw more light on Tindh. Its maharaja was popular with a certain strain of the colonial ruler. He provided to his visiting goras sumptuous feasts, and back in their palace rooms, little kids waited on their beds with their orifices covered in silk handkerchiefs. 'The Scholar had come to his friends in the south to recoup his strength.'

Appachchi shuddered. Worker Aunt told her brother, 'In future, don't tell me about such things.'

'How ridiculously funny,' continued BA Garu later to Appachchi, 'how unnaturally parasitical these creatures look, with their silks and pearls and jewels, and tinsel and kincob all acquired with the taxes they extracted from the labour of the poor and the deprived in their largely British bestowed territories. Nothing done to relieve even the material misery of their people. What a sinful life!'

The girls swore never to have anything to do with whites—men or women. And Worker Aunt kept her vow.

Seshacharyulu later updated for BA Garu, the career of the Scholar of Oxenford. The man had gone back to his original mission, looking for ancient manuscripts in Indian languages and precious artefacts in far-flung Indian homes, as some of his compatriots had gone raiding tombs in Egypt. One day, he thought he had hit gold. His guide took him to a sealed room in a house of pundits that had not been opened for generations. He opened the room, entered it, and sneezed and sneezed. A few days later he was dead. Miss Beston, a book lover, received his collection.

'Yet another martyr to Great Britain's India adventure,' said BA Garu.

※

She came from a family of sailors, navigators, and explorers of England. She had almost drowned once.

Occasionally, she recalled her roots. Her father was a sea captain. Her grandfather had been a sea captain. Her great-grandfather had been in the Royal Navy. 'It was not surprising,' she told her visitors, 'that I too loved the sea.'

Until she arrived in India.

Miss Beston had dropped out of school in England and arrived in India with her father in an Indiaman, *The Morrow*, and hardly looked back. 'Then the sea-faring girl turned a landlubber.' She laughed. The lush Coromandel became her home, her domain.

A visit to Miss Beston invariably boosted their morale, her guests said. The English nation, they felt in their bones, was the greatest in the world, as great as the Roman Empire. Oh, to be born in such a nation, in such an age, and to be young!

For the last decade, things had been changing on the ground, more and more in the white ruler's favour. The natives had been going in for revolutionary change. Macaulay, good old Thomas, was prophetic. Today, through her popular window, Miss Beston invited another batch of visitors to look at a Brahmin, the same boy she had pointed out to yet another batch of visitors earlier, the son of a ritual priest, now a head taller, 'That young Brahmin should be following his father as a ritual priest in his own right, but he now knows four European languages. How many do you know?'

They looked at each other like children in a classroom, wanting to impress the teacher and unable to do so. The boy had learned his foreign languages with the help of dictionaries. Not one of them knew the languages he had mastered: Latin, Greek, and Hebrew, besides English.

Miss Beston kept a watch on that boy over the next decades, occasionally inviting him for a chat. She herself had procured for him several books from England.

Miss Beston loved passing her books on to other readers, especially to her munshi, who learned over the decades science, geography, and geometry from her. He also enjoyed reading Adam Smith, Newton, and Wollstonecraft, and recommended them to his friends. Under the munshi's guidance Miss Beston developed an inner calm; she could go out with her latest rifle, shoot game, recite a few lines from her favourite authors, especially Shakespeare, and then, back in her living boat, with a sherry poised on a teapoy next to her, relax with a classic. Her routine did not falter, even when Mackintosh & Co. of Madras failed and Miss Beston suffered.

Her munshi admired her openly now. 'This is not any religion, this is the essence of all religions: spirituality.'

⁂

Things had gone badly for Worker Aunt—five miscarriages in seven years. Meanwhile, they waited, but Granny Appachchi did not conceive. Then disaster struck the family. Raghu, Worker Aunt's husband, caught the smallpox and died.

Granny Appachchi consoled her, stuck to her through day and night, attended to her like a patient nurse. But the first time she held her hand and led her to the bathroom, Granny Appachchi received a devastating shock: the series of miscarriages and abortions had torn her vadina to shreds; the desi midwives had used crude methods, played havoc with her, and disfigured her body. Appachchi reeled at the sight of Worker Aunt's body. She controlled herself somehow and did not disclose her feelings even to BA Garu; instead, she shut herself in the bedroom and sobbed and shook bitterly. Aiming at motherhood, at what cost! She held her head in her hands, it ached, it threatened to burst like a balloon.

Whatever happened, she resolved, she was going to stick close to her vadina.

Worker Aunt told her brother of an alarming development: Appachchi was up at midnight or in the early hours and squatting before the gods. She addressed them, particularly Lord Subramanya. 'What has she done to you, you have punished her so heartlessly!' Worker Aunt scolded her brother. After that, night after night, BA Garu would wait for a few minutes while Appachchi talked to the gods. Then he would gently raise her to her feet with soothing words and return her to the canopy bed. Now BA Garu managed two patients.

∞

A few days later, not yet recovered from the shocks she'd received, Worker Aunt, her head tonsured to signify her status as a widow, stood open-mouthed at the sight in front of her: Granny Appachchi was running, running away from something or somebody. She had never looked so crazy.

Later, Granny Appachchi explained to BA Garu:

'I had gone as usual to the cowherd Ramudu's hut for a chat. Ramudu was particularly nice to me; he enquired of my husband's welfare and he said he had creamy buttermilk that day as few of his usual customers had come to collect their share. Then he offered some of it to me, asking his wife to leave a good share of the butter in the buttermilk. He poured it into a pot for me. I blessed him with all my heart and called on Subrahmanyeswara to shower his blessings on him, to bestow upon the couple children—a boy who would support them when they grew old, and a girl to brighten up their household like a gold lamp.

'I had hardly covered a kos on the cart track when I found a rock right in the middle of the path. I thought that it might hurt a passing bullock, or branded bull or cow, and bent down, picked up the rock, and threw it into a ditch. That's when I spotted the serpent coiled up by the roadside. It uttered a cry of pain and slowly came out of the ditch, sighing like a creature so tortured that it did not have strength left for even groans and sighs. It was clear to me the poor fellow was in bad shape; he must have been starving. I felt my heart turning to water with pity, and so I addressed him with endearing words, and at last he raised his head slightly. He was quite a big fellow, his hood was as big as both of Ramudu's palms together, and he was as long as a toddy palm, but now he did not have the strength even to greet me properly. I assured him that I had the best buttermilk of the day, that Ramudu was the nicest cowherd anywhere around, and he had given me the most creamy buttermilk, and even if a share of it was given to him I could put some water in the pot and shake it well and it would still be the best buttermilk of the day. Only, he should in return bless Ramudu's wife with an heir, and I would see to it that they gave the little fellow his name, call him Subrahmanya. Believe me, the Lord Subrahmanya, though exhausted, still considered my proposal for a full minute or two and then nodded his head in assent, and with such beauty and dignity that no king in all his majesty could match him in splendour. He raised his head and opened his mouth—it was so pink inside and so deep—I would have fed him butter with my own hand, but I remembered the Lord's majesty, so I lifted the pot and poured the buttermilk slowly and steadily so that Lord Subrahmanyeswara could drink it in comfort. Before I knew it, there was no buttermilk left, but the Lord still kept his mouth open and demanded more, and then when I failed to pour, the Lord shrank and shrank until he became a common cobra.

'"That was good," said the serpent coolly, which surprised me: I had expected some warmth in his words. "But I have a grievance against you," the serpent said.

'I was shocked.

'"You picked up the rock and threw it blindly, without looking where it was going. As it is I have suffered at the hands of that inhospitable ryot; he has deprived my life of peace. And the rock you so recklessly flung would have knocked my brains out! If I had not ducked, I would have been a gone thing. Now you have also fed me with the creamy buttermilk which has revived me enough to think lucidly of the just and the unjust. I have pondered the matter to the best of my wisdom and have arrived at the conclusion that you still deserve a little punishment. And I have decided to give the choice to you. What shall be your punishment?"

'I shuddered and shook in terror and dropped the pot and ran, and when I looked back, panting, the serpent was right behind me. I ran and ran. Whenever I turned to look, the snake was right behind me. When at last I saw a young man going to his field, I stopped him and told him the whole story. The ryot looked over my shoulder and asked me, "Where is the snake? I do not see any snake." I turned round, still terrified, and there was no snake.'

Though Worker Aunt discounted the whole story as a figment of her sister-in-law's fevered imagination, BA Garu did not leave Appachchi alone the whole day. After she had gone to sleep, he pulled a blanket to her chin and went to his books. He mused the whole night on Appachchi's experience.

And so, he read. After all, knowledge dispels superstition.

BA Garu did not say, 'It's only a dream, forget it.' His way was to take things seriously. He read to Appachchi about snakes from old books. 'I want to know them, knowledge is the key,' he said. 'When you know, you lose fear. I shall teach you to handle the deadliest of snakes. But just listen to this.' And he continued.

One day, while BA Garu and Granny Appachchi were out on

a walk in the fields, BA Garu spotted a big snake. 'King cobra,' he said. 'The king cobra is very much part of our rich and variegated folklore, religion, and art. This is the only snake which builds a nest with dry bamboo leaves and twigs.'

He stopped the progress of the snake and held it down with his forked stick. It gave Granny Appachchi the creeps. He held the tail and ran his free hand along its glossy body and fondled it as though it was the baby they hadn't had, and said, 'You see how tall it is,' lifting the tail above his head, his eyes alert, the snake's eyes alert, its forked tongue restless. It hissed and lunged at him and he stepped away. Then he put it down ever so tenderly and let it move a little before stopping and holding it again, reluctant to let it go. 'It is at least 15 feet long, and that means it must be at least twenty years old.... You keep your distance.' Then, as the cobra spread its hood, he positioned himself before her, hardly two feet away from the deadliest fangs in the world, and holding up his left palm, as though it was a mirror, to distract the snake, he brought down his right hand and tapped it. Appachchi cried in shock.

'Go,' he said softly to the king, 'go, now. And thank you, Naja Naja.' And he let the snake go. Without a second look, to Granny Appachchi's surprise, the terrifying creature crawled away quietly.

He told his young wife, 'I have always wanted to tap a king cobra on its hood.'

The peasants rushed down with staves, asking, 'Has it gone, has it gone?'

'Oh, the heroes have arrived,' said BA Garu, and his young wife laughed with relief. The villagers looked sheepish. They had witnessed from a distance all that BA Garu had done, worrying not about themselves, not about BA Garu, but about their monsoon maiden, Appachchi.

One of them said gravely, 'The Naga king will lay a curse on you.'

Appachchi turned pale.

BA Garu did not even look at the man, nor at the peasants,

he just reached and held Appachchi's hand in his warm grip. He led her away.

'Don't look for it,' he told them, 'The king has vanished, he has left for his palace underground. Don't try searching for him, his followers will not like it. The king will not keep quiet, as he has with me. He knows you don't love snakes; he knows the touch of love, and you need a certain knack to handle snakes, you understand? So don't do anything foolish and take those staves and go back to work, back to work.' Suddenly, he exclaimed, 'Arre, what is that behind you folks!'

They jumped a foot or two and frantically looked around. When they turned, BA Garu had led his wife away.

∽

'Even God needed an adversary, after all.'

One Englishman in the Coromandel viewed Miss Beston's enterprise rather differently; for Mr Blotton, the architect of the great irrigation system of the Coromandel, who had also given special instructions to his surveyors to respect any aged tree: 'Old trees are beautiful with age.'

It is not as though he did not admire Miss Beston. He had known her from the beginning, since she was no more than a child. She was extraordinary.

When Miss Beston realized that Persian was used for government records, she had engaged Munshi Seshacharyulu, a local Brahmin who had mastered Persian under the Muslim rulers earlier; and had taught himself enough English under the new dispensation. Under his guidance, she picked up enough Persian to present and argue her own cases.

She had the advantage of history, she knew he knew.

'Every educated native I talk to,' she said, while her munshi nodded his head, 'is grateful to the white rulers; for under the Nizam the Circars had suffered; it had been the most successful depredation in Coromandel history. Not only the practice but even the remembrance of civil authority was wholly lost. There had been little protection from robbers and wild beasts alike: now the white rulers have given the people just that. Hanged the robber by the nearest banyan tree and left him to rot, and hunted the wild beasts. For the security of the people of India. For the common good.'

She had taken to India like a fish to water. For her, India was not 'a strange land with a strange people'.

Over the decades, Miss Beston had become a legend, a musical score in the repertoire of imperial India, a page-turner in British folklore.

Mr Blotton conceded she was extraordinary; even among the Europeans who had swarmed over the land for over a century now. She was a fish all right, but—and that is an important but—a fish that swam against the stream, against heavy odds: she was a rare salmon, a true-blooded English salmon. She laid her eggs in a vault.

Miss Beston retaliated: 'Carp Esq.'

Like any successful businessperson, she had built her career one step at a time. Before the canals came, she had transported her merchandise by road, and it had been a tedious process. But then the canal came as a real boon. She made the most of it until, by the end of the century, the railway simplified things for the Coromandel veteran by laying a special track to Sakhinetipalli.

A familiar business figure in the area, Miss Beston revived an old colonial custom: going out on business in a ceremonial procession. She had read and heard about it: the Dutch had enjoyed India better than the British of the time. A Dutch retinue invariably comprised two umbrella bearers, two torch bearers, sixty peons, two purebred grey Arabian horses, and two palanquins. The Dutch had even engaged in slave trade.

Later, with the Dutch out of the reckoning, the English now attempted to do one better: whenever a merchant went out, he was preceded by a bugler and two servants carrying banners. A swordsman preceded the procession. On either side were bhoochakra godugus, or parasols, followed by horsemen, foot servants, and a retinue in white and black. They even tried slaves—what would good old Macaulay think of that! Half the expenses every merchant incurred the Kumpini Bahadur reimbursed.

And they employed a whole lot of natives: clerks, maddathugarlu (assistants), omedvar (payless volunteers), sharabulu, peyshkars, and jawabneesulu (writers of letters) in civil jobs. In the police line were sardars, havaldars, nayaks, jawans, duffedars, and dawal bantrothu. At the lowest level were muchchees (for tying up ledgers and sharpening pens), masivallu (for making ink), masalji (for lighting lamps), torchbearers, paakkhaalis (for fetching water in leather bags), sweepers, and, exclusively for Brahmins, neella pandiri Brahmins or drinking water shed Brahmins.

It was this custom of going out in pomp and glory that Miss Beston revived. She grew tired of it quickly though. 'Things have changed since the time of the Dutch. The English people are a confident nation today, the nation is in charge, and there is no need for her to impress her native customers today.' She dispensed with ceremonial outings.

Prominent among the examples Miss Beston gave of casualties was Mr Blotton, Chief Engineer of the anicuts on the Godavari and the Krishna, or, as the natives described him, Lord Brahma of the great irrigation canal.

'Mr Blotton knows the Bible,' Miss Beston observed mischievously. Mr Blotton did not read any other books. He said he did not need any books other than the Gospels.

Though Major Blotton read the Bible every day before retiring to bed, and occasionally preached on Sundays to small gatherings of visitors and natives, she considered him a victim of India—a relict. The country was full of them—the cemetery crowded, packed. Their numbers seem to be coming down, however, thanks to the good sense that had dawned on the powers that be; now the delegates of her Glorious Majesty Herself were at the helm, not the 'Cheesemongers of Leadenhall Street'. The viceroy now believed that the top jobs could go only to the Europeans. Hastings had been hopelessly fond of these people! Incredible, isn't it! Respected their scholars. Cornwallis didn't, he knew better. Now top jobs only for whites. Hastings had picked up Indian languages, Clive did not. It was at Clive's request that the Nizam of Hyderabad ceded Northern Circars to the British in 1765, it was the most precious piece of real estate in the Deccan. And the great Munro wrote to his father: 'The most important public transaction since my last is the surrender of the Guntur Circar to the Company by which it became possessed of the whole coast from Jagannath to Cape Camorin.' Clive may have feathered his nest, adding a few eggs of sovereign gold to it, but he had also changed the history of this land and its people.

She concluded: 'Nations are carried forward by heroes, not by preachers.'

Miss Beston cited a success story, one of the numerous ones inspired by the legend that Clive was, though it was only a feeble replica of the great warrior himself. A young man had come as chaplain to Madras, renounced orders, entered civil services, amassed a large fortune, returned to England and was created a baronet.

Miss Beston had the plasticity and versatility of a true entrepreneur, Major Blotton remarked. Consider the way Miss Beston had changed her conversational style over the years: it was rife with India now. She talked of jewels and spices and weak tea. She used such terms now without bothering to explain them; she left it to the visitors to make the effort. She talked knowledgeably of right-hand castes: mainly agricultural, and left-hand castes, artisan—both branded as Shudras by the upper castes of the Coromandel.

Her visitors from the cantonment, army, and police, she told Mr Blotton, used a slightly different dialect: these gentlemen in kincaub trousers and with ladies on their arms peppered even their small talk with Latin and French; on dit, politesse, desunnaye, n'importe, enroute, plante, en passant, dandees. For them it was not dholy, but dhooly. Miss Beston listened to them—as she did to every one of her guests, Indian or European—with as much enjoyment and attention as anyone could expect or hope.

And the manner in which she could locate an appropriate quote at a moment's notice too was wholly admirable. Bandar/Masula, for example, had expanded under the Kumpini. Big and splendid city. She picked an old tome from the shelf at her elbow.

'To appreciate the accessibility of the Telugus to foreigners,' she said, 'consider the description of Masulipatnam in the words of a Christian missionary, Fernandez Navarette, as early as 1704.'

She read aloud to Mr Blotton.

> The City of Masulipatam is famous all along the coast of Coromandel.... The English and Dutch, and at present the French, have erected Factories there. Some Portuguese, Mungrels, and Blacks, who are Catholics, live there, and have a little Church.... Some English and Dutch, who have discharged themselves from their Companies, have settled there, and live with their Families....The city is singular, and there being such a diversity of Natives, there falls out something new every day among Persians, Armenians, Moors, etc. That city resembles Babel, in the variety of Tongues, and differences of Garbs and Customs, but I liked the natural inclinations of them all...met several people by the way, and they were all courteous and civil.
>
> The city epitomizes the recent history, with localities named after the Dutch, the French, and the English. Women in Masula wear long gold chains as ear ornaments and on the parting; and thick nose rings covering their mouths. When gentlemen meet they offer perfumes and betel leaves. The ancient town of Rajahmundry is in Masula division and is worth a visit, especially for a view of the river against a backdrop of hills.

She put the volume back in its place, sweetly ignoring a couple of hands stretching to receive it.

Her visitors were surprised she knew the difference between inferior proprietor and superior proprietor. She knew retti weight.

Miss Beston also knew the flora of the region, wild as well as cultivated: she was familiar with rellu, or flowering reed; and cow gram, cusa grass, doorba, and doova, or dub grass. She was familiar with the soils of the Coromandel. They were of various kinds: regur pure, regur loamy, regur sandy, alluvial, permanently improved, red clay, red loamy, red sandy. She might not have taken a liking for Mr Blotton but she had learned from him.

Miss Beston had actually acquired a conch; she blew on it to call her retinue for a hunt. In the hot season, she ordered khus screens and had them drawn and watered periodically.

Her visitors had heard that Miss Beston found time for everything. She maintained a regular correspondence with her husband in England; and with the Queen as well. She also maintained a diary for her family and had been very particular about her daily entry since her marriage. 'My child should know how her mother battled it out.'

In one of her letters to Her Majesty, Miss Beston confessed that she pitied most of the white women in India, mere housewives. 'Boredom is next only to the climate in the difficult exile of India, though servants took care of every possible manual task. They might be idle, dirty, and stupid, but even the humblest white establishment cannot manage without at least a cook, scullion, sweeper, water-carrier, washerman, maid, and outdoor staff.'

However, Mr Blotton soon realized that the young woman was heading in a different direction.

He was put off by Miss Beston's ways. For one thing, she had a most catholic taste in hunting: she shot at anything and everything that moved in the jungles of Guntur purganah, except humans. She had almost done that once, she confided to him, when she had mistaken a villager who was squatting huddled under a gongali—a rough blanket. More dangerous than her firearms, ever of the latest design—her friends and relatives dispatched them as soon as they were patented in England—more fierce and unsparing and undiscriminating were her companions, the hunting dogs.

In her first meeting, she had told Mr Blotton that she would confine herself to non-spiritual matters. She began with her kennel. Miss Beston was more proud of her poligar dogs than of her fine boats; she had received them from no less a person than Sir Thomas.

A poligar dog was the fiercest breed of dog. Before they turned into warlords, the poligars had been woodmen beating the jungle for hunters. But the chaotic conditions of the Deccan had helped them evolve from woodmen to warlords. Almost every village had its fort or was surrounded by walls; at the beginning there had been 30,000 armed peons under some eighty poligars, and the Kumpini was dependant on them for maintaining, sort of, law and order. It was the poligars who escorted the Kumpini bosses on their itineraries across the Coromandel.

And Sir Thomas had been gifted the dogs by the most ferocious poligar chief of them all. Sir Thomas had fought so well and vanquished the chief so conclusively that the chief knew it was all over, that the white people of the island were unbeatable. He surrendered with his coolie army and went to jail. Others among the poligars chiefs who did not have his wisdom simply perished. The pups presented by the vanquished chief were gifted to Miss Beston by Sir Thomas, and she raised them herself, forbidding any of the servants from coming anywhere near them. She bottle-fed them and the creatures repaid her care and affection. Not even a tiger could face the poligar dogs for long; big cats simply lowered their tails and ran into the farthest depths of the jungle. Only once would they fail her for no fault of theirs, almost finishing her, but that came decades later, on the threshold of the new century.

Mr Blotton recoiled at her canine extravagance. Miss Beston

had also a kennel of English hounds; ten imported English dogs had been added to the pack last year. 'It is disheartening to see those fine dogs die daily,' she told him. 'The price asked now in Calcutta for English hounds is considered too high, even by us Indians, being fifty guineas a couple!'

In the beginning they had been a source of a pretty mess on the floor of the boat; the stink alone had been enough to keep Mr Blotton away for a long time, until Miss Beston secured another boat exclusively for her kennels, and a bunch of dog handlers to keep them in good trim.

Now she had several kennels of these bloodthirsty dogs. Though she had not let them loose on her coolies, the threat still bound the natives to maintain law and order in her business establishment, Mr Blotton chuckled to himself.

Occasionally, she accompanied Mr Blotton to, as she put it, call on the great and noble river. 'It is a privilege to do so in the company of a river-friend,' she said with a charming smile.

'Do you know the Hindus have gender for rivers?'

'That I didn't.'

'For example, the Narmada—Nerbudda for the European—is a purusha nadi, a male river! When you reach a river the first thing to do is find out if it is male or female.'

Miss Beston could see he wasn't joking. Too much probing would only spoil the charm.

Each time it was a spiritual experience, she'd tell her visitors, there was nothing like this in Britain. Stags, of the chinkara sort, with small straight horns, came in to drink by the riverside; wild geese and herons flocked on the banks. She also saw six great crocodiles. 'For a riverine spectacle of these proportions you have to go to the Americas.'

A native bird catcher was trapping water birds, camouflaging his head with a mass of hedge and weeds. Miss Beston smiled, raised her rifle, and waved it over her head. The man frantically shook off the rubbish on his head and shoulders, rushed out of the waters, and ran as though his life was in danger. Mr Blotton chuckled, Miss Beston laughed heartily.

※

What punishment was adjudicated for Appachchi by the Naga? It appeared as though the whole village knew it, anticipated it, waited for it. What sentence was handed down by the self-respecting serpent? The villagers knew. Granny Appachchi was cursed with a mad husband—from that day her husband began behaving peculiarly, they told each other. 'Only a mad man will touch the hood of a king cobra.'

BA Garu noticed a snake's discarded skin in the fence next to the bathroom; it was so long it could have come only from a king cobra.

'This is nothing new,' both women told him. He knew, didn't he? Yes, he said.

Then, one evening, he spotted something stirring in the roof. When they brought the lantern, it turned out to be a snake.

'It is only a snake,' Worker Aunt said. Even this he knew. This was not the first time snakes had been spotted in the roof under the tiles.

The first BA of the district, one of the few university graduates in the province, he now lost his appetite, lost interest in his books, forgot how to dress neatly, to comb his hair. And he became a source of danger, a threat to her life. A God is never cruel, they said, he is ever just. BA Garu had returned from his higher studies, in Rajahmundry and then Madras, come fresh from the university with his gold medal, his picture in the newspaper, a handsome full-blooded young man. They had performed the nuptials; they were so happy, a parakeet–mynah pair.

And now this happened.

Worker Aunt consulted the Guru of the Freshwater Stream.

She took Appachchi along. 'Everything will be all right,' he assured them. 'No one is to blame,' he told Worker Aunt. 'Not Appachchi,' he said. 'Your duty is to support her in any situation.'

Worker Aunt did just that, sticking to her vadina through thick and thin, the villagers said to each other. Fortunately, she had the support of Nephew, a man who knew his way around the world, a manager of men and materials. He agreed to come and live with them and manage their affairs.

Over the years since the death of BA Garu, Granny Appachchi changed completely. Perhaps it was the grace of the Guru of the Stream, he had put his hand on her head, and something happened.

'I have done little,' said the Guru with a smile. 'I am just an instrument of the cosmic plan.'

What exactly happened when the global: Guru of the Stream put his hand on her head she did not tell anyone, until decades later, while escorting a young widow bride to her second wedding, Granny Appachchi became nostalgic and described the critical lesson gifted to her by the Guru of the Stream.

After that encounter with the Guru, she became a champion of life, all life, and loved any and all living creatures. And as though they had got wind of this change, the caterpillars came crowding back into her backyard garden.

Granny Appachchi would later use her newfound psychic power to protect a mature mango tree. For doing so, Worker Aunt called her a 'mad woman'. This is how it happened.

One day, her neighbour Lakshmamma's son Podumburra came running to her with a friend of his. Podumburra told her that they were about to cut down his friend's favourite mango tree in his father's mango grove. Why? She asked him. Because it was not bearing fruit. But it was a tree they both had grown up with—played around it, under it, on it.

'Plant a tree, dig a well, write a book, and go to Heaven,' Granny Appachchi quoted a Gujarati proverb.

When the boys held her hands and pleaded with her to go and do something, she said, 'I too love mangoes.'

She loved their very look and feel. For example, a banganapalle mango, with a crystal pimple of dried sap from the day it had been plucked by the farmer and brought down for fructifying. It was left cosying between two spreads of straw and a fraction of an inch of straw still sticking to it from the godown; a dark little birthmark here and there where a careless plucker, a tired fieldhand, had been ungentle with it, had violated its sensitivity with his plucking crook, or where a neighbouring twig had brushed inadvertently, without any evil intention, it was the wind; a subtle swab of pubescent green still survived the spreading sunshine of the fruit.

Amla leaves in June: pale green of the tips, and tender green of the delicate fingers.

Appachchi left. Without a word even to Worker Aunt, she left with the boys. What she saw shook her. There was a huge group of coolies brandishing axes and hunting knives and saws, preparing to execute the condemned mango tree—convicted ex parte, as her father would have remarked.

The boy's father did not appreciate the visitation: the Brahmin woman was renowned for her legendary powers. He glowered at his boy, suggesting he could expect a memorable whipping later in the day.

'What am I going to do, Amma,' he said to Granny Appachchi, 'this mango tree has gone barren.' He checked his tongue, immediately regretting using the word. 'It has not borne fruit for the whole season. I promise you I shall plant a new sapling in its place. What is the use of feeding a non-productive tree?'

'Simply because a member of your family, say, one of your own children is not being productive, will you cut his throat?'

She sang an Odia song of the Dewar tribe which highlighted the sacredness and the love with which the tribals treated the mango tree:

You have cut a banyan,
You have cut a peepul,
But why did you cut the mango tree?
It was as if you were carrying
A cow's leg upon your head.
Why have you cast away your virtue?
Why have you killed your nephew?

She went near the condemned creature, touched its leaves tenderly, and patted its trunk.

She whispered something in its ear. Only Podumburra could hear it because he had stuck close to her. Later, he breathlessly recounted to his mother the whole episode. 'Granny Appachchi said, "Mamidamma, mamidamma, aren't you being unfair? Is this the way to repay all the trouble this man has taken to rear you, nurture you? If you reward him with fruit, he will take care of his large family. His wife is a breeding machine, I wish she were a mango tree. Now, their children need you. I love you. Love you."'

Amazingly, though he resented the intervention, the farmer respected Granny Appachchi, the favourite disciple of the Guru of the Stream. He professed now that he was always one for non-radical solutions.

The following summer, the tree's branches almost touched the ground with the weight of its fruit. The farmer took a whole basket of the best mangoes and went with his beaming boy to present the fruit to Appachchi. She took only a couple; Nephew, the man of the family, was a sugar patient who could not resist a mango, she told him. She took the rest of the mangoes to the banyan school and distributed them among the pupils and their teacher.

More than ever Worker Aunt was worried that her vadina would one day be stoned to death for witchcraft. The field hand had reported to her the rumours and tales circulating about Granny Appachchi. She casts multiple shadows morning and evening, they said.

Nephew laughed away her fears. Ever the rationalist, in spite of decades with the Guru, he had no explanation for the phenomenon of the rejuvenated mango tree. About the rumour of Appachchi's multiple shadows, he replied, 'So what! Several selves in one?'

Granny Appachchi went on merrily with her work. And children loved it, especially the story of Rain Murthy.

> Long ago, the Rain God Varuna was pleased with Murthy's devotion and blessed him. Whenever he remembered Him, it rained. Then, he tried not to remember Varuna. He avoided Varuna, but it did not help. Whenever he remembered any god, it rained. It just rained. Wherever he was, even if he was under the most leakproof roof, tiled or terraced. It was a bit of an embarrassment. Particularly that year, for the god had chosen the wrong time to confer such a gift. That was the year of cyclones and storms and floods, and the sun god had hardly shown his face. Rain Murthy had a harrowing time, his people had a terrible time. Before they could link him to the heavy rains, he fled the region. The storms stopped. He went to the driest region of the south and performed the severest austerities. When Varuna appeared with a benign smile on his face and enquired how his great devotee was faring, Murthy replied sullenly, 'Not at all well.'
>
> 'How come?' the god asked with concern.
>
> 'I know you know.'
>
> 'Tell me all the same. There is no greater pleasure for a god than to listen to his devotees.'
>
> Murthy narrated his woes.
>
> 'They are not your woes, they are your neighbours' woes!'
>
> God Varuna was getting into a puckish mood.

'Please do not prolong my agony, Lord, please take back the boon.'

'All right, if you insist.'

Varuna waved His divine hand and suddenly Rain Murthy felt light, for the rain dropped from him and now he was just Murthy, his old self.

'Anything else?' the god asked affectionately.

'I will think and come back.'

'Good idea,' said Varuna and vanished.

The moral was, Granny Appachchi said, when you are in the company of gods, watch your tongue.

Part III

BA Garu

'The practical goal in life,' BA Garu said, 'is to keep one's sanity intact.'

It was the nuptial night, which had been scandalously delayed. BA Garu had decided to start family life only after the completion of his higher studies. Appachchi broke free from his arms; she was crying. This inauspicious talk on the very night of their union had alarmed her. Worker Aunt, who had joined her husband after her first menses, had gone through five pregnancies and miscarriages. Even the lady doctor in Rajahmundry could not help her deliver one healthy baby.

BA Garu lifted her chin, gently wiped her tears, and held her face in his hands.

'We are not little children, are we?' he said. 'I am only telling you there is a need to understand things, understand life, understand our lives, ourselves. And our mind is the key.'

He mused aloud, 'Not as practicable as practical.... Uncertainties keep up our interest in life, and at times, keep us on the edge.'

Something was disturbing him. His Madras sojourn hadn't made him a happy man. He also quoted an English poet:

> How soon hath Time, the subtle thief of youth,
> Stol'n on his wing my three-and-twentieth year!
> My hasting days fly on with full career,
> But my late spring no bud or blossom shew'th.

'Why talk of such inauspicious things?' said Worker Aunt the next day.

He was most disturbed by the pillage. He was, however,

relieved somewhat, he said, that the Queen had taken over the subcontinental responsibility; he told the women that recent events would undoubtedly affect future history. Being the first graduate of the Coromandel, on the way back home, BA Garu had been stopped by the townsmen of the district headquarters of Rajahmundry to celebrate. The city elders took him out in a procession and felicitated him at a public meeting, where almost the whole town turned up. Not just the local newspaper, even the Madras papers reported it.

As BA Garu approached the village from Madras to set up home with Appachchi, the first thing he noticed was the hill slopes which provided a backdrop to Sakhinetipalli. They lay bare. The forest cover had receded obscenely, like a bad case of alopecia. 'They are like the Vetapalem weavers,' he told Appachchi.

'The Boat Woman is a latter-day Tataki,' he told the two women. 'She is just one. The demons have covered almost the entire country. When will we get rid of them?'

But then, as he settled down to a householder's life, he noticed a change for the better. And he hoped the Boat Woman would keep moving up. He did not want her to return; whatever he did not want, neither the two women nor the villagers did. After the first few weeks of brooding, he pulled himself together. He changed his sartorial style: he put away the north-style kurtas. Now whenever he went out, he wore the local cotton banian with a pocket on the right, and on top of this peasant style garment, he covered himself, like the commoners again, with a blanket. He retained his ear studs, like most men around him. He spoke of the multiple benefits of ear studs for men and women.

And soon, he was absorbed in just one mission.

When the village had fallen quiet, he put Appachchi on his horse, and walked it to a field by the river. He softly mumbled an English song, softly at first, and full-throated as they returned. Milton, the stallion, a poet at heart, paid complete attention. BA Garu did not notice that his celebratory solo in an alien tongue was disturbing the field hands and the peasants—'That mad Madras man,' they muttered and went back to sleep.

He whispered these lyrics sweetly while he made love to her on the banks of the Godavari. The river gushed through granite boulders, as though after a long separation, eager to merge with the sea. Grand and noble, he called the river. The sight of the wide-backed, deep-hearted river always inspired him, and he sang out like a koel in March. But now there was another source of inspiration. Now he recited for her benefit. The very sound of his voice warmed Appachchi's heart. BA Garu went on like an intoxicated bumblebee. The first fragrance of the mango blossom had overpowered the air to stillness.

> Let him kiss me with the kisses of his mouth: for thy love is better than wine....
>
> A bundle of myrrh is my well beloved unto me; he shall lie all night betwixt my breasts.
>
> His left hand is under my head, and his right hand doth embrace me.
>
> Behold, he cometh leaping upon the mountains, skipping upon the hills.
>
> The flowers appear on the earth; the time of the singing of birds is come, and the voice of the turtle is heard in our land;
>
> My beloved is mine, and I am his: he feedeth among the lilies.
>
> Until the daybreak, and the shadows flee away, turn, my beloved, and be thou like a roe or a young hart upon the mountains of Bether....
>
> But I found him whom my soul loveth: I held him, and would not let him go, until I had brought him into my mother's house, and into the chamber of her that conceived me.

On the banks of the Godavari, the great and large-hearted river, which had echoed for centuries with Vedic chants of the

Konaseema pundits, now rang snatches from the *Song of Songs*.

> Thy lips are like a thread of scarlet, and thy speech is comely: thy temples are like a piece of a pomegranate within thy locks.
>
> Thy two breasts are like two young roes that are twins, which feed among the lilies.
>
> Until the daybreak, and the shadows flee away, I will get me to the mountain of myrrh, and to the hill of frankincense. Thy lips, O my spouse, drop as the honeycomb: honey and milk are under thy tongue; and the smell of thy garments is like the smell of Lebanon.

On evenings when the couple stayed home, Worker Aunt, her husband Raghu, and the others in the family kept away from the backyard for the night.

> This thy stature is like to a palm tree, and thy breasts to clusters of grapes.
>
> I said, I will go up to the palm tree, I will take hold of the boughs thereof: now also thy breasts shall be as clusters of the vine, and the smell of thy nose like apples;
>
> And the roof of thy mouth like the best wine for my beloved, that goeth down sweetly, causing the lips of those that are asleep to speak.
>
> Let us get up early to the vineyards; let us see if the vine flourish, whether the tender grape appear, and the pomegranates bud forth: there will I give thee my loves.

Granny Appachchi managed to leave behind one jewel or more in the bath shed at least once a week, and the maidservant would come and inform Worker Aunt, who promptly collected them and chided Granny Appachchi. In pointful contrast to her sister-in-law, Worker Aunt dressed meticulously. Even as a little girl, she had never come out of her room without finishing her bath and putting on her clothes and jewellery: the kantey, the vankis, the katlakasulaperlu, the big danglers, and the outsized papidi pinnu, not to speak of the bangles and bracelets. She was particularly upset the day after BA Garu's first nocturnal outing with his youthful bride, for they had both forgotten to retrieve Appachchi's jewellery.

Simhadri, a toddy tapper and sharecropper, discovered the jewels. He recognized who they belonged to and bundled them up in his upper cloth. He handed them over to Worker Aunt, who rewarded him with a silver Victoria rupee. She was as upset with Granny Appachchi's shamelessness as with her carelessness—and with BA Garu's violation of age-old customs and ceremonies. She spoke to them, even though she knew it was useless. Dondu dondey!

Said Worker Aunt to the incorrigible duo:

'You know, in every precious stone resides a spirit—anyone of them can inflict incalculable harm on anyone lacking due respect; it's better you make them your allies through your adoration. If you manage to please them you will receive their support; they will then be with you like playful kids, even hug you and give you spontaneous kisses. They will come to your aid when you are in need, provided they are convinced you have given them the attention and respect they deserve. If you offend them with your carelessness they will leave you, once and for all. Don't do it again.'

BA Garu was stunned: Appachchi was delighted. She looked at her husband, waiting for him to speak.

BA Garu, who sported minimum ornamentation, discoursed on the subject. He talked of the metaphysics of jewellery: 'The philosophy of ornaments cuts across caste, region, and religion. It is man's earliest attempt at creating an object of art.

'In the course of time, jewellery expressed the whole spectrum of human emotion, the whole breadth of class, caste, and gender. Even black magic. And medicine. Stones and jewellery are also indices of social strata and status. Royalty evolved their own unique forms of jewellery; for example, a gold crown studded with rubies and emeralds. The crown went with the sceptre and the orb. They were associated with aristocracy, the "right people". The principal preoccupations of mankind—power, wealth, religion, and health—have all given rise to their own forms of jewellery.

'Jewellery has played a significant role in our classics. For instance, in the Ramayana, recall Sita's chudamani, which Rama had received from Kubera himself. In the Mahabharata the jewel that Yudhishthira first loses in the infamous gambling is a pearl. In *Sakuntalam*, the signet ring; in *Silappadikaram*, the golden anklet; in *Manimekkalai* the jewelled girdle....'

༺༻

The great Godavari, the Southern Ganga, was flowing a stone's throw away, with the spectacular Scorpio dangling in the southern sky like a goddess's hair ornament. They were in the backyard, which was almost a one-acre field of black cotton soil, with the byre to the west and a huge haystack next to it rising above the mud-brick compound wall. To the east were his favourite rose bushes, a whole field of amaranthus greens, their stems round as your wrist, and a clump of banana trees, one of which had put out a huge bunch which Worker Aunt had covered religiously with an old gunny sack. BA Garu recited:

> Thy plants are an orchard of pomegranates, with pleasant fruits; camphire, with spikenard.
>
> A fountain of gardens, a well of living waters, and streams from Lebanon.
>
> I sleep, but my heart waketh: it is the voice of my beloved that knocketh, saying, 'Open to me, my sister, my love, my dove, my undefiled: for my head is filled with dew, and my locks with the drops of the night.'
>
> My beloved put in his hand by the hole of the door, and my bowels were moved for him.

At home, he arranged a sturdy teak cot near Appachchi's favourite jasmine bush. Though in the beginning the young woman was scared stiff of stripping in the open, he slowly coaxed her into it.

On their nuptial night, the very first time he met her, even before he touched her, Appachchi's scent had appealed to him: an aroma of marigold garlands exposed to humid heat, occasionally with the gentle pungency of turmeric freshly touched with water. And now, there appeared another bloom in the bouquet, her love fragrance.

BA Garu did not want her to conceive early. They were still newlyweds, he argued, time enough to make babies, and of course he loved her fragrance, but Granny Appachchi did not allow it.

∞

One night when BA Garu opened his eyes, his bride of a year, in her white sari, looked to him like a crumpled jasmine under the moonlight. He slowly and softly got out of the bed, took a thick blanket from beneath his pillow, and spread it over her. He retrieved a mat from under the bed, spread it on the ground, and went to sleep on it. At some time in the night, without waking her up, he put her on his shoulder, entered the house, and took her to their room with the four-poster bed. The click of the backdoor latch carried to the members of the family a clear signal.

'What has come of all this lovemaking yagnam?' Worker Aunt said to her with rare spite. She had conceived in the first month itself but after a year, Appachchi still hadn't.

When Appachchi mentioned the matter to him, BA Garu whisked her into their room, kissed her, and made love to her.

He said later, 'And if we are fated to have a child, we will.'

Still later, 'All the same I shall talk to a lady doctor.'

'Nothing wrong with her,' said the lady doctor across the canal in Rajahmundry. 'Why don't you go to Madras for a sperm test?'

BA Garu was taken aback. That was unimaginable.

'I shall think about it,' he said.

But he never went for a check-up. As time passed the matter weighed heavier on his mind. All the more because Appachchi never reminded him of the doctor's advice.

※

'India is the most fascinating place in the entire world to work in,' she said.

The Boat Woman's home was a chain of boats: a houseboat followed by support boats and luggage boats. First a very fine pinnace, containing two excellent cabins, fitted up with glazed and Venetian windows, punkah, and two shower baths. In this vessel, Miss Beston and her husband—when he visited India—were accommodated in one room and their child and her ayah in another. The second was a dinghy which housed the cook and provisions for the home. The third, an immense baggage boat, which contained all their furniture. The fourth, a vessel for the washerman, his wife, and the dogs. The fifth was a large boat for the horses, and the sixth had more dogs.

Miss Beston's dynamism was not limited to her business interests. She took care of her food; over the years, her table came to be mentioned with respect in the Coromandel. Initially, she had offered to her guests the three great luxuries of Anglo-India—wine, cheese, and ham. But she found that in this climate it was impossible to ingest dishes prepared by her Indian cooks in the English style. So, encouraged by her guests, she banished all English dishes from her table. After all, the natives had their own regional cuisine. They had discovered tamarind, for example, and tamarind was such a big help in countering the humidity of the Coromandel coast. Her kitchen underwent a sensible culinary reform that yielded her sound health and strength to withstand the Indian climate and cultivate her commercial interests. She valued her munshi's praise: 'In ideology European, in cuisine, Indian—she is wise.'

She had also discovered the local flora, not just the fauna on which even the Zoological Society consulted her now; she introduced her daughter Jane to these. The very flora of the land was enough to make even Miss Beston superstitious. The stories they told her about the peepul, and the ridiculous marriage they performed of the peepul with the neem! Their anthropomorphism made sense... almost.

She particularly loved eavesdropping on the peepul in a breeze. How many silks can compete or compare with the peepul's rustling! The whole tree swayed in gentle restlessness, as though going through bouts of quiet ecstasy.

'Sattvic flutter,' said the munshi.

Both mother and daughter listened avidly to the munshi recounting local tales about various trees. He had a tale to tell about the magnificent banyan. Jane loved his tales; it was she who inspired him with the idea of collecting his tales in a book, which was published in Madras towards the end of the century. One of these tales was about how the banyan tree nourished man:

> Nirantali, the first keeper of the world, was sent by the gods to live in Saphaganna. She brought with her some banyan seeds, wrapped in leaves.
>
> When the earth and the clouds were ready, men were born. Both the sun and the moon shone upon the men, and they felt very hot all the time. They had no shade for their mud houses. So, they took the banyan seeds from Nirantali and planted them. These grew into slender trees with very tiny leaves that provided no shade at all.
>
> Nirantali tugged and pulled at the leaves till they were large. Then, she stretched the branches till they came down to the earth. And so, shade was provided.
>
> But men still did not have proper food to eat. So, Nirantali told the banyan tree, 'Feed men with your milk.'
>
> The banyan replied, 'I have only blood in my body. Where

should I get the milk from?'

Nirantali swung her axe, hit the trunk of the tree, and said, 'Let milk flow.' And so, it did and men lived on it till grain came to the world.

∞

Winter in the Coromandel—a gossamer veil drawn briefly across the face of the southern sun—is the only time you live like a European; the rest of the year, said a visitor, is mere leather and prunella. Some of the visitors from England went overboard in Coromandel winter; a particularly scholarly dame referred to good old England as 'fuliginous'.

'Visitors can enjoy the luxury of extremes; but we "Indians" have to accept. Acceptance is not just a Hindu principle; every good European businessperson in India is a Hindu in acceptance. Don't hope to do commerce with this dusky land without some metaphysical grounding and philosophical strength.

'I discovered this early; thanks in part to my father, before he fell victim to the smallpox that broke out in the Kondapalli garrison. India is in my blood. So don't be too awestruck at my abilities and exploits in the Coromandel.'

Mr Blotton regretted again the gulf that was widening between the European and the native. 'Where was the old intimacy,' he sighed rhetorically, 'the old intimacy of the pre-Mutiny era!'

Miss Beston countered him, 'Nostalgia is the first sign of weakness in a ruler or a businesswoman.'

She fell silent for a minute. Her audience waited. Miss Beston was a great giver, even Mr Blotton agreed. She was a pleasure to listen to.

'We are missionaries, the real missionaries, not the Bible wielding tribe, but masons laying the solid foundations of the new empire.'

Miss Beston prided herself on one achievement, though: 'I get on very well with women in India, white or brown, black, or brown-black. Unlike men, they never feel threatened in my presence.'

She had realized early that women became larger than life in certain situations. In this imperial environment, away from home, assailed day and night by a hostile climate, surrounded by aliens of all kinds, white men respected their women more than in England. Miss Beston did not see this as a radical change. But it was a striking difference from back home. Being a woman of status came so much more easily in India. It possibly had something to do with the military culture, the ethos of the garrison and barracks; but the civilians were, equally, more receptive to their women. Or it had—this might sound most improbable—to do with their routines: working before sunrise and working late into the nights.

She also drew satisfaction from another achievement, just one more, Miss Beston disclosed to an exclusive batch of civilian probationers. She had absorbed the shock, the 'people shock' of India. A strange, awful experience awaited all of them. Too many browns and blacks in the bazaars, that's a shock, but equally so, as they travelled on horseback, in bullock carts, with 'kites skirling in peevish tones', is the very loneliness of the vast stretches, where you long for a human face, black or brown if not white, and often begin to mistake a movement in the bush for human presence; even a mirage of men is welcome.

∞

Once again, a Brahma Kalam decision. The two sisters-in-law, now housewives, took some time off and went out together. Worker Aunt was still recovering, but Appachchi wanted to take her mind off the worries at home.

The stench hit them from far off. They pitied the little girl. 'If you are born into it, it won't affect you,' said Worker Aunt.

Ten years had seen such change. Now, there was no danger of anyone being surprised by a big cat—the Boat Woman had eliminated all of them. Earlier, in a clearing of the jungle, BA Garu had said, with trees you could not identify all around, you felt like an amateur actor on a hostile stage. No longer. There were others at work.

Covering their nostrils with their sari hems, ignoring the birdcalls, pushing aside the swaying cobwebs, they progressed slowly, cautiously. Hiding behind the bushes, they looked at the elegant white and blue passenger boat in the canal, towing a flat bottom heaped mainly with two commodities. Worker Aunt whispered: 'Hides and sandalwood.'

'How the sandalwood must feel in the company of those hides!' whispered Appachchi.

The Boat Woman's backyard rivalled the demoness Tataki's courtyard. There stood a huge mound of bones, with vultures and kites and crows hovering over them.

'How can anyone dead feel anything? Even sandalwood. Wood is wood. Dead is dead,' Worker Aunt said.

'Dead may not be dead,' said Appachchi. 'Nothing is dead.'

After a while, they identified another kind of lumber in the loot: red sanders.

'Two or three trips she will make to transport the bones. Especially the tiger bones.'

It was risky; there were fierce-looking hunting dogs on board, though chained. They observed that carcass after carcass was carried from the last boat to a large yard where the Boat Woman's helpers cleaned out the flesh and threw it to the dogs and the coolies, they took the raw hides out into the field and left them in the open air; others brought them in after tentative treatment and stacked them in one of the rooms. The Boat Woman was tall and still very strong; she lifted an antelope without help. She also helped the coolies with lifting the big cats. The two women kept covering their noses with the sari hems and watched. Worker Aunt regretted coming. She wouldn't have spent a moment at the spot, if Appachchi hadn't wanted it.

A villager they knew came around and startled them.

'Dorasani wishes to see you.'

They looked around: the Boat Woman was waving to them. They got up and rushed home.

They were invited again. This time, the Boat Woman herself came down with her little daughter and without her gun. She had calculated perfectly: both Worker Aunt and Granny Appachchi were enchanted; the child was a Cinderella doll in a muslin frock with golden curls. The girl put her little hands together and said, 'Namaskaram'. The Indians were bowled over. The Boat Woman could talk sweetly in almost fluent Telugu to them. She was charmed to meet them after such a long interval. She invited them on board. Worker Aunt wasn't interested; though Appachchi was excited at the prospect, she too declined politely. They had a visit to make. Neither of them took their sari hems away from their noses. Miss Beston apologized sweetly, 'What to do, it is business.'

On their next outing, Appachchi relented and went alone as Worker Aunt still refused. She said she would wait until Appachchi took a look and returned. Though both had been drawn by the image of the little girl, only Appachchi went on board. However, by then the daughter had gone home to be with her father; she was going to school in England.

The dorasani took her around the boat. Appachchi was surprised that the boat was not just a boat; it was a whole house, an establishment. When Appachchi turned to leave, the dorasani said something to the gomastha and he rushed to the kitchen and fetched some oranges for her.

There was something about the boat, the women didn't like it. Later Appachchi and Worker Aunt wondered what it was.

'Death,' said Appachchi.

Perched on every corner of the boat.

They debated the Boat Woman experience with BA Garu.

Those Women of the Coromandel

The two women didn't want to go back for anything. The Boat Woman was also the boar woman, the bone woman, the hide woman. The canal was full, even overflowing at places. The water was clear mostly, except where the garbage from the freight boats had dropped carelessly before floating briefly and washing down the canal. Miss Beston had given clear instructions: no pollution of the waters; but then there was a limit to what one could do in such a matter, especially out here. The sisters-in-law looked at each other, their village, which was downstream, had got used to bathing and offering worship to the Sun God. Now they could see they had all been doing it standing in polluted water.

'I would like to go and see the Boat Woman,' said BA Garu. 'I like to jostle death.'

Both women covered their ears with their hands.

※

Mr Blotton winced when a kind-hearted officer confessed to Miss Beston:

'We shot, I am ashamed to say, many harmless monkeys of the "green" or "pagoda" species. About a half gunshot off, the Subs had, it was reported, the time of their life. In the way of sport, I myself shot one only, and was so horrified at the humanlike expression of its dying face that I decided never to shoot another. Otherwise, we had a good bounty, especially with florican, quail, waterfowl, waders, and other congeners of the marshes. One drawback was the great number of poisonous snakes which infested the grasslands.'

They discussed the virtues of ducks versus quail.

Miss Beston's visitor did not share her interest in this difficult land. 'A further spell of service in India is threatening me…it has been my misfortune during life to be obliged to wield the pen far oftener than the rifle.'

This man would be a martyr, thought Miss Beston, not to India, but to boredom!

Mr Blotton nodded. He could read her thoughts by now. For him, Chief Engineer, her tale lacked moral appeal. Though a rifle had always been part of his baggage, he had not fired a shot for decades now.

Sir Arthur Blotton was disgusted at the sight of the Boat Woman's mess.

'How I fought the bureaucrats in Madras and London to get the anicuts built and canals dug! And this is the use we make of the waterways in India! Have a thought for this country, lady, have a thought! What are you in need of, pillaging the land of its flora, fauna, and precious metals?'

The Boat Woman retaliated, 'Don't preach, old man. Thank you very much for gifting us a means of reaching the interior of this land. He who has the gun will rule, and we are the rulers. Your job is to keep the anicut in good trim, and the canals flowing. Make sure of that. If you don't, you may lose your job and go back to the highlands you come from. For the railway will be here, sooner than later.'

The old man reflected for a while.

'I dread the prospect of the railways.'

'I love the prospect of the railways. Transportation by canal is awfully slow. And the load ceiling too is low, too low. Now that you mention it, I shall ask my friends back home to press the prime minister to process the papers more quickly—ahem, more expeditiously—than they are used to. And then I won't have to face your ill-tempered talk, your annual rigmarole.'

At this point it was time to bring in Her Majesty. Miss Beston read out to her audience a line or two from the gracious Queen Empress's letter; she even allowed them to hold the fine sheet of Whatman paper with the royal insignia.

∞

Before BA Garu's arrival, a ryot had brought every year, in early summer, a load of raw mangoes for making pickles. BA Garu would not think of abbreviating an everyday joy. He asked Appachchi if she would accompany him to the mango orchard. She looked at Worker Aunt for support but didn't receive much help. BA Garu went to the byre, yoked the bullocks to the cart, and brought around the double bullock cart to the front door. The floor of the cart carried a trough made of bamboo laths; it could easily accommodate a thousand mangoes.

BA Garu was very good with cattle, a match to his young bride in handling mute creatures. He had won the approval of the villagers with the way he drove the bullock cart, without once using the lash. It gave him more satisfaction than his academic distinction and honours. 'Hang on, tightly,' he cautioned his wife now, seated in the cart right behind him. The rains last year had created potholes in the cattle paths. Jolting and knocking against the wall of the bamboo bowl, Appachchi hung on gamely to the cart's stanchions.

When they reached their mango orchard, BA Garu unyoked the bullocks and unravelled some fodder from the apron of the cart. He patted them and whispered some loving words to them; they swished their tails in happiness.

He went looking for the entry point in the thorn fence, Appachchi following him. He couldn't find the opening, so they called out a few times in case anyone was inside. At last, they heard a responsive echo. A wizened ryot materialized around a bend in the distance and waved them to his right. There, they entered the orchard through a makeshift nettle thatch gate which BA Garu lifted with a staff and pushed back.

The ryot suggested that for the mangoes to make the best pickles they should move further into the orchard. They went by a narrow footpath, stepping clear of occasional caravans of fierce tree-ants.

'Here it is,' said BA Garu, and patted the ryot on his back for bringing them to the right tree. The man shrank back; no upper-caste person had touched him. What would Worker Aunt say? He had heard of the strange ways of her brother and his wife, though.

The tree was decked with green mangoes almost the size of coconuts. BA Garu could just barely cover the green fruit with both his hands. With a harvest sickle the ryot cut a piece each for the master and the mistress. He said, 'Good, lots of fibre and the right taste. Just right for avakkai.' He was satisfied with their response: both crinkled their noses and made faces like monkeys that had eaten one tamarind too many. The ryot's creased face relaxed into a smile and swelled with pride.

When he could operate his tongue again, BA Garu said, 'Yes, good for avakkai, you are right. Now, what is your name?'

'Appadu, ayya.'

'Just hand me the plucking crook. Good, you just stand there and tell me where you can see the most fleshy fruit. I am going to climb the tree.'

The ryot's face fell. He could foresee Worker Aunt scolding him severely.

The ryot's family, who had been standing deferentially at a distance so far, now stepped closer for a ringside view.

'What will I tell Amma garu, ayya?'

BA Garu noticed that Appadu had ignored his seniority, and he knew that Appachchi had noticed it as well because she was smiling mischievously. Power hierarchy had nothing to do with seniority among siblings, it seemed!

'You have duly warned me, haven't you? And you have a witness here, am I right?'

He ignored the apprehension in the ryot's face.

'I am going to go up with you,' said Appachchi.

The ryot's jaw fell open. His children were delighted. A spectacle awaited them.

Women in his family, his own daughters, were of course known to climb, and occasionally, fall and break their bones. But he had not so far heard of an upper-class lady, and that too a Brahmin and his own landlady, climbing trees. BA Garu felt sorry for him. He had received too many shocks for one day.

BA Garu assured him, 'It's all right, I am there to take care of her,' he said. 'You just guide us. By the way, are you girls going to school?'

The children nodded their dishevelled heads.

'Don't remove them from the school,' said Appachchi. 'Next time you come to us, bring them along.'

But there was only one plucking crook. So BA Garu said they should take turns, or he would use the crook to reach the top branches and she could pick fruit from the lower branches as far as she could reach. 'Watch out for wood ants, they are zealous guardians of the tree goddess.'

Granny Appachchi tied the ends of her sari around her waist and climbed up the tree. She plucked and threw each fruit to the ryot and his children, who joyously participated in the tamasha. BA Garu nicely nicked the stalk and dropped the fruit in a satchel. He emptied it gently on the bed of dry and green leaves arranged by the ryot's family.

When it was all over—they had collected four hundred mangoes by the time the sun had climbed to the top—the ryot went up a toddy palm and cut bunches of palmyra fruit. He came down, chopped their tops, and gave them the luscious kernels filled with delicious clear juice and jelly. BA Garu gave a rupee to each member of the family.

'You need anything, Amma garu will—I will talk to elder Amma garu.' And he himself would keep a tab on the daughters' progress.

✸

BA Garu had come back from Madras with plenty of books, and with the white man's evil ways. 'But then,' he reasoned later to his friend John, 'which nation or people can say with pride that they haven't contributed their mite to collective misery? History is a bottle of horrors.'

For Appachchi and Podumburra's benefit, he chose however to look at the unexpected and unintended dividends of recent history.

BA Garu said that it had all started—if a beginning of something can be definitely fixed—with the Dutch supplying spices to the British. Like good neighbours, the English and the Dutch had scant respect for each other. One day, the Dutch suddenly raised the price of pepper from three to six shillings a pound. That was a hundred per cent raise, and on a commodity on which the English had been hooked. But, of course, food habits are important only as a source of profit; the merchants were no sentimental lot, they never were, and never are—is Ringworm Subbayya interested in our family or in the hard and ready cash you shell down promptly every time you visit his shop and buy groceries from him?

First to seek the new learning were the upper castes. Obviously. He talked at length of Telugus who had made it big by learning the language, mostly on their own. A nation is built on a foundation of unsung heroes, like Ranganatham—a product of a primitive school system.

Appachchi could never learn enough about Chennapatnam and the college there. And her young husband would never fail to satisfy her. He told her that among the first to profit from the white man's dominance were the Brahmins. Either in Bengal, or here. Private munshis not only tutored white officers in Telugu; they also helped them in every other way, short of giving their daughters to them. The famous English pundit, Peterson, learned his Telugu alphabet from Velagapudi Kodandaramayya garu and Peterson later got his teacher the head examinership in Fort St. George. 'I was examined by him. Peterson told me that a book written by a munshi had got his friend Mayo 1,750 rupees from the Kumpini. And you know that's a lot of money for a pundit! Many civil servants try their hand at compiling dictionaries and are rewarded by the Kumpini.'

But sadly, BA Garu continued, English language and literature were one thing and the board of examiners in Chennapatnam was another. 'They were interested in manufacturing mere English teachers, not lovers of English literature.' He opened his personal file and out fell a loose, dog-eared sheet. He looked at it sadly. 'There is no better way of finishing off your interest in the language than appearing for this examination.'

It was an old question paper from his FA examination of Madras University.

'But look at the syllabus,' he said. 'The question paper gives us an idea of the General English syllabus. Look at the questions, the English board of examiners think they ought to vie with the Sanskrit pundits. Instead of making Sanskrit easy like English, easy for us Indians to learn, they make English as complicated as Sanskrit grammar....dukhrun karane, dukhrun karane.'

Appachchi laughed with BA Garu. She knew the allusion. Once the great Sankaracharya had come upon a scholar on a riverbank, committing to memory a bit of Sanskrit grammar, 'dukhrun karane, dukhrun karane'. Sankara went to him and told him that dukhrun karane was not going to help him; it was only the Lord's name and His worship which would carry one across the river of life.

'Apart from its prestige as the language of new rulers and as almost the sole passport to government service and public or professional careers, English had the historical advantage of coming to India at a time when Sanskrit and Persian had long played out their mission as languages of enlightenment and had become mere custodians of past glory and sanctuaries of orthodoxy.

'The administrator, the missionary, the imperialist—each wanted English introduced for his own narrow purpose.

'Though a taluk office had been established at Bhimavaram as early as in 1817,' he said, 'the Kumpini started the first English college in the Coromandel only in 1853, and it was started at Rajahmundry.'

As for Indians themselves…they knew which way the wind was blowing. They had whole-heartedly taken to Persian some centuries earlier, with the Muslim conquest, and had mastered that language. It was obvious to them that a similar strategy with regard to English was now called for…. BA Garu said with pride that Indians had a tongue for languages, 'a tongue of tongues'.

Soon, BA Garu set about the ambitious task of improving the English of his young wife. He convinced her of the need to learn the language of the white people. He did not have to try hard to get her to agree; she had been taught the alphabet and been introduced to a couple of readers printed in Chennapatnam.

'You have it in you, you'll learn it fast,' he told her.

In just six months Appachchi had picked up enough English grammar to appreciate his comments on the question paper.

And with her by his side, BA Garu analysed the question paper.

> What is case? Name and explain the functions of the different cases of the noun.

Impossible.

> Write down the plural forms of:
> father-in-law, genus, series, alkali, deer, phenomenon.

Possible.

Another interesting one:

> Convert the following—addressed by Brutus to Cassius—
> into the indirect speech, modernizing where necessary:
> That you do love me, I am nothing jealous;
> What you would work me to, I have some aim
> How I have thought of this and of these times,
> I shall recount hereafter, for this present,
> I would not, so with love I might entreat you,
> Be any further moved.

Murdering Brutus, slaying Shakespeare. Later, later.

> How are the words rebel, august, minute, contrast affected by the position of the accent?

This question must have been smuggled in by the English pundit's British boss. We Indians must be taking a toll of the English officers' patience. But then, is accent as important?

Appachchi decided then she could never do it. But BA Garu was on her side, and everyone said he spoke like an Englishman. 'I shall help you, speak to me in English as often as you can,' he told her.

Months later, when they had had enough of the English language, BA Garu regaled Appachchi with stories from Greek classics: the exploits of Achilles and Odysseus, and the terrible fate of their comrade, Agamemnon. Overnight, Clytemnestra had entered Appachchi's demonology.

∽

BA's photo appeared in *The Chronicle* of Madras for the second time. He had written an article, 'India at Crossroads'. The editor mentioned that he had been the first from the river district to graduate from Madras University.

BA Garu's article in the scholarly journal brought a good friend of his from Chennapatnam to the remote village of Sakhinetipalli.

John Pathappan surprised his best friend; he simply materialized in Sakhinetipalli, and his cart was escorted by a sizable crowd of villagers. John was not in the cart; only his luggage was.

In his friend's presence, BA Garu seemed to do nothing else except quote from the Bible—not Solomon—and English classics. He ceaselessly recited English poetry, line after line from Shakespeare—in particular from *Macbeth* and *Othello*.

And he quoted from *Hamlet*:

> There are more things in heaven and earth
> Than are dreamt of in your philosophy, Horatio.

'Do you believe it?' John asked him.

'I don't know.'

∞

Towards the end of the century, on her way back to Sakhinetipalli, Miss Beston too got hold of a copy of a question paper of Madras University; so many in England had mentioned the prestigious institution. She sat down with her munshi and Jane and scrutinized it.

If a horse falls down, I miss the train.

This is pure fantasy, an adventure for the closet paper-setter. As though he travels by train every other day, as though it is his way of life. Going to Madras by train must have been the very pinnacle of his life's ambition.

Supply the future auxiliary for each person.

Possible.

How would you recast the conditional clause, if it is to express a supposition opposed to the actual fact, employing first that 'the horse did not fall', and secondly that 'the horse did fall', and what corresponding changes would have to be made in the consequent clauses?

This is what I call pedantry, showing off scholarship. We will take this up later, later.

The stream was very shallow. Consequently, I could not swim in it.

Express the thought of these two sentences (1) in a simple sentence, employing (i) the expression 'too shallow,' (ii) the correlatives 'so'—'as,' and also (2) in a complex sentence, employing the correlatives 'so'—'that.'

Not bad, can be considered.

> Mark the accents on development, executor, incapacitated, committee.

Put off, put off.

> Mark the feet and accents in:
> The first of gold which this
> inscription bears,
> 'Who chooseth me shall gain what
> many men desire.'
> Russet lawns and fallows grey
> Where the nibbling flocks to stray.
> 'It's the voice of the sluggard;
> I heard him complain
> 'You have waked me too soon,
> I must slumber again.'

Unless you wish to write poetry like Wordsworth, keep off this area.

> Point out in what respects the language of the following extract differs from the language ordinarily employed in prose:
> All in a moment through the gloom
> were seen
> Ten thousand banners rise into the air,
> With orient colours waving, with
> them rose
> A forest huge of spears and
> Thronging helms
> Appeared.

This is what I call an invitation to adventure. An attractive proposition. In other words, he is asking us to tell him the difference between straightforward prose and creative writing. You can do it at various levels, analyse various aspects of creative communication, and benefit from the exercise. Very good question.

Write out the following, carefully punctuated:

Tell me not in mournful numbers life is but an empty dream for the soul is dead that slumbers and things are not what they seem life is real life is earnest and the grave is not its goal dust thou art to dust returneth was not spoken of the soul.

Yes, yes, yes! Punctuation is not just signposts used by a writer to guide the reader; at its best it can make your style terse, creative. We should aim at that level of mastery.

∽

John was quite a sensation in the settlement of untouchables. Black BA Garu, the villagers told each other in wonder.

'MA garu!' corrected BA Garu.

'That's enough!' laughed John. 'These innocent people have done enough damage to my ego already!'

They could not believe their eyes and ears, an untouchable! John was of the fifth caste! But this man looked like a dora, dressed like a dora, smoked a pipe like a dora, talked the tongue like a dora, while speaking Telugu like a Tamil. Scores of field hands, peasants, and others flocked to take a look at him. The toddy tapper and peasant sharecropper, Simhadri, who had returned Granny Appachchi's jewellery to Worker Aunt was there as well; as was Appadu, with his wife and daughters.

After the first day, John said that his tongue felt like rubber; the cuisine from Worker Aunt's famous kitchen impressed him without satisfying him. BA Garu commissioned Simhadri's services. The mutton and egg and fish, shot through and through with Telugu spices, from the tapper's hut overwhelmed the city man.

And not just that. When the young man from Chennapatnam

spoke to them in their own tongue, Simhadri and his neighbours insisted on washing John's clothes. Appadu's wife, Punyalu, washed his garments and pressed them with live coals in a brass chembu. John had only one message for them: never ever rely on the tender feelings of the upper castes; the panacea for all your ills is education. They all turned and looked at BA Garu; he had said this to them umpteen times, but now they had before them an example.

'Send your children, boys and girls, to school. My own father was a cobbler; even now he is, and he sent me to the mission school; now, of course, there is no need for him to earn wages.'

BA Garu agreed. 'The weapon of weapons to end all our social ills is education. Give any community, however backward, a couple of generations of education, even just one. And see what the result will be.'

At the turn of the century, when John started his political party, as many as seven young men from the region joined him. Young Podumburra, on vacation from the English school in Rajahmundry, and a camp follower of BA Garu, was an avid member of the audience. Podumburra started the largest and best co-ed school in Rajahmundry.

He was enchanted not just by John Pathappan's words but also by his smile; he recalled it always with pleasure. He came to know from his own personal experience with various gurus, especially the Guru of the Stream, that Divinity in man reflects itself in the human visage. Decades later, during a social reform campaign, when Podumburra went back to Granny Appachchi for help, he found the same light in her visage. Judged by the best examples, the Guru had said, all religions are the same; the very base is the same: spirituality.

John honoured Podumburra by addressing some of his remarks to him. John was the second man in Podumburra's life who made him feel that he could go on listening to him forever. It was thanks to the two Madras University graduates that Podumburra pursued seriously his interest in history, in the Bible and the Indian scriptures, and did law from the same university.

He loved listening to the two men debate.

They were discussing the two most touching scenes in the Bible: Peter's denial of Jesus, and Jesus's last moments on the cross. Peter the Rock! The Rock on which the Church was founded later. 'You cannot ask for a better understanding of human nature,' said John Pathappan. 'The First Disciple's infidelity lies very close to the surface. And even with divine impulse, man is not able to resist temptation,' said John. 'Peter's conduct is a striking demonstration of common human weakness; but Peter wept bitterly: Peter neither concealed it nor excused his lapse.'

Said BA Garu: 'Repentance is the best form of sadhana. Incidentally, doesn't Pathappan mean Peter?'

'Yes. Pathappan is Peter in Malayalam.'

On Jesus's last words on the cross, John said, 'These words of Jesus are quoted from *Psalms* 22:2, the opening line. Matthew quotes the psalm partly in Hebrew and partly in Aramaic. It was used by the early church as a psalm of the Passion. As such, it is used by Matthew as a prophecy, not as a cry of abandonment expressed by Jesus.'

Though he did not really need help, Podumburra was back the next day with his maths notebook. He sought the visiting scholar's help in solving a problem or two. BA Garu was surprised: 'You know I am not good at maths, but how did you come to know John is as good a mathematician as he is a historian?'

Podumburra smiled shyly.

John Pathappan was a Malayali. He had gone to college in Calcutta. BA Garu had told Appachchi that graduates of Kumpini colleges denounced their own religion. Granny Appachchi said, 'Don't tell vadina.'

Worker Aunt stoutly refused to entertain the visitor at home, especially when BA Garu told her that John's father was a cobbler.

'For one seru, a seru and quarter.' Dondu dondey. And she could not understand why her brother expressed such affinity with his friend.

So, Granny Appachchi suggested lodging the friend away at a safe distance in the farmhouse on the banks of the great wide-backed river, not far from the untouchable settlement. The friend considered this a particular favour; the place so charming, and the untouchable colony not far off—its people so simple, so different from the city types. And Appachchi eagerly listened to their discussions and debates; recitations of passages from the Bible and English literature, especially Shakespeare, were melodious to her ears.

'Leave the two men to themselves,' Worker Aunt advised her. And Granny Appachchi stayed put in her room, but BA Garu brought his friend to the veranda, from where she could hear every word they uttered.

The two men discussed everything under the sun.

'History is the worst adversary to proselytization,' said John. 'When we Indians are taught to question the validity of our own gods, we, English-educated Indians, question also the validity of the Bible and the truth of its narrative.' He gave the example of Raja Rammohun Roy's book on Christianity.

'Do you?' BA Garu asked.

'Of course, not,' John responded. 'The moment I lose faith in the Book, I shall leave the fold.'

They both agreed on the importance of sadhana, spiritual striving. John quoted Eckhart: '"If thou do not fail in intention, but only in capacity, verily, thou hast done all in the sight of God."' He added: '"Whoever strives and labours, him may we bring redemption."'

John said, 'Knowledge leads to devotion.'

BA Garu cited the *Chandogya Upanishad*: '"The devas and the asuras are both born of Prajapati." In each man are these two kingdoms of light and of darkness.... The Mahabharata says "Nothing is wholly good or wholly evil." The Gita lists the qualities of a true devotee: freedom of spirit, friendliness to all, patience, and tranquillity. He is not a source of grief to any; no one can make him feel grief. He renounces the fruits of all his actions. His acts are skilled, daksa—pure and passionless. He does not lose himself in reverie or dream but knows his way in the world.'

'That's the opposite of me,' BA Garu continued and chuckled. 'The saved soul grows into the likeness of the Divine and assumes an unchangeable being.... Compare: "Be ye therefore perfect, even as your Father which is in heaven is perfect."'

'Matthew Chapter V verse 48,' said John. 'This has implications. This can lead to the greatest sin of all, the sin of Lucifer, the claim to be godhead.'

On the caste system, BA Garu quoted from the *Dhammapada*: '"Not by matted hair, nor by lineage, nor by birth is one a Brahmin. He is a Brahmin in whom there are truth and righteousness."'

'John, you are a Brahmin,' said BA Garu with a smile.

'No, thank you, friend, I am happy with what I am, a lowly Indian.'

'"Those who believed and led a righteous life are the best creatures,"' Podumburra, who had been silently listening to the conversation, quipped.

'The Koran?' asked John. Podumburra nodded.

The following day, they turned to another topic.

'How many languages have you learned in Madras?' Appachchi asked John.

'Only six.'

'Six!'

'Yes, that is because I am lazy. And then I clutter my brain with junk. But that is no excuse, it just so happens some of us have a flair for languages. I know of people in the districts who have picked up several languages just from dictionaries.'

Said BA Garu: 'Local scholars have always interacted with white officers of the Kumpini and have been encouraged suitably by them.

Look at Seshacharyulu and the Boat Woman. All that they have in common is an interest in books and English poetry. Of course, it is also a kind of challenge the white scholars brought to our pundits. Take Alladi Ramachandrayya, for instance.'

'Ramachandrayya of Nellooru?'

'Yes, the same. He was employed by an influential white officer. Rama didn't believe a word of what his master Wilkinson told him in geography and astronomy but kept on arguing for six years that what the Gita says is the only truth. Then he was converted to modern thought, the English ways of thinking. Thinking changes first, then costume.'

'Of course costume can come first, and thinking never! The same old cobwebs fill some minds. There is no physic for false ideas.'

'Gajula Lakshminarasu Chetty established Madras native society,' said John. Because the natives, pundits, and merchants, uneducated in English education, believed that the white officers of the Kumpini in Madras were supreme; they didn't know of the Board in England. The redoubtable Chetty conducted a tour for an influential politician from Britain, what they call a Member of Parliament, and the dignitary was shocked to see outside the taluk office tax defaulters hung upside down from trees, and in various other ways tortured.'

Added John with a wry smile: 'He also opposed and protested missionary activity and the open support of missionaries by Kumpini officers and judges who propagated Christianity in courts. Ran a paper called *Crescent*.'

In the days that flew by, too quickly for Podumburra, John and BA Garu strolled along the embankment of the river and discussed other authors: Adam Smith, Newton, Wollstonecraft, and Macaulay.

BA Garu had known John Pathappan as the scholar who had read Macaulay better than anyone else in Calcutta or Madras. All that he needed was to trigger the scholar in him. BA Garu said quietly, 'The English colonialist perspective is exposed in Macaulay's Minute'.

John took his cue.

'This extraordinary man—amazing energy!' said John, 'believed in educating Indians in English medium because their native dialects were "so poor and rude that, until they are enriched from some other quarter, it will not be easy to translate any valuable work into them."'

'Let's accept the English language, Western education,' said BA Garu.

John Pathappan nodded.

'Still, his ignorance does not impress me,' continued BA Garu, 'his arrogance does. The English colonialist perspective lies just below the surface in the Minute.'

'Who is to blame?' asked John Pathappan. 'Where are the translations?'

'That's true, but why dismiss what you do not know?' asked BA Garu.

'He didn't, your own co-religionists did. Not just Raja Roy, but your own fellow Telugu, Soob Row.'

'I am not just thinking of his attitude to Indian classics. See what he says: "The literature of England is now more valuable than that of classical antiquity".'

'That certainly is not true,' John went on, 'and this attitude of praising something at the expense of something else irritates me. And Macaulay himself had said earlier that behind today's English literature there was the nurturing of classical antiquity.'

'Besides,' John Pathappan went on, 'in perhaps the most engaging part of the Minute, Macaulay stated his goal for English education in India, to "form a class who may be interpreters between us and the millions whom we govern; a class of persons, Indian in blood and colour, but English in taste, in opinions, in morals, and in intellect". And these people were to then aid in governing and civilizing the natives of India, in order that they would conform to British rule.... Now look at yourself; you have been an outstanding product of Macaulay's dream, his mission. How anglicized are you? And look at me: I may look so, but am I?'

BA Garu conceded his friend too wasn't a dream child. 'We are the exceptions. The vast majority may prove the old Whig right.'

'But it is the exceptions that change the destiny of a nation. What we Indians seem to overlook or forget is the other Macaulay, the British politician and parliamentarian.'

'Macaulay was a radical. He inherited this streak of humanism from his father. Macaulay pleased his father with his role in abolishing the British slave trade in the West Indies. Thomas is a good specimen of the British middle class. He came to India to make money and clear his father's debts. He succeeded. Indians owe the Minute to personal circumstance and middle-class morality.'

'Whig in England,' said BA Garu, 'imperialist in India!'

John cited another, a more imaginative, creative Whig: Defoe. 'Daniel Defoe!'

'Robinson Crusoe!' exclaimed Podumburra.

'Yes, that great middle-class guardian of the English nation: Defoe. He had complained that Indian cloth had "crept into our houses, our closets, and bed chambers; curtains, cushions, chairs, and at last beds themselves were nothing but calicos or India stuffs."'

'Nationhood is the dream child of the middle-class! It is a figment of their imagination. Earlier, it was the aristocracy, in future it will be the mythopoeic middle-class making and marring nations,' said BA Garu.

'True! And well said,' replied John Pathappan. 'But Macaulay was creative, he had the right instincts, and that included the English instinct for what works. He offered his countrymen a clear choice: reform or revolution.'

'What do we call it? Instincts or statecraft?' asked BA Garu.

John savoured Macaulay's prose:

Governments, like men, may buy existence too dear.
Propter vitam vivendi perdere causas, To lose the reason for

living, for the sake of staying alive.

The mere extent of empire is not necessarily an advantage. It would be, on the most selfish view of the case, far better for us that the people of India were well governed and independent of us, than ill governed and subject to us; that they were ruled by their own kings, but wearing our broadcloth, and working with our cutlery, than that they were performing their salams to English collectors and English magistrates, but were too ignorant to value, or too poor to buy, English manufactures. To trade with civilized men is infinitely more profitable than to govern savages. That would, indeed, be a doting wisdom, which, in order that India might remain a dependency, would make it a useless and costly dependency, which would keep a hundred million of men from being our customers in order that they might continue to be our slaves.

'Substitute slaves with customers,' said BA Garu, 'you gain all round'.

'My dear friend, note the candour: "the most selfish view", he says. And it is.'

'Now I know the fountainhead. Thank you, John. You should write a book on him. I was under the impression it is we Indians who have been affected by the Minute; thanks for the perspective. We are being ruled by intellectuals and philosophers sold on the Macaulayesque vision. It is Macaulay's philosophy which has inspired the best of the British administrators in India so far. He must have been the great influence on even people like Munro: help India, govern India well, so that they can be a good market for British merchandise and manufacture....'

'Perhaps,' said John, 'that's vulgarizing human nature.... The best administrators, like Munro, however powerful this commercial prospect in their minds, must have governed well because that was the only governance they knew. Give them credit. It is something in the imperial air. The best of them are humanists and loyal subjects of Her Majesty at the same time. No, there is no contradiction as far as the English nation is concerned. They would have done whatever they have, Macaulay or no Macaulay.'

'The worst administrators haven't read Macaulay, or haven't understood him. Macaulay promoted British middle-class commercial interests in India as no one else had.'

'True,' said John. 'But I have fallen for his rhetoric. His rhetoric must make sense to every sensible Englishman today.

> Are we to keep the people of India ignorant in order that we may keep them submissive? Or do we think that we can give them knowledge without awakening ambition? Or do we mean to awaken ambition and to provide it with no legitimate vent? Who will answer any of these questions in the affirmative? Yet one of them must be answered in the affirmative, by every person who maintains that we ought permanently to exclude the natives from high office. I have no fears. The path of duty is plain before us: and it is also the path of wisdom, of national prosperity, of national honour.

'Which nation?' asked BA Garu. 'The English! At the expense of India and the other colonies, the English are painting the world red, the pale red of penury.'

'That's a little unfair. The English have given us our own scriptures; it has given me the greatest book of my life.'

'That's true. English has given me the Bible as well our own scriptures. Nothing is wholly good or wholly evil, as the Mahabharata says.'

Podumburra nodded his head vigorously.

For BA Garu, recent British Indian history was another bottle of horrors. And in a hamlet like Sakhinetipalli, with how many people could he discuss such topics of intellectual interest, especially when he held them with such sentimental fervour? Yes, occasionally,

Nephew was there; but then, the elder's interests and opinions were rather different.

The young boy Podumburra occasionally joined them; he was a listener, soaking up ideas and views, storing them away for future, when he would himself graduate and sit down as an equal with intellectuals like John Pathappan. For now, Podumburra experienced the joy of listening to John expounding on recent British Indian history.

'Come to Madras,' John said to Podumburra, 'for your higher studies.'

BA Garu looked fondly at the boy, and Granny Appachchi caught that glance.

'Consider the drama,' John said, 'The drama of British conquest of India: by 1818, the entire Indian subcontinent, except the Punjab and Sindh, had been brought under British control, now free to "reach out to the natural frontiers of India."'

'Substitute: natural resources,' chipped in BA Garu.

John had the gift of perspective. He took Macaulay back to the beginning.

The British completed the task of conquering the whole of India from 1818 to 1857. Till 1813, the British had followed a policy of non-interference in the religious, social, and cultural life of India, but after 1813 they took active steps to transform Indian society and culture and create markets for their industrial goods.

'I agree, the methods of the old brigandage are changing,' said BA Garu. 'It is the British industry, it is English capital, which will be the future instruments of change here.'

After Muslim havoc in the last century, John reminded them, a famous deity surrounded Himself with bees: it was change for the better for the natives of the Coromandel. Under the chaotic revenue system earlier, not more than one-fifth or one-sixth of produce had been retained by the ryot. And until Sleeman put an end to them in the North, the thugs, like sound entrepreneurs, converted rupees to pagodas.

'However,' said BA Garu to Appachchi, 'some of these whites were no better than pindaris; the British engaged in looting Bengal and Bihar. John Sullivan, president of the Board of Revenue, Madras, wrote to his underlings: "our system acts very much like a sponge, drawing up all the good things from the banks of the Ganges, and squeezing them on the banks of the Thames."'

He noticed the concern in his wife's eyes. He added: 'But of course, that's what so many nations have done, and will do, to those who are not so fortunate. They have just started on Africa now.' He pressed her hand gently. Podumburra relaxed.

BA Garu was not happy with Lord Cornwallis. This man was the inspiration for the post-Mutiny Englishman: he began systematically keeping Indians at an elbow's distance, methodically excluding them from positions in government; what the delegate of the Queen started, her loyal servants and families emulated with expatriate zeal. They distanced themselves steadily, studiedly, conscientiously from the natives. Even that great Coromandel scholar Mr Black went out of his way to claim, to the surprise of everyone, his Indian friends as well as his colleagues in the government, that he had never associated with the natives. This was further compounded by a general and profound sense of racial arrogance. Europeans had very little connection with the natives of any religion.

BA Garu concluded what John had begun. 'And the French Revolution, changing European thinking—new attitudes of mind, manners, and morals—are appearing in our midst now. Young Indians are confident India will rise again.' He turned to Podumburra and said, 'Am I right, young scholar?'

The little man nodded bravely.

'Another Mutiny!' exclaimed John.

Podumburra turned to BA Garu.

'No,' BA Garu said. 'The Mutiny was mindless violence; the whites were more brutal, though; violence was their credo.'

He added, reflectively, 'The old, free, and unselfconscious relationship between Indians and the British is rapidly disappearing.'

He was not complaining.

∽

John showed interest in the Guru of the Stream. And when they made the journey to meet him, Podumburra tagged along. They listened to the Guru's teaching along with his devotees:

> The seeds of wrong behaviour will not germinate and grow into painful events in our life if the wrongdoers engage in loving service to those who are in need of sustenance, courage, love, and help…a lifetime of good deeds will cover a multitude of past sins. If you're constant in your service, the bad seeds may die away.
> Loving service to those who are in need is the form of devotion most pleasing to the Divine.
> 'He Himself is a flame of love.'
> He tells us: 'He who selflessly renders service, sweetened with love, to My creatures, he who sees Me in everyone and in everything; he who remembers Me at every moment is the yogi nearest to Me.'
> Deserve the grace of God by helping the weak and the poor, the diseased and the disabled, the distressed and the downtrodden.... More than listening to a hundred lectures or delivering them to others, offering one act of genuine service attracts the grace of God.
> How far are you practising the precepts of the Bhagavad Gita?

'Or of Jesus?' whispered John.

> Devotion must find expression in dedicated service to the Lord. When you look upon the world as a manifestation of the Divine, you are bound to receive the grace of the Lord.

Be simple and sincere. It is sheer waste of money to burden the pictures and idols in the shrines and altars of your homes with a weight of garlands and to parade costly utensils and vessels and offerings to show off your devotion. This is deception; it demeans Divinity, imputing to it the desire for pomp and publicity. I ask only for purity for heart, to shower grace. Do not posit distance between you and me; do not interpose the formalities of the guru–shishya relationship.... You are waves; I am the ocean. Know this and be free, be Divine.

Service can instil more intensely than any other activity the sense of the basic One.

Service broadens your vision, widens your awareness, deepens your compassion.... No other sadhana can bring you into the incessant contemplation of the oneness of all living beings. You feel another's pain as yours, you share another's success as your own.

The sick man, the poor man, the suffering man, the illiterate man, the wicked man are all limbs of the same body, of which you too are parts.

You are not alleviating the distress of that other person, you are offering worship to the Lord, in that form, in that body. There is no place in the world that is not filled with this bliss. Every object in the world contains this innate bliss.

Your imaginings, your inferences, your judgments and prejudices, your passions, emotions, and egotistic desires muddy the consciousness and make it opaque. How then can you become aware of the Atma that is at the very base? Through service rendered without any desire to placate one's ego and with only the well-being of others in view, it is possible to cleanse the consciousness and have the Atma revealed.

So, for whose sake are you performing service? For your own sake.

By saturating the service with love, work can be transformed into worship—nishkama-karma.

Service without idea of self is the very first step in the spiritual progress. For it trains you to transcend all the distinctions artificially imposed by history and geography and to realize that the human community is One and indivisible.

BA Garu was moved, there were tears in Podumburra's eyes. 'Jesus,' said John, 'this man has taken me to the Mount of Beatitudes!

> Blessed are the merciful,
> For they shall obtain mercy.
> Blessed are the pure in heart,
> For they shall see God.
> Blessed are the peacemakers,
> For they shall be called sons of God.

'Be free, be Divine,' John repeated. He looked at Podumburra, reached out his hand, and patted the boy's head.

Subdue the senses, do acts of charity, be compassionate—says the *Brihadaranyaka Upanishad*.

Podumburra nodded.

It is indeed the mind that is the cause of men's bondage and liberation. The mind that is attached to sense-objects leads to bondage, while dissociated from sense-objects it tends to lead to liberation. So they think—says the *Amritabindu Upanishad*.

After his sermon, the Guru of the Stream called them in for an interview.

∽

Miss Beston and Mr Blotton too debated to an audience of civilians and soldiers.

'No doubt,' said Miss Beston, 'some of the English women consider themselves ladies forever, whatever the circumstances.' She didn't mention names. 'Take the woman who amused herself when her husband was on tour by shooting tigers and then returning to camp and sitting down to do exquisite needlepoint. In the earlier decades they hadn't exposed Englishwomen to the horrors of the Indian hot season. But now that so much unemployment is there in Britain, India is more attractive than, say, West Africa....

'There is a change taking place in the mind of the white woman in India. Without being conscious of it they are building and relying on inherited wisdom about India; they are coming to rationalize the convictions and prejudices of their own culture towards others that it considers to be less developed, an attitude that comes all the more easily when they are dealing with a subject race. They are part of an elite; they are a superior race.'

Mr Blotton gave grudging praise. 'Unlike Miss Beston, most British women in India had never really adapted to India. Then came the Mutiny; the horrors of the North, though far away, have terrified even the most sober Englishwoman in the Coromandel. The Mutiny has resulted in moral ossification. Racial superiority is no monopoly; scratch the local pundit, he will pour scorn on the white race. Not surprising that perfectly sensible European women are exposed these days to the cheap temptations of racial superiority. To gold lust and racial superiority, add imperial policy: the result, a heady brew. These perfectly sensible ladies deride anything Indian in India, a bewildering world, a world so dangerous.

'And the Brahmins return the compliment: "mlechchas", they call the white rulers; they have experienced a good sample of them, including the Dutch and the Portuguese.'

Miss Beston recalled to every visitor the experiences of a more volatile Englishwoman she knew.

A servant had actually saved her, his venerated memsahib, from snakebite by pulling her back. As it was a king cobra, she agreed that he had saved her from certain death, but, she was still convulsed with horror: 'He had touched me!'

'…Then?'

'Then what? The native was turned out, turned loose like an old horse no longer useful.'

Miss Beston resumed introspectively. 'Sadly, in the land of the blazing sun, we are all—male and female, ladies and gentlemen—we are all made to believe that we are the top people.'

'Not just in India, but anywhere.'

'What about you, do you feel the same way?'

'While in India, be an Indian!... Joking apart, it is sensible to conform in matters that do not cost you, that do not affect your commerce. Once in a while a maharaja may be invited for tea…but except those who contribute to the exchequer of your business….'

'Living in a semi-native style,' she said softly, as though to herself, 'had been slowly going out of repute among English officers even before the Mutiny.'

She lifted her arms. Mr Blotton noticed that there were no bangles on her arms, no bangles or bracelets to jingle.

Mr Blotton asked for the hookah.

∞

The Guru came and sat right opposite John.

'No need to take out your scrap paper of questions.'

John was taken back; he had worked on a list of questions to shoot at the Guru. BA Garu smiled, Podumburra folded his hands reverentially.

'You have thirteen questions on your list, you burned that candle down last night. Your first question: "How do you materialize things?" Let me show you.'

The Guru pulled his right sleeve up to his biceps, closed his shapely fist, swung it about three times, and turned his palm up. John's favourite sweet! The halwa was not fully formed yet; at the centre was a semi-solid mass and water was fast flowing into it from all around the palm.

'From the finer elements to the coarser elements,' BA Garu whispered.

The Guru smiled.

In a few seconds, the halwa was ready and he put it in John's hands. John winced: it was hot.

'Eat it,' the Guru said.

'May I share it with these friends?'

'No need, there is more in Baba's confectionary.'

Gulab jamun for Podumburra and jalebi for BA Garu and Appachchi.

'Now, your second question...' He methodically went over every question John had planned to ask.

As the Guru came to the end of John's invisible list, he said, 'Why haven't you shown the photo to your friend yet?'

For the first time, John blushed.

He fumbled a bit.

'Left side, inner pocket, next to the heart!' the Guru said. 'No more hesitation. She is a good girl. A good mate for you in your social service programme. Go ahead and marry her. And then she will be your comrade in your social reform campaign.'

As they moved from the ashram and across the clear stream rippling past, John turned to Podumburra and quoted *Hamlet*: 'There are more things in heaven and earth than are dreamt of in your philosophy, Horatio!'

BA Garu continued his sessions at home with an audience of two. He was charged up and the colloquies at the riverside had not satisfied him.

BA Garu warned Appachchi and Podumburra to guard themselves against what he called the 'Parallax of History'. An Englishman writes an English-biased history; an Indian, one favourable to Indian. European historians could not be trusted on India yet; they were still too close to the trauma of the Mutiny. Nor Indians: the punkah puller on the Boat Woman's staff used to be a Muslim noble! What all this land and its people have gone through!

'But how things are changing! Accept history,' he urged his audience of two.

In the Telugu districts, non-Brahmin munsifs are growing powerful and the influence of wily karanams (village officials) is declining; so, they are now sending their sons to English schools. Niyogi Brahmins are rising as district officers with English education; Niyogis seem quicker in learning to respond to the new English teaching: clerks, munshis, pundits working with whites are contributing greatly to the change in thinking.

'The possessor of learning becomes the possessor of wealth.'

BA Garu reflected for a few moments.

'Vaidikis next, perhaps—can the other castes be far behind? The new century will see them at the helm of affairs.' He turned rhetorically to Podumburra, who smiled in eager gratitude.

'Let us note the twofold service of the English language in India. Politically, it is already fostering and strengthening a sense of oneness more fully and more profoundly than ever before in the country's history. And instead of thwarting the development of Indian languages, English is acting as a powerful stimulus; all the major languages of India are being fertilized by this contact and will yield, some sooner, some later, rich harvests of their own. As a result of the encounter, India, a withered trunk, is suddenly shooting out with foreign foliage.'

Podumburra, nursing literary ambitions, privately resolved to write in Telugu, the people's language.

'Yet, village life of India in general will change far more sedately. The village payroll still remains what it has been for centuries: reddy, karanam, talari, thoti, neradi, purohitudu, schoolmaster, josi, vadla, kammari, kummari, chakali, mangali, medic, and prostitute.

'The first heap of grain still goes to servants of the village. When paddy is pounded, the pounding women still share the broken ones garnered at the end. While the gold hunters muddy the pool, down below is stirring the Indian psyche. The hills will be green again.'

⁂

John had offered a different view of the Indian village. 'The Indian village is but a sink of localism, a den of ignorance, narrow-mindedness, and communalism.'

By the end of his stay, however, John was charmed by Granny Appachchi and Worker Aunt; he loved the villagers and their ways and was amused by the reverence and awe in which they held any man in suit-boot.

'This village is an exception,' he concluded.

One of the many things on which the friends agreed was that one ought to have at least a few relationships unaffected by ego or filthy lucre.

John left by bullock bandy for the nearest railhead at Bhimadole to go to Rajahmundry. He had a first-class ticket; the Madras Mail had to halt for a minute or two exclusively for him—a nerve-racking event for the local stationmaster. From Rajahmundry he would go to Bandar; by boat from there to Madras, and then travel cross-country to Coimbatore.

'When will you show me a train?' asked Appachchi.

'Whenever you and sister are ready. We just have to go to Bhimadole, our nearest railhead.'

'You come with me, let's all go to Chennapatnam,' said John.

'No, not now,' said Appachchi. 'Later, perhaps,' she looked at BA Garu.

'You can take my outhouse if you don't want to live in my house.'

'A good idea, Meenu,' said her husband. 'Needs planning and preparation. We must persuade Chelli too.'

BA Garu and Granny Appachchi saw him off.

'Goodbye, John,' said BA Garu. 'Take care. Come next time

with your family.'

John patted his pocket. 'Of course!'

'You take care, too,' said John. 'You have a pretty wife, take care of her. And goodbye Meenakshi, goodbye Podumburra. May Jesus the Good Lord bless you both.'

'Goodbye, John,' repeated BA Garu. 'Take care.'

'What are the good omens?' John asked.

BA Garu looked at Appachchi.

'A bell chimes, an ass brays, a married woman walks towards you, or a corpse, any flowers, a toddy pot.'

'I know. And the evil omens?'

'One Brahmin, two Shudras, a widow, oil, a snake, or a sanyasi. A bad omen ought not to be mentioned.'

'I know. Now get out of my sight, one Brahmin. I want this married woman to walk towards me!' said John. They laughed.

Appachchi went ahead, turned, and walked towards John's bandy.

'Thank you, so much, Meenakshi,' he said.

As the bandy receded slowly, and disappeared behind the hills, BA Garu broke into a smile. He pointed to the sunlit hills for Appachchi to notice: the hills were sporting light greenery.

'BA Garu!' said Appachchi, almost breathlessly. She held his arm and pointed at Podumburra. The boy's upper lip too was sporting a delicate down. As the two adults gathered him in their embrace, Podumburra blushed.

∞

For a man supposed to be yearning for a child, BA Garu had a peculiar dream one day in Brahma Kalam.

It was a wisp of a cloud, like a melting fragment you see some days, all alone in the blue sky, floating along and so absolutely solitary, like the ghost of a piece of bark torn away from the tree by an elephant. But then the dream recurred, and it made him wonder what its significance could be. He narrated it to Appachchi. In the dream, there had also been a little girl, 'his daughter', but somehow he did not treat her like one—he harassed her, not physically torturing her, but went after her the whole day.

'You are so kind-hearted,' Appachchi said, 'how can you even think of such a possibility?'

He asked her to keep the dream to herself, but they worried over its significance.

Another day, it was a boy, his son. He had asked the child not to do something, but the boy disobeyed him. He walked away. BA Garu followed him quickly, shouting, 'Stop, stop!' Worker Aunt followed her brother, and he sensed why. She didn't want him to punish his son. So, he determined not to be physically violent, but to be gentle and firm, like all ideal fathers. When at long last the son did return to him, BA Garu held his arm so hard the boy winced, and he kept on hitting the little fellow until Worker Aunt rushed and rescued him. And this dream was too shameful, too intimate, to share even with his own Appachchi.

BA Garu concluded that God did not want to give him a child. Who knows, as a father he may really turn out to be a child-tormentor. 'Let's stop thinking of a child of our own,' he told Appachchi. 'Your sister-in-law is going to have several more, let's treat one of them as our own, We can adopt her.'

'How are you certain it is going to be a girl?' Appachchi asked him.

'I know,' said BA Garu.

As it happened, not much later, Raghu caught the smallpox and died.

Somehow, whenever they had thought of a baby of their own, both of them had thought of a female child. Now, after the dream, they stopped going to shrines and temples and mathams and holy places and sacred groves, worshipping and praying for the boon of a child. Worker Aunt had suggested all these rites and rituals; they owed her an explanation. At first, they hesitated to disclose the contents of his dream. But then one day BA Garu told his sister that he had had a dream in which God Subramanya appeared and said he should not think of a child of his own, but treat his sister's offspring as his own. And that was that.

She was terrified. 'It is a curse.'

'But the god was so benign,' said BA Garu. 'He gave me such a delicious smile, and he began and ended our meeting with the abhaya mudra. If it is a curse he should have behaved differently.'

And the following night, at the same time, Lord Subramanya appeared again in his dream and he said, in so many words, that he was pleased with the couple and what they were giving him or not giving him—not giving him was not not-giving, but was actually giving. And the god appeared in the dream of others too at the same time—all of them, including Worker Aunt—and it was the same unambiguous message: he was pleased with BA Garu and Appachchi and whatever he was doing was not to be misinterpreted. That was that. All talk about a baby stopped in the family and in the village.

Decades later, Granny Appachchi would play 'mother' to a 'girl child', a young woman, who had been married away at three and widowed at eight. This girl's marriage would be the first widow remarriage performed by Podumburra as a part of his social reform campaign.

And then, Granny Appachchi had her terrifying experience with the serpent, and BA Garu read up everything he could lay his hands on snakes. He sat with her and Worker Aunt, after meals, day after day, and told them what he had read.

Granny Appachchi approached Worker Aunt.

'Let's go to the fair,' Appachchi said. 'It will divert him.'

'It is not a place for decent women to go,' said Worker Aunt.

'BA Garu will come with us there.'

'Have you asked him?'

'Yes.'

'And he is willing?'

'Yes.'

'He must be crazy.'

'What do you say?'

'I won't. If I go with you to the fair, I will have enough trouble watching you and your funny ways to enjoy the fair. And I am in no physical condition to walk around the fair. The dust will only give me another cough.'

'Vadina, I promise, I shall behave myself.'

'How many times have you made that promise?'

'And broken it?'

'And broken it.'

'Only once or twice, that's all,' Appachchi laughed. Though Worker Aunt couldn't hold back her smile, she didn't change her mind.

It was a festival fair, in the Dussehra season. A cattle fair was also on, BA Garu was as much interested in it as Appachchi. There were excellent milch cows from the Godavari delta and heavenly bulls from Ongole. It was Appachchi's turn to educate her husband. 'The Ongole cows show much maternal love. And they keep a watch on their surroundings. Even after a long separation, they can recognize their masters with great loyalty and affection.... Ongole bulls are heavy; they're good as draught animals. Majestic in looks and gait. They have a long stride. Ryots believe that the hoof mark of the hind leg should fall ahead of the hoof mark of the foreleg. The longer the distance between the two the hardier the bull is.'

The peasant loved his animals; his language shows his affection for his life-mate. For example, in the lingo of the rural folk, 'eththu padadam' meant a bullock or cow gone too old to work or yield milk. At this stage, the ryot did not send it off to the butcher. Instead, when a bullock grew too old for service, it was retired from agricultural labour. The peasants oiled its neck and washed it well, and then applied oil and turmeric again.

They enquired how much the bullocks cost: each was priced between 10 and 20 varahas, or pagodas, or 3 and ½ rupees each; in the new rupees the price of a bullock was between 35 rupees and 70 rupees. That was a lot of money!

A huge pandal thatched with toddy palm fronds had been set up, and various stage shows were on.

At the bioscope, there was a big crowd waiting to buy tickets; they had managed to block the window of the ticket booth.

'Tuck your sari, and get on to my shoulders,' said BA Garu. 'And keep a copper ready. Don't put all the money in the ticket man's hands,' he warned her.

BA Garu raised Appachchi on his shoulders and approached the ticket window. He pushed away the people in his way; a few of them recognized him, and tried to squeeze themselves into the path he'd created.

Appachchi shouted at people to get out of the way. When they reached the ticket booth in the wall of the tent, the ticket master bent low and looked up with surprise at the young woman who towered over the others. He gave her two tickets.

They watched the moving pictures.

That was not the end of their adventure. By the time BA Garu returned home with his wife, he had become a hero. And a source of anxiety for the two women and Nephew.

Suddenly, a young bull had gone out of control, snapped her tether and ran, scattering the crowd. It butted fiercely whoever came in his way. People had shouted, 'Get out of the way! Get out of the way!'

'You wait here,' BA Garu had told Appachchi.

He had tucked in his dhoti, surged forward and grabbed the bull by its horns, and though the bull slowed down, it wouldn't stop, kicking up clouds of dust. A couple of men joined him and they had managed to subdue the intransigent beast.

'Meenu,' BA Garu had called. Appachchi was startled. His

voice was feeble. 'Meenu,' he'd whispered, 'Promise me. If anything happens to me, you will marry again.'

With that he had sagged to the ground. And, in no time, a red patch had formed in the dust. By the time they carted him to the government hospital at Rajahmundry, BA Garu had bled profusely. By the grace of the Guru of the Stream, he recovered. It took two months for him to recover fully.

One morning, the visit to the fair still giving her nightmares, Granny Appachchi opened her eyes feeling disturbed. Something had woken her up, a sixth sense, a superior power guarding her, and she opened her eyes just in time. It was her eyes that saved her, for her eyes held her husband's, and he froze as he stood there, over her, with a stone pestle in his hands. She said to him, 'BA Garu, what are you looking at me like that for?'

Her voice startled him. He came back from some other world, looked at himself and the pestle in his hands, and he was filled with alarm and overcome with shame.

'Ayyo, Meenu, I didn't know what was happening. What was I doing? What is this stone doing in my hands?'

Appachchi gently took the pestle from his hands, rose from her bed, and returned it to the kitchen. Then, she took him by his arm and led him back to their room, and giving him a glass of pot-chilled water, put him in bed. He fell asleep. A man who had never snored now snored like an oil mill and muttered in his sleep.

Appachchi got used to it, like the lion tamer gets used to putting his head in the beast's mouth every evening.

After BA Garu's death, Nephew, the only surviving elder male of the family, came to live with them. He turned out to be a practical counsellor for them and the villagers as he had been to his special clients, the Kshatriyas of Singapuram near the Papi Hills.

But then.

Death came again.

The second time in hardly a decade.

Lord Yama came calling again. This time, however, he took a long time leaving. Yama had actually climbed the steps, put one foot across the threshold of the ornate lion door, and stopped there. Nephew took a long, long time to die.

And the one memory, above all, the one image that haunted him, was dust.

Its mastery was a mystery.

Part IV
Nephew

It was dark under the lamp.

In the beginning, it was a new experience for the two women that Nephew, the man of the house, was at home most of the time. He seemed suddenly to relax, as though there were no more chores to do, no more engagements to attend to, no more visits to make, no more arrangements and litigations. And, he talked to them, his family of two women. He talked about his experiences in the construction of the Godavari anicut. He recalled fondly how he had been the right-hand man of the big man, Sir Arthur Blotton before he returned finally to Sakhinetipalli to manage the lands and properties of the two ladies.

But not all his tales were tales of satisfaction, of a life fulfilled. His pride was soon overshadowed by terminal frustration. He was like a bookkeeper, trying to match accounts: only, this time, for the first time, for the only time, he could not coax or coerce them to toe his line. There were too many knots and kinks; his life had been too tangled. There had been too many mysterious entries; the Great Inspector would spot them straightaway. The laws of karma will grind on, no matter what.

He was soon confronted by a terrible truth: barring Blotton's project, and the service to his brother-in-law's family, and the two ladies since the passing of BA Garu—and yes, the veranda school—all positive, above-board entries, redounding his credit of good karmas, whatever he had done had not been worth doing—worse, ought not to have been done.

The women tried to reason with him that that was not how they perceived the situation.

He would not be convinced.

'All is midhya, maya,' he said.

He now found the world cold as a well.

Appachchi debated with him.

The man had read the Gita, hadn't he? He had.

And he had attended discourses of the Guru of the Stream, he said, and he quoted the Guru. He had never missed a discourse.

The Guru had said:

> At the gates of liberation (moksha) and self-realization (sakshathkara), three guards are posted to ask you for your credentials. They are peace or mental equilibrium, joy or contentment, and inquiry or discrimination (shanti, santhosha, and vichara). Even if you make friends with only one of the guards, the others too will facilitate your entry. First in the series is peace. If you make peace yours, contentment (thrupthi) will automatically become yours!

Hadn't he! They knew as well as he did.

It was dark under the lamp.

Nephew had been the first to greet the Guru when the young fakir had reached the outskirts of Sakhinetipalli. Nephew, a confirmed atheist at the time, the Secretary of the Rationalist Students Association of Rajahmundry, had been the one to welcome him and help him settle down near their village.

Nephew's friend had lost a cow and he and his field hands were searching frantically all over, when this man, in a fakir's kafini and with long flowing hair, built like an athlete, sitting quietly on a boulder in the jungle, hailed him and said the dappled cow he was looking for was over there beyond that clump of babuls. And they had found it there. As they gathered before him, he asked for a few coals for his hookah; they had said they would rush to the hamlet and fetch some. No need, the fakir had said. He'd struck the earth before him with his kamandalam (holy water pot) and tiny flames had risen.

In the conversation that followed, he said he had no home. They'd invited him to go with them and settle there by the side of the dry nullah to the north of the village. And the Guru had agreed. When they all reached the place, the Guru had chosen a most unlikely spot: a dry rocky area abutting a dry nullah. They witnessed another miracle: the young fakir stepped into the dry sand bed of the nullah, tapped it, said, 'sweet water,' and looked up. They had turned and looked in the direction and then gasped in surprise and joy. Water came rushing from afar, from the cliff sides. It had been a hill stream—how long it had flowed, no one knew—it had thinned and gradually lost its way in the dust, and then dried up; all that the villagers could notice were the dark stains on the cliff where it had come from, like streaks of dried tears on a child's face.

Then, with the Guru's words, the crags shimmered with water veils.

Water, clear, crystal, had come rushing down the nullah, pushing aside everything in its way, like a child racing to meet with her mother as she returned from a long journey. The fakir had stood in the dry bed, bent down and gathered some sand in his hands; he had taken fistfuls and sprinkled it on the villagers, on himself, and all around. He had played with the water; the villagers also had jumped in. They'd danced and shouted in joy, especially the womenfolk. For, until then, the only source of potable water had been the well in Worker Aunt's home, and, for the vast majority of the villagers, a step-down well about two-and-a-half kilometres to the north of the hamlet.

It became a feeder canal for the fields of the villagers; they could now raise even paddy. It was almost as if the villagers had received new life.

His friends of the Rationalist Association in Rajahmundry had been incredulous; only a few of them had come along with him to verify his reports. And they'd gone back still incredulous. The

Guru had also helped him experience an out of body experience. Nonsense, they said!

Looking back, Nephew said to the two women, he still considered this phase as the most fruitful in his life: the Guru had been the best thing to happen to him, to the villagers and the entire village, as to countless thousands in the land.

He now acknowledged that the Guru had chosen him and made him his instrument. But that hadn't mitigated his negative karma. Couldn't the master have erased it? Mitigated it? He himself had declared he could, and did in several cases, when he cured terminal diseases. But in his case the Guru hadn't. Nephew was not bitter about it; it was just a matter of fact.

'It is dark under the lamp.'

'I am only a weaver,' the Guru had said.

So, Nephew had known the Guru and served him, right from the beginning. Discourses are one thing and disciples another. He had been a part-time devotee! The Guru himself had called him so. It was dark under the lamp.

Granny Appachchi quoted the Guru:

The Gate of the House of God is always open.

We are bound to reach our destination, attain perfection, but the journey is slow—painfully slow. Everyone has hope, there are no irredeemable sinners. Keep at it, keep labouring, working, accounting, counting, pounding, weeding, tilling, sowing, weaving, hammering—your own chosen vocation is enough to spur your progress towards ultimate perfection. No effort is wasted. And death is not the end of life. The relations we form and the powers we acquire do not perish at death. They will be the starting point of later developments. Everyone will be redeemed, sooner or later. There are no unforgivable sins. All of us are pilgrims, of not just the Silver Pilgrimage, and the Golden Pilgrimage, even the Diamond Pilgrimage.

The Guru had concluded his discourse as usual with a chant from the *Brihadaranyaka Upanishad.*

> From Untruth lead me to Truth.
> From Darkness lead me to Light.
> From Death lead me to Immortality.

The two women served the family elder, the man of the house. If loving service was enough to tend back a sick man to health, Nephew would've recovered. He had gone, however, beyond the reach of love and affection. He was not just sick physically, not just mentally, he was sick inside—his inside was cold as a well when its waters had diminished to its lowest ring. The man of the sturdy heart was heartsick.

Of what? Was there something he was keeping from them?

He knew, with great tact and affection, they had doctored his list of successes and achievements. They had left out his role as the legal counsel and bookkeeper and litigator to the Kshatriyas of Singapuram. They consoled him with fond reminiscences. He had been the master of management for the family, for friends, for the villagers, and, like his brother-in-law, for Mr Blotton. And of course, he had run things for the Guru of the Stream for a decade.

In better times, a long while ago it seemed now, Nephew had been as zestful in carrying out simple tasks of everyday life, such as cutting fruit and distributing them among the family members and the servants. He had inherited this passion for fruit from his own father. He had learned it all from his own father. His father had bequeathed, not just land and houses and cash, but also several kinds of knives. Of course, his relatives had appropriated all his properties and effects: the only things left with him were the knives. A knife for every fruit. For example, a knife for cutting the pineapple. Another for cutting the jackfruit. A knife for every season.

Whenever a field hand discovered that a jackfruit had ripened, he plucked it from the tree and brought it eagerly to Nephew. And

Nephew would reward him with a copper and a smile. Then, he would stop whatever he was doing and go about the ceremony of cutting the jackfruit. He insisted on doing it on his own. He called for a cup of gingelly oil to coat his hands and the knife and keep the sticky sap from his hands. He first cut it in two; sometimes, he had to exert great strength, while the ladies warned him to mind his fingers and thighs. Then, when it lay open, he dipped the knife in the oil, while inhaling the aroma of the delicious fruit, commenting aloud on the tree's cleverness in packing its seeds in such scrumptious thonalu—pouches.

Nephew then cut into the central ridge, carving it away carefully from the syrupy thonalu. Then, when the rind was removed, he turned to the casing of the thonalu and detached the fruit one by one. He separated the seeds, accepting the help of the ladies of the house at this stage. And they appreciated his gesture by making a curry of the seeds or roasting them in embers. All the neighbours received a share of the thonalu as well as the seeds. A jackfruit was a tough job for one but a feast for many. What a curse, they said when he became ill, a fruit lover like Nephew kept away from these delights by the cursed disease.

The spiky rind of the fruit and the golden tassels were carried away by the field hand to feed his pigs. How is it different from carving up a hog, the field hand wondered. This Brahmin landlord would make a good carver of pigs, a great butcher. Or of people! He had done it to many at Junction. Ruined even that innocent tapper. God saw everything!

Another domestic chore Nephew had enjoyed throughout his active years was drawing water from the well. Sometimes, after the rains, when the river swelled and broke its bunds, the water in the well rose close to the third ring, and he could actually put his hand in and touch it. He personally supervised the cleaning of the well, sending for the field hand who was an expert at this job. In the summer, the water level receded, as though it sought a retreat to aestivate undisturbed; and if there was a drought, the level dropped even further, but still the well never dried up completely.

Granny Appachchi was attached to the river; Nephew loved the well. Granny Appachchi would say that it was much simpler to bathe in the river any day. And it was running, flowing water. Nephew replied that well water too flowed: you drew the water and filled the gangalam, the large brass storage vessel. The cattle trough and the cauldrons were filled with water for washing the kitchen utensils. The water in the well level went down, but by the morning it was up again. The well renewed itself continually. Where had the water come from? It had flowed in through the underground water table. His point was well taken; all the same, Granny Appachchi wouldn't bathe with the well water if she could reach the river.

Once they realized they had a difficult man of the house to feed, very finicky, with a declining appetite, the two nieces took special care with cooking for him. They consulted each other on the choice of the vegetable and the recipe; they put their own preferences aside. As he was a chronic diabetic, they preferred bitter gourd, but Worker Aunt ruled out Granny Appachchi's naïve suggestion that they have bitter gourd every day.

They discussed not just the choice of the vegetable, but the manner of cooking it, and of course the very method of cutting the vegetable. And, more often than not, preparation begun the moment Nephew returned from the weekly santa, followed by a coolie with a filled basket on his head. They knew even from the western room he had arrived; the aroma of the mint leaf he was fond of eagerly explored every room of the house, like a young woman home for the first time after a year at her mother-in-law's. Worker Aunt examined the contents of the basket and their condition; occasionally, she offered her opinion to Nephew on the selection of a vegetable, though he was already getting to work at his desk in the front room, planning his next move to bail out the Kshatriyas of Singapuram who, ever a law—rather outlaw—unto themselves, got into so many scrapes that it was his legal guile that had saved them from trial after trial.

Now Nephew acknowledged, even appreciated, her observations. Even the menu was finalized between the women, though tentatively, with a decent number of alternatives, and submitted to the man of the house for his final decision.

Appachchi carried the vegetables to the backyard, drew water from the well, and bathed them as though they were human; if Worker Aunt had permitted it, she would have used soap. And though both women agreed that what is pleasant to the eye is good for the stomach, in the matter of cutting, there often rose bitter differences between them. How large each piece of the brinjal had to be? Or the bitter gourd? Or snake gourd? Usually, Worker Aunt preferred to shred them large; Appachchi, small. 'Left to herself,' Worker Aunt complained, 'she would make chutney of every curry!' When they could not resolve the dispute, they appealed to the man of the house. He almost always curbed a smile and gave a verdict that did not make either feel small. Or, if he was too preoccupied, or too hassled with court work, he was less considerate, brushing them off. The debates, on such vital matters like whether a vegetable should be cut into large pieces or small, extended through the cooking and into the lunch session when their sole guest—they ate after he had—was a distracted, though tolerant, auditor.

When the women realized what was happening, what was looming ahead, that his life breath had reached the throat, Worker Aunt broke down in the western room, and Granny Appachchi held her in her arms and wept. Appachchi worried about the impending event, and its effect on Worker Aunt. She realized the urgency of preparing for the event. The importance of the state of mind at the moment of death was emphasized by the Guru.

They learned soon not to bother him if they sensed he was in no fit condition or in one of those higher Biblical moods. Not the Gita, nor the New Testament, nor the Koran: the scripture he preferred was *The Ecclesiastes*.

'Pray,' said Appachchi.

'Yes, pray to God,' urged Worker Aunt.

The Guru of the Stream had talked at length of prayer.

> There are various forms of prayer, ends of prayer, all earthly goals. We pray to avoid emotional suffering (artha), gain practical advantage (artharthi), obtain intellectual advantage (jijnasuh), or gain wisdom (jnani). All these are noble.... Prayer is the effort of man to reach God.

No such ambition for me, joked Nephew.

> Prayer is a form of self-help, you put yourself back on the track. The ultimate goal is integration, a harmony of body, mind, and spirit.... Besides, prayer takes you away from your own self, above your self. It assumes that there is an answering Presence in the world....

There is only Absence, with a capital A, Nephew said; Silence, he said, silence of a deserted palace. In the Pleasure Palace, echoes lurked like bats from the high dust-layered cornices, from the crystal chandeliers behind cobweb veils, poised to attack you; assault your inner self.

Granny Appachchi and Worker Aunt sat on either side of his bed; they took turns talking to him and reading to him.

Worker Aunt read the Upanishads to Nephew.

> That which indeed is the Infinite, that is joy.

Nephew completed the slokam from the *Chandogya Upanishad*.

> There is no joy in the finite. The Infinite alone is joy. The Infinite indeed has to be sought after.

'Every stage of man's life—and human history—is important,' Nephew quoted the Guru of the Stream: the charms of childhood, the antics of adolescence, the ambitions of youth, its passions, the self-important plans and acts of manhood—nothing goes to waste. All phases are stages in the journey of journeys. No one is forever, nothing is forever: only the Self is immortal.

Nephew grew introspective.

He was not mocking the two women; he deeply appreciated their concern. Intellectual exercise was one thing; inner realization was quite another. And how could anyone help relieve him of his karmic baggage? The Guru hadn't, for reasons best known to Him. He alone knew all the three kalas, past, present, and future.

Worker Aunt quoted from the Gita:

> The path of devotion is most suitable for him who is neither very tired of nor very attached to the world.

'I am tired, very tired,' said Nephew. 'The days of distress are black.'

He concluded: 'My dead are better than your living.'

The women left him alone.

It took some time, but gradually, the clouds cleared and the sun came out; Nephew opened up more. He wanted to clean up his karmic account book himself—as far as possible—and in this birth so that at least in the next he would have a better tenure.

As though prompted by his inner voice, a counsellor within—the Guru, no doubt—he dug out his inmost secrets; among them his service to the notorious Kshatriyas of Singapuram. He confided to his two nieces how his legal expertise and worldly wisdom had contributed to the prosperity of these landlords; and to the ruin of sharecropper ryots.

We are all subject to finite fascinations.

And obsessions and preoccupations.

As his physical powers diminished, Nephew recalled memories and images associated with Singapuram, inlaid like grime in the grooves of ill-used kitchenware. He was haunted by one element: dust.

Dust.

Ochre-coloured, fine as snuff, it was insidious. How on earth it had come and covered that stretch of a kilometre or so, next to the Kshatriya palace, no one knew: some said it had come from the same desert which had given birth to the treelike cactuses the all-powerful proprietors of Singapuram had brought for their newly constructed Pleasure Palace that overlooked the Grand Trunk Road. Some said it had oozed up, like water in freshwater wells. The horse carriages and bandies, the marching columns of soldiers of the Kumpini, on the Grand Trunk Road between Calcutta and Madras, lifted whole loads of it, high over their heads. Each time something roused it, by a carriage or a lashkar column, it rose, alert, poised in the air, instinctually overwhelming it—and then, its own weight, burden, sieved it; it settled on the toddy palms, the cactus hedges that lined the crops in the fields on either side of that north-south artery of the Coromandel. Those cacti could not be found anywhere else in the Coromandel; they had come from far away, from a desert country, sparsely populated, with their dower of dust, the dust of eons; and they thrived even in the new environment. The beedi and cheroot shacks and the toddy shacks lay covered under layer after layer of dust, though they still catered gamely to the needs of wayfarers. Passing passengers still swallowed the fare they offered—crunchies, bananas, tobacco, spectacularly brewed tea, and toddy—all with a hint of dust. Passengers did not seem to mind, one way or the other. They simply held, if they had one, a towel or upper garment against their faces, and eased down from the carriages and bandies and fumbled away from the bus like unsighted people lost in a fog. Everyone, not just literate passengers, called this place 'Junction'. Just 'Junction', for a mufassil road from south to north heading towards the famous temple at Srinivaspuri and the hills crossed at this point the Grand Trunk Road which lay across the Coromandel like a varicose vein. You had to go there to catch a contract carriage plying on the Grand Trunk Road.

Junction was also the abode of his friends, the most powerful Kshatriya family of the river district, contractors to the Kumpini. The Kshatriyas of Singapuram had come there for white business and twisted pleasure, had sojourned there for the winter.

Now, in the season of lengthening shadows, Nephew remembered Junction and his association with the new Kumpini rajas more than he thought of and recollected his contribution to the Guru of the Stream. He also talked to the two women about friends gone, lost and gone—and what a way to go! For every man there are only a limited number of ways to arrive, but many more of going. For some, heavy.

We are all subject to finite fascinations.

Nephew recalled his last visit, a sentimental journey to the Pleasure Palace. He had got into a conversation with a tea shack worker at Junction. The man was too young to know him, and Nephew did not disclose his identity. Like the clever vakil that he was, the most successful ever for the Kshatriyas of Singapuram, Nephew got the popular version of the story of the Kshatriyas of Singapuram; and at the end of the day, when no more passenger carriages were expected, the tea shack worker escorted the visitor to the Pleasure Garden.

The sight shocked Nephew. The depression had not left him since. The palatial buildings in ruin, the garden a stage property that had witnessed such drama, their theatre of Six Foes now overrun by weeds and wild creepers. The final shock came with the artesian well: the water now dropped in a thin trickle, like an old man's pee. Nephew sat down on the broken concrete rim of the shallow pool, crawling with worms and insects.

He fled home to Sakhinetipalli.

Nephew recounted the story to the women, in fits and snatches, over the months and years he was confined to bed, while they did their best to keep him from bedsores and gangrene.

As children, what first attracted me was talk of a five-headed toddy palm near the Junction. The trunk of the palmyra was slim, like Cleopatra's neck, and how it had managed to bear so many heads, become a demi-Ravana, was a matter of wonder and speculation. An inauspicious trademark.

This aberration was a popular attraction. For most of the tourists the weird toddy palm was like a signpost to the Pleasure Garden of the Kshatriyas of Singapuram. But the whole place had started its career as an ashram. The elder Raju's father had cleared the place for a saint and built a group of cottages around the central hut for his ashram, and with the blessing of the holy man performed the miracle of the artesian well. When the saint passed away, and the elder Raju's father too passed away, with little patronage from the next generation the disciples scattered. The new owner pulled the cottages down, and with marble fetched all the way from Rajasthan, erected a beautiful palace to entertain the white officers and their Indian friends.

Now, from the freak palm and the palace we children were drawn to Junction because though it was most of the time storms of dust, we still liked the sight of passenger carriages and horsemen cantering up and down, with an occasional bonus of marching lashkars, trailing chaotic curtains and ragged trains. The draught bullocks and horses plashed the dust as though the thoroughfare dipped suddenly into a hill stream, and it was not dust now under their hoofs but crystal-clear gurgling water.

The immediate attraction was the freak. Once we took a look at it, our curiosity satisfied, we felt thirsty. And our friends led us to the Pleasure Garden. The caretaker readily allowed us to approach the bore pump for a drink of water. The first time I saw it I was more amazed than I had been by the freak palm.

The shiny spout was the largest I had seen anywhere, as

large as an elephant trunk, and the water poured out with quiet full-cheeked force in a jet that was as thick. Later, I admired the saint who had assessed the size of the unseen water table. So much water below the ground, and such dust above! The dust too, people said, had leaked, surged from some secret source below. The Lords of the Garden had taken over black cotton soil and left it a dust bowl, and he, Nephew, had been a collaborator!

And it had flowed on and on, the gardener said, just like this ever since it had been bored years ago. The water fell in a cement trough that was big enough for us kids to swim in, and from the tank it went in two opposite directions in open channels and fed a huge variety of plants and trees. The whole place was dense, tropical, uninhibited; the sun even at midday merely speckled the rich black cotton soil of the garden. Beyond the sounds of the cicadas we could hear the passing vehicles on the Grand Trunk Road.

We could glimpse the palace through the foliage; we dared not go anywhere near it. The gardener had admitted us on promise of not disturbing his master. He was all alone there; his family lived in their native town of Singapuram twenty-five kilometres away.

I did not know then that I was fated not much later to witness the goings on inside the shuttered palace. Vidhivihitham buddhiranusarathi, Mind follows what Fate has decreed.

Father was posted as the Revenue Officer of the district and came to know its biggest landlords quite well. In course of time, they treated him as their counsellor and guru. They came to him for consultation even on the most personal matters, and they took care of our needs and problems. They offered financial support; through their munificence, Father gradually built his own properties. An official connection had developed into a personal nexus, and friendship. Friendship with a snake is like fencing with a scimitar. Not surprising, on my father's death, his brothers and daughters seized whatever they could; leaving nothing for me. Poetic justice.

I still remember how I looked forward to the rupee or two even the younger brother, Chinna Rajus' wife, Chinnamma gave me; how when Chinna Raju came to call on us in town, I followed him around like a pup until the last moment when he gave me a fistful of coins from his pocket before getting into his horse carriage, and how I did not even wait to wave at him but ran out to the shack shop for peppermints and jaggery sweets.

Some years later, when I next met Chinnamma, and I was now into my teens, I stood away, staring awkwardly at her. She looked at me in her serene way and said, 'He has grown up'. Time had changed our relationship.

Chinnamma was childless, and she grew fond of me. She persuaded my parents to send me every vacation to their place in the small village. I looked forward to the summer vacations, when I was sent to Singapuram and put up with Chinna Raju and Chinnamma.

She was slim, in her youth she must have been quite a beauty. I had a fleeting glimpse of her when I suddenly returned from an outing and found her bathing in the backyard; she wasn't embarrassed, she just asked me to go into the front room and play with the empty matchboxes near the grandfather clock. I loved to join empty matchboxes—Chinna Raju for some reason never threw away matchboxes but preserved them in a chest in the hall of their home—and I spent hours playing with them, making a long train out of them and gliding it around on the polished granite floor.

Though she was childless, her husband respected her as few husbands in that male-ruled society did in those circumstances. The couple did a round of pilgrimages. Finally, they went and sat listening to discourses by a guru from their caste who lived in a cottage in their farm near their family graves.

They ate fish and chicken only on special occasions, though they were Kshatriyas. Chinnamma sent me for my meals to the temple pujari's home. The field hand preceded me with a cup of creamy curds and announced me at the house. The lady of the house welcomed me with a warm smile; both husband and wife made me comfortable on the swing and asked me all about the town and my parents while the lady lay a leaf plate and served me a meal of many courses. For every meal it was the same, our procession of two.

The fidelity and loyalty of the couple brought honour to the village. Before they both passed away, they had adopted Sekhar Raju and the entire property passed on to the young man. Young Sekhar Raju, their nephew, was handsome, and he looked quite fetching in Western clothes—he had a three-piece suit even before he was ten. I remember how enviable and happy he appeared as he came back from overseeing the harvest, escorted by a long caravan of paddy carts, perched on top of the hay in the first bandy.

Two brothers, and what a contrast!

Chinna Raju's elder brother, Pedda Raju, the master of the place, was held in awe. He rarely raised his voice, but the servants ran to execute his commands. Of course, he suffered from his middle-age priorities: women, cows, and Brahmins. And he grew to be a misogynist: nauch girls should only stand on the stage and not sit. 'Are women eligible for Moksha?' he would argue with father. 'They will do well to attend to their hearth, in service at home.'

...The crookedness of this fagot the fire alone will correct.

He was the kind of man who could hear the movement of an ant on the floor. And he was short-tempered. As his legal counsel, I remember, once one of his clerks was with him;

he was checking the accounts. I had suggested he should give a few minutes of personal inspection of his account books. Suddenly, he reached out and gave a resounding slap to the clerk; the man screamed and blubbered. The Master didn't demand any explanation; he quietly closed the incriminating record and showed the door to him.

Of course, when it was our turn, we hoodwinked the best revenue officials with our parallel sets of books I maintained for him. *What need of economy in telling lies?*

One of his liaisons, the worst-kept secret of the Coromandel, disturbed me most. Pedda Raju started an affair with the wife of the principal priest of the Lord's temple at the famous pilgrim centre of Gopalapuram. She was a stalwart woman, always clad in pattu saris, and loaded with jewellery. I remember the most impressive of her jewels, her vaddanam, or girdle belt, which must have weighed, looking back, at least five kilos. The diamonds in her nose rings, earrings, rings on her fingers, and in her necklaces were the first thing anyone would have noticed. At any time of the day, she was gorgeous, especially when she accompanied her husband, who looked like two paddy bags filled and sewn up into one.

I was a friend of both the men, but my moralistic preaching did not make any difference; Pedda Raju respected my advice in every other matter.

When the head priest passed away peacefully in sleep, Pedda Raju openly set up the woman as his mistress in a bungalow in the town. My father too had passed away. The affair did not end. It was she who passed away first, leaving Pedda Raju to mourn her loss publicly. And then his own wife passed away, and he married again, a much younger woman. She turned out to be his nemesis. As he grew old, she took lover after lover and in the end openly carried on her liaisons. The old man could not do anything: he had lost control of the estates and was dependant on her for everything.

I remember one of her lovers. We were out one day in the jungle when we heard a gunshot and went in the direction; there this man was, hunting waterfowl. He was a broad-shouldered, handsome man. When I turned back, he hailed me to join him. I found him a jolly sportsman.

Even the humblest of the housemaids did not escape Pedda Raju's notice; service was compulsory. A complication arose when his eldest son, Sekhar Raju, took after his father. *Yada pitha tadha puthraha*—as the father, so the son.

One night, the son went to the maid servant's hut. Her kids were asleep; the husband pretended to be asleep. The young master took her out to the malli bower. They heard approaching footsteps. She raised a finger to her lips; his father too was approaching the hut. She rushed back to the hut, not a minute too soon. The elder Raju strode in and raised her by her upper arm. He took her to the malli bower and asked her, grimly, 'Who was it?'

'Why don't you finish your business and go?'

He slapped her.

'My man,' she said, sobbing.

'I had warned him. Next time he touches you I shall flay him alive.'

She nodded.

He left.

The son returned.

She said to him: 'Aren't you sleeping with your own mother?'

He froze.

'I am going to shoot him,' he said in a rage.

The son could not get himself to carry out his threat. He did use the double-barrelled gun—against himself. The bullet ricocheted, broke the ventilator pane, and dropped in the lush lawn, next to the artesian well. I reached in time to relieve the old man of all worries, though not his shock and grief. I will remember to my last day the broken glass in the ventilator where the ricocheting bullet flew. The police came, I talked to the officer in private and he briefed everyone. An autopsy was conducted. The only surviving heir of the estate had taken his own life.

Pedda Raju never recovered. He got into his bed and lay there, until they removed his body for his funeral rites.

One day, around midnight, the watchman, faithfully keeping watch for months now, heard some sounds from the master's bed. He raised the wick of the lantern. The old man had turned to the side of the wall, how he had done it was a marvel to the watchman. The master's eyes focused on the wall and he blabbered, salivating like a yeaning cow. The servant called for help from the tea shacks of Junction. The neighbours needed some urging to come, for the place was only fit for ghosts now. They all wondered what the old tyrant was worried about; then they put it down to delirium. The family physician gave him a shot of morphia. 'Let him rest,' he told the watchman. The crowd dispersed, happy to get away from the premises.

The watchman discovered him the next morning—dead, his eyes still and stark: ants had discovered them.

I attended the funeral.

Shortly after that, the Pleasure Palace was abandoned.

Only the watchman and his wife were left behind until a decision was taken about its final fate. Even they did not stay on for long. For one thing, the suicide's ghost frequented the place and the grounds, and almost everyone in the family had sighted him at one time or other. For another, the watchman's elder son was taken in by a missionary school; he did well and went on to do his college in Madras. The other children followed the eldest; every one of them did well, joining the provincial government of Madras. He and Podumburra are great friends in Rajahmundry. Now the parents also moved to Madras, rejecting a pension granted reluctantly by the heirs. The ghost kept everyone else from the place.

The grounds and the garden grew weed-ridden. The water fountain thinned, hiccupped, and coughed, and finally gave up. The rose bushes withered, and the malli creeper too dried up; the grass followed. Everything joined the famous dust.

There was a sequel. The deceased had written a will: every piece of immovable property he had left to the Missionaries of Madonna in Madras, who had adopted the watchman's children. As the legal counsel, I got in touch with the bishop. The Diocese of Madras decided to demolish the palace and erect an orphanage, the first in the river district. The watchman was put in charge of the operation. When they tore down the master's bedroom, out fell a cache of gold from its eastern wall. The watchman gathered them in a gunny and took them all the way to Madras to hand them over to the bishop.

It was the biggest surprise of my life: the old man had kept not two, but three parallel books.

That gold hoard gave the Coromandel its best mother and child hospital.

On another day, Nephew recalled something more pleasant. He remembered the weddings. Both Granny Appachchi and Worker Aunt had been married at the same time. He had been in charge of the whole show, the grandest ever witnessed in the village.

A marriage may be performed with a maund of rice, as well as with a maund of pearls.

The parents on both sides had sold the best lots of their lands to meet the expenditure. They erected palmyra pandals covering whole streets, with mango leaf festoons hung all along the pandals, and plantain trees tied to every post. The wedding dais itself was decorated with cartloads of jasmine and chrysanthemum and davanam and maruvam.

The chief cook had come from the Konaseema. He came with select assistants, one of them a specialist in making kazas, another in making payasam and booreys. The chief himself was known as Kali Yuga Bhima, famous for delivering without fail a delicious feast every time he dug up a hearth trench and put his vast cauldrons on the roaring fires.

Bags and bags of rice had arrived, which were stored in the main hall and kept under lock and key, as well as groceries, baskets and baskets of tamarind, etc.—a whole caravan of jaggery and red-hot chillies from the Godavari district.

Kali Yuga Bhima got the backyard swept clean until it resembled an eating leaf laid down for a special guest. He and the Vedic pundits offered up chants and hymns and went through a ceremony which threatened to be as long as the wedding itself. Then, he had five hearth trenches dug, their walls cut clean. Firewood that crackled and almost peeled off in their hands was put in one of the trenches and Lord Agni was invoked. Not to forget Lord Varuna, so that it did not rain. There was quite a crowd when the chief cook lit the first trench fire. As the water boiled in immense cauldrons, they lifted whole sacks of rice and emptied them into the bubbling water while a muscular cook kept stirring it with a long wooden ladle, keeping away from the flames but still close enough to pour with sweat and roast to a dark tan. Teams of assistant cooks cut up mounds of vegetables on wooden planks—brinjals, cucumbers, gourds.... And pulusu was boiling with the fragrance of coriander spreading all over the place. Two trenches were allocated for preparation of sweets and sweet dishes, for which all the fresh milk that could be procured from villages all around had been carried in huge brass pots.

From time to time, over the buzz and din, someone or the other shouted, and another shouted back. The chief went round the trenches, keeping everyone on their toes.

As Granny Appachchi was too young, her father put her in his lap and went through the ceremony. Worker Aunt went through it all herself, as though she was already sixteen.

The mothers helped the grooms in tying up the mangalasutrams.

The great Carnatic singer Tanjore Krishna Bhagavathar had come with his accompanists from Chennapatnam by steamer and a special covered cart. His concert spanning all the five days of the wedding was a treat the district did not forget for generations; on the last day, he sang devotional songs composed by a friend, a saintly man of Tanjore called Thyagaraja, sung for the first time in the Coromandel. At the end of the final session, the two fathers decorated the celebrated singer with a gold medallion, gold bracelet, and gold anklet, and bestowed on him a gift of varahas.

A team of Vedic pundits from the famed Konaseema recited the Vedams, and they were honoured with Kashmir shawls and sumptuous dakshina and tamboolam.

When everyone had left, including the grooms and their families, singing the praises of the hospitality of the fathers of the brides, the village felt lonely, as though the whole place had been deserted.

After a few days, Appachchi got tired of carrying the heavy gold mangalasutram and put it away in the bhoshaanam (wooden chest); her mother pleaded with her that it was inauspicious and she should not be seen without it in public. However, she refused to wear it—'With it around my neck I feel like a branded bull,' she said. Worker Aunt wore hers without any problem.

∽

When Worker Aunt prayed for Nephew's health, the Guru created vibhuti and gave it to her: 'Rub it on his chest and back, he will be all right.' It worked, thought the two women; 'No power worked for me,' said Nephew.

The Guru of the Stream quoted from all scriptures of the world. In the season of dimming lights, dimming eyes, Nephew recited verses from only one book of the Bible. He had read the Indian scriptures, but gradually, he began to prefer the Bible, and even in the Bible, just one book.

> …but if a man live many years, and rejoice in them all; yet let him remember the days of darkness; for they shall be many. All that cometh is vanity.
>
> Truly the light is sweet, and a pleasant thing it is for the eyes to behold the sun:
>
> All this have I seen, and applied my heart unto every work that is done under the sun: there is a time wherein one man ruleth over another to his own hurt.
>
> But it shall not be well with the wicked, neither shall he prolong his days, which are as a shadow; because he feareth not before God.

When Podumburra called on him, Nephew turned to him and said:

> Rejoice, O young man, in thy youth; and let thy heart cheer thee in the days of thy youth, and walk in the ways of thy heart, and in the sight of thine eyes: but know thou, that for all these things God will bring thee into judgment.
>
> There is a vanity which is done upon the earth; that there be just men, unto whom it happeneth according to the work of the wicked; again, there be wicked men, to whom it happeneth according to the work of the righteous: I said that this also is vanity.

Podumburra recited to the old man:

> Vanity of vanities
> > Sayeth the Preacher
>
> Vanity of vanities; all is vanity.
>
> All things have I seen in the days of my vanity: there is a just man that perisheth in his righteousness, and there is a wicked man that prolongeth his life in his wickedness.
>
> The thing that hath been, it is that which shall be; and that which is done is that which shall be done: and there is no new thing under the sun.
>
> I have seen all the works that are done under the sun; and, behold, all is vanity and vexation of spirit.
>
> That which is crooked cannot be made straight: and that which is wanting cannot be numbered.
>
> For in much wisdom is much grief: and he that increaseth knowledge increaseth sorrow.
>
> The sleep of a laboring man is sweet, whether he eat little or much: but the abundance of the rich will not suffer him to sleep.
>
> And this also is a sore evil, that in all points as he came, so shall he go: and what profit hath he that hath laboured for the wind?
>
> All his days also he eateth in darkness, and he hath much sorrow and wrath with his sickness.
>
> Remember now thy Creator in the days of thy youth, while the evil days come not, nor the years draw nigh, when thou shalt say, I have no pleasure in them;
>
> And further, by these, my son, be admonished: of making many books there is no end; and much study is a weariness of the flesh.

Appachchi and Podumburra turned away and wiped their eyes.

To curb the menace of an exploding rodent population—they were worried that one of them might bite Nephew's feet and he wouldn't even know—Appachchi hit upon an idea: get a cat. Worker Aunt accepted the proposal, on one condition: no one was going to feed meat to the cat. Appachchi agreed, curbing her misgivings.

It was a cat with a pedigree. The kitten had been gifted by a zamindar from Konaseema. His zamindari had been founded on pindari pillage. He had a reputation for severing in public the hands of thieves. Appachchi imagined that the kitten had taken birth in an appropriate environment; it too would be merciless. The kitten arrived and was duly received with martial honours appropriate to a warrior about to save a whole township from the scourge of dacoits. The treatment the kitten received matched Appachchi's grand plans. It warmed her heart when on the second night after its arrival the kitten grabbed a rat, pinned it down in her claws and meowed to her with a twinkle in its eyes. She gave it an extra helping of payasam.

In just a few weeks, however, Worker Aunt's diet worked a radical change in the world view of the kitten; it allowed rats to pass by without harassing them; a couple of weeks later, she looked with benevolence at any stray rodent. Appachchi suspected that the transformation had reached unprecedented sattvic proportions when with her owns eyes she watched through a chink in the door the cat engaged in a quiet chat with a mob of mice, as if conducting an arugu (pyol) school session with neighbourhood rodent goons. The moment Appachchi cleared her throat, the kitten pushed the whole lot under its large hold-all chest and turned to her with a sweet smile painted on its face.

'How can a vegetarian cat kill rats?' said Nephew with a feeble smile, opening his mouth for the first time in weeks.

'That's what I had said, but,' pleaded Appachchi with Worker Aunt, 'you wouldn't allow me to get the field hands to cook some meat for it. Even now it is not too late.'

After much further deliberation, and with scriptural support marshalled by Appachchi—you could get anything from Worker Aunt as long as you could produce evidence from the scriptures—Worker Aunt agreed that the tamasic cooking be done fifteen kilometres away, not one inch nearer, in the extreme right corner of the vast backyard of the farm hand's hut in their paddy field. The field hand was given proper and meticulous instructions: he was to fetch the abominable packet to the backyard wall, vault over the wall and cover the whole thing prudently—Worker Aunt had her renunciant reputation to consider. No one was to know about it; if anyone accosted him on the way to or from the shandy, he was to make up a story for them, never disclosing the real identity of the beneficiary of the explosive packet. You could utter falsehoods in a good cause, the Scriptures said, as cited by Appachchi. Worker Aunt nodded vaguely: it could signify agreement or disapproval, whichever way you were inclined at the moment.

Before this elaborate plan could be carried out, however, scriptural support was found to allow cooking of meat in an orthodox Brahmin household. While the cooking was on, Worker Aunt sat in the front room of the house, the farthest possible distance from the polluted region within the house, worried all the time that Nephew might notice the stench and laugh at her. Appachchi hovered hopefully all around the house, as though she herself was being subjected to a bout of spiritual enlightenment. Finally, the field hand—he was under oath not to speak a word about the whole mission—whistled a melody he had learned from a passer-by who had been trained in it by a noose-gang, Warlu Wandlu, the South Indian species of the Thuggee. He also raised his hand, Appachchi rushed in headlong, her heart pounding against her ribs, with the privileged kitten in her hand.

She was in for a shock. The cat simply sniffed the meat dish from a distance, made a face, and almost retched; and though the field hand coaxed it, whispering patiently how nice the stuff looked and smelled, the cat turned its head with sattvic disdain, quite insulting to a conscientious field hand. With mincing steps, the transformed soul in feline form moved away quietly but firmly.

Nephew lay on the carved and canopied wooden bed, shrivelled up like a banana peel exposed for long to the blazing summer sun; and, in spite of their best efforts, smelling like a goat that had missed its annual bath for the fifth year running. He suffered the humiliation of incontinence. Blubbering the moment he was greeted by a visitor, he shocked anyone who came to see him, for the 'tiger' of Sakhinetipalli had never been seen with moist eyes, saying, 'I am a sinner, a sinner, no one should bother about me, and no obsequies for me, either, just cremate me in the same spot where I cremated my sister and brother-in-law.'

The two women racked their brains. They had to keep him happy: for happiness is half strength. They thought of various delicacies to help him regain his gastronomic morale. They thought of roasting for him a dibba rotti.

Everyone in the family loved dibba rotti, especially the man of the house. Occasionally, he had even asked for it, enjoying now no more than a shadow of his earlier appetite. Then, the two women collaborated in complete harmony to produce, as Nephew put it on one happy and contented occasion, the best dibba rotti in the river district.

Take a cup of black gram, wash it and soak it for a couple of hours, then remove the skin by stirring the contents with your hand. Drain the water; don't throw it away; mixed with the bran feed, the cattle in the byre will love it. Simultaneously, take two cups of rice ravva—that is the proportion, one to two—and wash it in water. Drain the water somewhat, let some of it remain to soak the ravva. Now, the most important part: grinding the black gram. The women took turns. Once they sat at the grinding stone, no one should or could disturb them; they hardly paused in rotating the grinding stone. While the left hand swung the stone, with the right they pushed the gram back into the hollow of the grinding stone; even the man of the house in his office in the front part of the house could hear the rhythmic whizz of the rotating stone. From time to time, they paused, tested the texture and consistency—too much water will make it thin and then you end up with the vulgar dosa; the secret is to manage to grind it to the consistency of home-made butter. Salt and cumin seeds are now added for taste and flavour.

Once they both agreed that the gram had been properly and nicely ground, they moved to the kitchen. Because the open hearth was undependable—unless you kept a close watch, the flame sometimes grew feeble and almost lay curled on itself like a heartsick cat—they lit a charcoal brazier. This part of the programme was entirely monopolized by Appachchi. She arranged the coals in the brazier as though they were chess pawns or precious stones, selecting each for size and looks. She put a few old papers in the lower chamber and lit it up. At this juncture, the women always offered a silent prayer. Perhaps the prayer had some effect; in no time, fanned by Appachchi, the coals were ignited; first the edges grew pink, then the colour spread autonomically—soon coals turned into ruby.

At this juncture, they put a frying pan on the brazier; and added some gingelly oil. Just as it started heating up, they emptied the contents of the vessel into it, sending off a peal of whistling that could be heard into the street, soon followed by the fragrance of the dibba rotti being processed. Then, the whizzing softened to a steady whisper. The rite was on, and they left the brazier with its precious burden alone; it was now a matter of time. But that time was the critical factor; as they went about their other chores, they returned every now and then and nudged the lid ajar and took a peep inside, taking care that they didn't disturb the creative colloquy of the roasting bowl.

At the appropriate time—only the veteran, only the culinary expert, would know what was appropriate—they lifted the rotti to see how far it was done. The underside was to be a tawny gold, without the slightest speck of black; black was burnt, not roasted; the man of the house would not touch it.

Finally, dibba rotti is best eaten while it is still hot. So, they either hustled the man to the rotti, or the rotti to the man.

Unlike in earlier times though, Nephew now looked at the steaming dish without interest. He broke off decorously, self-consciously, as though he were a Collector who had never played football inaugurating a tournament under the public eye by kicking a football, a little piece of crackling crust, and chewed it without relish. His time was up. Still, he mumbled, he loved to watch people eat.

The women didn't need more encouragement.

One day, when Granny Appachchi had gone to Ringworm Subbayya's with a list, Nephew turned to Worker Aunt and mumbled, with great difficulty, a name which had been a taboo word for a long time. And their emotions poured out from within their depths, exploding like hot lava from a volcano that had lain dormant for a long time. That one act of Appachchi they could never forget; she had disgraced not just the memory of her husband, but their entire family and the village itself. They wept again. For Nephew, it was worse; he looked back with late lucidity on the injustice perpetrated on a fellow soul.

After the death of BA Garu, Granny Appachchi had refused to shave her head, refused to change into white, refused to drop her bindi. Worker Aunt supported her; after all, that was what her brother had himself enjoined on her. BA Garu had taken a promise from her: 'It's time women lived a full life after the death of their husbands; a widow is still a woman, a woman alive. Wear all your jewellery, especially the toe rings, mattelu, which are an Andhra ornament.' Granny Appachchi continued to wear them. Worker Aunt, widowed, didn't, though she had changed several notions she'd held on to after her Kasi yatra.

When the obsequies for her husband were over, Granny

Appachchi called on the Guru and received his blessing.

The water of the feeder channel still sang its consoling pallavi, sweet and soothing to the ear. The Guru was old, very old; still, he was fit enough to attend to his chores, and discourse to the devotees. He received Appachchi with a reassuring smile and sent her to the room she had occupied last time. Not one word was exchanged, a whole discourse had been delivered.

> When there is earth to lie upon, why trouble about bed? When one's arm is readily available, why need pillows? When there is the palm of one's hand, why seek for plates and utensils? When there is the atmosphere, the bark of trees, etc., what need is there of silks?

Still, Granny Appachchi had experienced an oppressive vacancy. Gold is known by the touchstone and a man by living with him.

When Granny Appachchi wandered into their room, everything, every personal effect, hurt: his writing table; his glass lamp with a fine flower of a chimney, his gold-nibbed fountain pen, his favourite books lined on the table against the wall, the tiny blotch on the tablecloth where her pen had dripped just a few days before his death...such a neat man, but he had not allowed Appachchi to change the cloth. A memento of happiness past.

But the room itself felt deserted, a shell just vacated by the soul. The byre, the backyard, the village had lost its substance. The air was oppressive. The world was soonya. She had entered nothingness, and nothingness had entered her, through every pore. She cried.

She chewed and chewed each morsel of her meal, and went on and on, until Worker Aunt sat next to her and fed her. Appachchi retched, and was sick all over.

'Does not matter,' said vadina. She cleaned her up, led her to the bed, and laid her down carefully.

'Sleep now. Sleep, Amma.'

Worker Aunt advised Nephew to move her for some time away

from the village. When the matter was broached, Appachchi recoiled at the very idea. She burst into tears. She could not live away from Worker Aunt. Worker Aunt suggested she could retire for a year or so to any place of her choice. Nephew supported the proposal. Finally, when it became intolerable, the very sight of the slates and the pencils and the books and the back numbers of periodicals, all neatly arranged as he had left them, Appachchi decided to move from the village and into their island farm. She took with her only the cutting from the issue announcing his death, and what the Vice Chancellor had said about this scholar in an obituary notice. He only is dead whose name is not mentioned with respect.

Worker Aunt had instructed the tenant who lived on the island farm, sharecropper and toddy tapper Veeranna, of Appachchi's impending visit. He quickly erected a cottage for her in the midst of the fields, away, far away, from any human habitation; all that she had for company was field mice and snakes. But she was no longer afraid of wildlife, neither the serpents nor scorpions held any terror for her. And she could never keep from activity, from sheer manual labour. At the farm, she gradually went back to adolescence. The great open was once again her domain.

All her life, Appachchi had marked seasons by their scents and by their sounds. Appachchi's strongest sense was the olfactory.

She had particularly enjoyed the neem in bloom. For weeks before Ugadi, New Year's Day, she would roam around the neem grove like a bee totally distraught by the load in the air. No one can ignore this, she would say, the unmistakable infusion of the neem in the air. For some days it hung a little up in the air, you had to stand up to catch it, then you can squat on the arugu and enjoy it. A little later, it waited for anyone leaving the house; and then, as though encouraged by Appachchi, it would enter the door and settle in the hall, pour into the bedrooms through the casement windows when they were opened once a week to clean up. How come people did not notice its presence or took it for granted? A little after the

Ugadi festival, its reign ended, the tiny blossoms, in thousands, lay on the ground, faded brown, the wind casually shovelling them to the roadside—a springy mattress, the dust of generations.

She would suddenly stop on the goat path in the jungle and look around. There was nothing much to see, BA Garu would think, but she would pick her way through the thorn bushes and reach the little jungle shrub bearing tiny but thick, creamy scented flowers. 'Don't pluck,' she'd say. 'They die, fade, and dry.' The only cause that justified that kind of violence was adorning the gods. And that was one of her quarrels with the gods.

In priority, the neem came after the mango. The neem was sattvic, the mango bloom was sensual, and rajasic. The whole village ought to have gone into a frenzy when the mango tree bloomed, but to Appachchi's surprise, it didn't. The mango blooms had enough to satisfy everyone; the honeybees had had their fill; still there was much more, so much more left for humans, if only they had Appachchi's nostrils.

Every season had its compensating scents. The perspiration, the heat, the discomfort, the mosquitoes, and other evils of the summer were offset by the malli. Then in winter appeared the lovely akasa malli, with its creamy flowers over long necks. Both flowers filled the rooms with their perfume throughout the night. The old ladies were right: the flowers were perfect for the nuptial chamber.

Granny Appachchi remembered his description of the monsoon: like wild elephants, BA Garu had said, intent on marauding a peasant's corn field on the edge of a hamlet, the thorn bush hedge of no use against pachyderms that had developed a taste for cereals on the stem.

Toddy tapper Veeranna was built square and sturdy, but at times he reminded Appachchi of BA Garu. For example, he allowed her to sit on the manch while he went after the boars with a spear. Miss Beston had used a horse, Appachchi remembered. 'Why spend money on the upkeep of a horse?' Veeranna replied. His spear was effective, and his voice was thunder itself. Between them they kept the wild beasts away. Thank God the elephants hadn't crossed the river to the island; their hands and nights were full. But so were their fields now. Occasionally, he went into inspired discourses like BA Garu; but the scholar wouldn't have been able to discourse on some areas that he talked about—for example, fish fry. His intellectual passion too held her.

And Veeranna alias Simhadri Venkanna had a few professional tips for aspirants on tapping palm liquor. 'These are an uneducated toddy tapper's views, don't be offended,' he'd say. But he was the champion tapper of the region.

Paring a palm for tapping the amrut is like sleeping with a woman. Search with your finger for the three-sided beauty. Work on it nicely with your chisel till it becomes tender and soft and throbbing. And then harden it till it becomes tough as mortar milled to a nice paste. Both tender and tough. You drive your vuli into it at the base.

All this labour is worth it. If it is a strong palm, tall as a toddy palm should be, a challenge to the gownda, then it can take four or five shaves or tappings every alternate year; leave the pots alone for the night and by the morning the liquor floors a man in no time. It is bitter as poison. A country date palm is shaved in the morning, no second shave in the evening, unlike a toddy palm. The pot stays on the palm till the next morning. Bring it down. Then, rest the country date palm for one day. Thus, alternate shaves. The country date palm is a delicate lady. But, the toddy is a real wonder, like a robust woman, and can take continuous taps throughout the year, unlike a country date palm which obliges only in winter. Each country date palm can take me for only one month; each toddy for a year.

A country date palm must be delicate leafed for easy drawing. It is difficult with thick-leafed big-thorned palms, but once you succeed she yields full pots. Venkanna the expert, they all say. Drove the vuli, they say, straight in.

In the countryside, Granny Appachchi realized that monsoon felt different. The youthful passion of the first hit, the well-timed nuptial of the sky and the earth. The passionate youth of the monsoon, frenzied lovemaking after a prolonged separation. Its grandiloquence, its profusion, rolling down immense crystal bead curtains, drilling dimples in the sandy soil. The morning after: fine soap-rinsed sunlight, the peace, the clarity of the sky. Nature in languor, dreamy relaxation.

There is the workmanlike steadiness of later visits, the deceptive unobtrusiveness of the subsequent moves, from a drizzle to needlework, an almost imperceptible buzz, like white ants, diligent proletariat just below the surface of the earth. The gods overwhelm with overflowing streams, rivulets, and rivers, flooding whole districts, a divine frenzy.

Word reached Nephew that there was something unseemly going on between Appachchi and Veeranna. Worker Aunt would not believe it: Veeranna's hair was funny, like a jute cap on his head; the man smelt like a flock of unwashed goats, or he probably bathed once a week and in his own fermented toddy. She did not pay any further attention to the rumour. But when Veeranna boasted to the company at his toddy shop that Appachchi had signed a document giving away the rights of the fields to him, all that belonged to her, Nephew went and convinced Appachchi that she could not be so thoughtless. How could she be unkind to her own family? He escorted her home. She never returned to the island.

Worker Aunt regretted sending her vadina to the island farm. 'When her fortune would have her govern a kingdom, her misfortune would have her graze asses.' At any rate, she said, her belief was confirmed: 'You should not trust the one who writes, or the one who cuts, or the one who pares.'

Nephew talked to the village elders and they sent for Veeranna. He showed the document to them: it was perfectly valid. They suggested that he surrender the papers as well as the fields to Nephew. He refused. Nephew returned home and filed a suit. Veeranna was not allowed to rest or enjoy the fruits of the fields and orchards; the visits to the court in the taluk town took all his time and energy. First, the hearings were adjourned. Veeranna's lawyer connived with Nephew; after a year, Veeranna's patience ran out; he shouted at his lawyer and almost roughed him up. Not just his lawyer, but the whole community of lawyers of the taluk town boycotted him. And Veeranna was left to face Nephew's lawyer all alone. As Nephew had bribed the judge, he had to face often the ire of the judge as well. He wanted the judge to call Appachchi to testify; but she had already been 'certified'; she was in no condition to testify. Veeranna tried hard to meet Appachchi and talk to her, but he was not allowed to go anywhere near the Brahmin street. Nephew sent word to him that a criminal case would be filed if he disturbed the peace of the household. His strong sturdy face now bore the impress of subjection, and almost of servility.

Nephew seemed to know the verdict beforehand; he had prepared a prospective buyer for Appachchi's share of the property. The day the judge restored it to Appachchi, he left on horse. Horse and man boarded a special flat bottom boat for the island, where Nephew sold it away for hard cash. When he briefed Worker Aunt, she said, 'Good'.

Worker Aunt couldn't swallow what her vadina had done. Not much later there was a petty quarrel between the two ladies and Worker Aunt left for Kasi.

∽

Though ashamed of their good health, the two women kept Nephew company in his last days.

The broken man kept talking to Worker Aunt about his past, his frustrations, his discovery of a 'philosophy': 'All is illusion.'

Worker Aunt tried to match his esoteric quotes with her own

Sanskrit scholarship. All this is gatajalasethubandhanam, trying to build a dam to store water that has already flown down. And on the mystery of the passage of time and man's life, she came up with another: kalaha kridathi gachchthyayuhu: time sports, life goes on.

Granny Appachchi quoted the Guru of the Stream:

> God is not involved in either rewards or punishments. He only reflects, resounds, and reacts!... Do good and have good in return; be bad and accept the bad that comes back to you. That is the law, and there is really no help or hindrance.
>
> He has endowed you with the faculty of reasoning (viveka) and detachment (vairagya). With a sense of awe and wonder, you have to use these for attaining Him. Though bound, you not entirely incapacitated.... Do not blame fate or siro-likhitham, writing on the forehead, for your condition. The likhitham has been done by yourself.
>
> The seeds of wrong behaviour will not germinate and grow into painful events in our life if they are covered deep with loving service to those who are in need of sustenance, courage, love, and help. A lifetime of good deeds will cover a multitude of past sins. If you're constant in your service, the bad seeds may die away.

Nephew heard her out.

'Service for me? Now!' he smiled wryly.

Worker Aunt too got into the spirit. She quoted the Guru of the Stream.

> Total adherence to truth, absolute selflessness, universality, and the spontaneous outpouring of love are to be seen only in God and nowhere else.
>
> God desires only your ananda.
>
> Work done without the thought of self and eschewing the craving for name or power pleases Him most.

Granny Appachchi added:

'This is no religion of despair; it is a religion of hope, of assurance, of encouragement to lead an active, useful, beneficent life.'

'Be free, be Divine,' Appachchi concluded.

Nephew, whose mind had wandered off early, now paid attention to the words. He glanced at Worker Aunt and said to himself, 'Enough of freedom for me, divine or human.' Unlike Shakespeare, a favourite of his, and in spite of the Guru of the Stream who had given him ample access and more attention than he had conferred on many other devotees, in spite of all those miracles he had seen the Guru perform before his very eyes, he receded as his end neared, as though some unseen force had erased selectively the later phase of his life, retaining only the Kshatriyas in his account. He went back to his sceptical moods, not for him 'more things in heaven and earth....'

In the last years of his life, Nephew paid a heavy price for his fondness for sweets and mangoes. When diabetes nibbled at the nerves with a thousand ant jaws, and they moaned and groaned through the day and through the night, he prayed to God to take him away.

He still recited from the Bible, a book he had started reading at the English Mission School of Masula.

> A good name is better than precious ointment; and the day of death than the day of one's birth.
>
> Sorrow is better than laughter: for by the sadness of the countenance the heart is made better.
>
> For as the crackling of thorns under a pot, so is the laughter of the fool: this also is vanity.

In the season of lengthening shadows, the two women held together, uncomplaining, playing the mother, nurse, companion, and counsellor to Nephew, and managing the house, the byre, the fields, the field hands and sharecroppers, and the numerous visitors who called, but whom Nephew, the dying man, did not want to see. He had turned away from his community, from this world, but without another world to depart to, to look forward to, feeling stranded like fish on a sandbar, exposed to the heat of memories. He believed he was unwanted though cared for—he could not say that he was uncared for; the ladies cared for him. They tended to him not out of gratitude but out of their affection. His irritability grew; nothing satisfied him, not even his own favourite dishes cooked with great care and love by the two old women. His appetite declined steadily, his big frame shrivelled and shrank. All conversation ceased; he hardly opened his mouth. He lay on the canopy bed, eyes drooping most of the time. He was all bones now, his skin hanging on his frame.

The big grandfather clock in the front hall kept marking the hours; its chimes rang through the night and could be heard even in the street, and at night, even at the end of the street. The head of the family wound up the clock. On the dial, they had marked 'WED'; every Wednesday, Nephew wound it up as his brother-in-law had done for decades. As Nephew declined, Worker Aunt took over the duty. And even the very week of Nephew's death, she did it, and kept doing it. Granny Appachchi offered to do it for her, but Worker Aunt said, 'You have no head for mechanical things, you will end up breaking the spring.' The clock was kept going; it never stopped.

The man kept hearing a sound: the sound of water, dripping, dropping, rushing over rocks, water gurgling in his throat. He gulped it down every now and then. And then, the sound of rain.

The suffering made it difficult. In the early days, when he was still in the mood or had the energy, he reported rapacious ants at work just beneath his skin; the women had to press his limbs all night. He complained of a stench, of the dust he waded through so often on his way to Junction.

He would sit on the beautiful sitting plank covered with silver flowers, lean against the carved wooden plank, and groan and fidget and suddenly shuffle off.

'What's it?'

He was too distraught.

The two women looked all over, swept the place clean, and then laid the planks again. They brought his eating plate and drinking pot, and he sat down for a meal he no longer enjoyed. He fingered the rice and the dal, ate a little, and then pushed the plate away.

The villagers themselves and everyone around, family and friends, even those who had called upon God to punish him for his sins, wished him release. Only Worker Aunt and Appachchi, decades younger, kept working quietly. When it happened, they themselves cremated him and performed the last rites, spurning the idea of only a male having to perform the obsequies, Worker Aunt all the same strictly following the Vedic rites, doing everything possible to make the onward journey of the spirit smooth.

'There is medicine for a disease, but is there a cure for fate?'

And when he died, at last, taking ages and ages to go, not because he wanted not to go, not because his desire for this life was strong, but as though something somehow held him—not back but down, like a man in the dark, his dhoti caught in the fork of a fence picket, tugging desperately, in growing panic. There was no doubt about it; it was one of those cases where Yama took His own sweet time carrying out His duty, not because He was remiss in His duty, but because some force greater than Him held His hand.

The two women recognized it. It was universal: the fear of death. Fear had made the going tough.

'What is this dust? Have you seen any near Junction? I haven't.'

'Nor have I.'

'Then?'

'Remember what he had said? Clouds of dust, the dust of eons.'

Part V

Worker Aunt

After the death of BA Garu, the two women eventually decided to dispose of his personal effects. It was Granny Appachchi's idea. They gave away his kurtas and dhotis, his towels and handkerchiefs—they were as big as hand towels, some of them embroidered by Appachchi herself. 'I cannot stand the sight of these,' she said. They sent away his stallion to a relative in Rajahmundry.

But the books were a different matter. Everyone in the village remembered the day they had arrived. There had been a procession of passenger carts with strong rainproof thatches, little huts on the move, covered on both ends, as though some women of upper castes were travelling in purdah. BA Garu had sealed them and he had personally supervised the unloading, one cart after another, of books in several languages.

'You know, Meenu,' he'd said to Appachchi, 'I could not afford to be lax or careless. So many youngsters around who would not touch a single dammidi, one-twelfth of an anna, of another do not mind filching a book.'

'They must be mad,' Appachchi had said.

'Yes, they are. All kinds of madness is possible, Appachchi. After all, we are human beings, not devatas. And book-reading is a rare form of the malady.'

And he'd managed to infect his young wife with it. Soon, Appachchi and BA were both found lost for hours in their room. Appachchi had tried to get Worker Aunt interested; she did not succeed. Worker Aunt had taken her brother and Granny Appachchi to her own modest library, which had in all five or six books of bhajans and prayers, besides the two epics, and some puranas, the Gita, and the Upanishads.

Sometime after Worker Aunt had left for Kasi, Granny Appachchi called on the Guru of the Stream. The first time, the very sight of the crystal-clear water, bubbly, cavorting, whirling, rushing forward with such spirit, revived her; it always reminded her of schoolchildren rushing out after the long bell in the afternoon, yearning for release. Today, it moved serenely, quietly, with hardly a gurgle.

The Guru was alone. It was the afternoon hour, siesta hour for everyone, but the Guru was working at his loom. Tears poured down her cheeks; the sight of her Guru had cleansed her heart again.

The Guru did not say a word, he blessed her and pointed to the arugu. She sat there and went into meditation immediately. The Guru returned to his loom.

When Worker Aunt returned from Kasi, he received both sisters-in-law together as always; without a word exchanged the two women got the message. Their sadhana had resumed. Woven into the warp and woof of everyday life, their spiritual practice continued. The Guru of the Fresh Stream had warned both of them. All the same, when it came, Worker Aunt was shocked.

Now, something happened again. Appachchi changed. She underwent a radical transformation. Granny Appachchi became a champion of life, all life, of all and any creatures.

Love for little ones came naturally to both the women. Podumburra, and every one of the boys and girls of Granny Appachchi's arugu school, remembered her flying visits to the town with or without BA Garu. Later, while Nephew lay dying, Worker Aunt was stuck to his bedside, but Granny Appachchi did not turn away children from the arugu school. She spent more time with them.

Very early, she had introduced them to sweets. Every week, a new variety of sweet was bought from the best sweet-maker of the taluk town.

'We came out, all of us,' recalled Podumburra to his children, 'not just the kids of the family visiting for the vacation, but every kid in the village, on to the arugus and waited. We strained our ears to hear the first tinkle of the bullock bell. Losing patience with the waiting, we came out on to the street and looked at the other end, the right end. The bullock cart should appear at this end. But you never know, the cart may have taken a detour, so we turned around, and standing right in the middle of the road, we looked and strained our eyes to spot any movement at the end of the street. Passers-by noticed us immediately and said in greeting, "Who is coming? Who is coming?" They were all either neighbours, or friends of our father, or our relatives in some branch of our family or other. "Granny Appachchi," we shouted joyously, "Granny Appachchi!"

'Because every time she came she brought us snacks, sweets, and savouries.

'When the bullock cart turned into our street, we raced to it and almost got in its way. Granny Appachchi was at the rear of the cart, grinning away with satisfaction, her deep-set dark eyes twinkled and moistened with love. She halted the cart. We clambered onto the cart; those fifty yards' rides gave us as much satisfaction as going by a single bullock cart bandy to the town to watch a circus show or the biscope. By the time we reached home, covering those few yards, each of us had his mouth full, munching something or other, shelled chestnuts, and sweets!

'Ladoos—boondi ladoo, Bandar ladoo, ravva ladoo; nuvvundalu, sunnundalu; kazalu—kakinada kazalu, madatha kazalu, badsha; kova kajjikai, kova puri, kajji kayalu, pootharekulu; halva—Bandar halva, Bombay halva; Mysore pak; soan papdi; jangri, jalebi; ariselu, boorelu; kaju kathali; savouries—pakodi: jeedi pappu pakodi, vullipai pakodi, gatti pakodi, mettha pakodi; chekkalu; the most delicious cheygodies all fried in pure ghee, they just melted in the mouth!

'In no time our mouths were so full we could not utter a single syllable, but we didn't have to announce the arrival of Granny Appachchi.

'"The kids will all fill their bellies with this junk," grumbled Worker Aunt, "it will be a blessing if they don't fall ill. And what's the point in my cooking any rice, it will remain uneaten." Granny Appachchi behaved as though she had not heard. Releasing herself from the mobbing kids, she went quietly to Worker Aunt and held her and gave her a sweet smile, asking, "How are you, vadina?" Worker Aunt melted like a pure ghee sweet, and said, "First wash and change into decent clothes, the meal is ready, you can eat with me and tell me about your experiences"—she almost said "your adventures". "Yes," said Granny Appachchi like a docile daughter once again, and pulling some clothes from her jute bag, she rushed to the river.

'The kids waited, with their bellies full, not heeding Worker Aunt's call to come eat. We waited with one eye on the backyard door, and the moment she appeared, we mobbed Granny Appachchi and gave her a hug, a kiss, a hug again, a kiss again. Worker Aunt commanded us to keep off, 'If you don't want to eat, let me and Granny Appachchi eat.' So, the kids retreated to the front hall, its sideboard a treasure trove now, and helped the field hand sort the purchases and fill various tin cans with them, unpacking more and more of them from Appachchi's luggage. She had bundled them up in her own saris! Worker Aunt could only sigh in resignation at the way her vadina continued to recklessly ruin her sari collection. Worker Aunt rewarded the field hand with sweets and savouries to take home to his kids; later, the helper's family was there to welcome Granny Appachchi whenever she carried these shipments. She also gave away all the rice she had cooked for the kids, and the vegetable dishes and mukkala pulusu (tangy vegetable stew) in a mud pot she had kept thoughtfully for such a purpose. The kids of the field hands too came to cherish Appachchi's visits.

One day, it was the tamarind tale Miss Beston narrated to Jane after dinner. Now that her munshi had collected his tales in a manuscript, she enjoyed this experience of holding Jane's rapt attention.

Once upon a time, there lived a king of Central India. He was handsome, but very vain. He looked at himself constantly, in mirrors, in pools of water, even in other people's eyes when they spoke to him. 'I am the handsomest king on Earth,' he said to his courtiers. He paid less attention to ruling his kingdom than he did to having his hair styled and his body oiled. As a result, his people grew poorer and unhappier.

But the king did not care. 'Why!' he boasted one day in court, 'I am probably more handsome than all the gods.'

Unfortunately for the king, a particularly ill-tempered god happened to be flying by and was incensed at what he heard.

'Something will have to be done about this king.' He searched in his mind for an appropriate punishment. Then his eyes fell upon a bull. 'Horns!' the god clapped his hands with glee. 'I'll see how His Handsomeness likes himself with horns.'

When the king awoke the next morning, he followed his normal routine. First, he drew his mirror out from under his pillow and gazed into it.

Suddenly, the guards outside the king's chamber heard a loud shriek. They came rushing in to find the king sitting upright in bed with a large pillow on his head.

'Out...out...' he waved a trembling finger at them. As they backed away, he shouted after them, 'Send for the royal barber immediately.'

The royal barber was a cheeky talkative little man. He came in briskly.

'You're up early today, Your Majesty, but why the pil—'

As the surprised barber drew close, the king said in his

most commanding voice, 'Barber, I am about to show you something. But if you talk about it to a single living soul, I will have you flogged and hanged.'

The king slowly removed the pillow from his head.

'Oh!' The barber clapped his hands to his mouth in horror.

'Well, don't just stand there,' said the king impatiently. 'Do something to cover them up.'

The barber had worked on several men with thinning hair; he had developed expertise in covering up open spaces. Now, he gathered the king's strands and reshuffled them this way and that and managed to cover the horns partially. The king put his nightcap on to hide the rest. 'Now go and tell the court I am unwell. I will not see anyone.' He sat up and glared at the barber. 'And remember my warning.'

The barber fled. As soon as the door of the bedchamber closed, he started laughing. The palace attendants stopped him and asked him the reason for his mirth but the barber only shook his head helplessly and fled laughing through the halls.

'I will die if I don't tell someone,' he groaned. 'My stomach is swelling with the secret.'

The barber left the town and roamed all over to find a way he could relieve himself of his burden. He remembered an old tamarind tree on the south side of the town. Its bole looked like the belly of an aged elephant, thick and gnarled. He found a hollow in its trunk, made sure there was no bird nesting there, and breathed his secret into it. 'You know—how would you?!' he chuckled. 'If you promise to keep it a secret I shall tell you the best-kept secret in the kingdom.'

The tree nodded; at least, that's what the barber thought.

'The king has grown horns.'

Call it the burden of the secret; the very next day the tree collapsed. And a passing musician cut a limb and made a drum of it.

The tamarind tree yielded the drum, which proclaimed the secret to the whole world. The king confiscated the offending instrument and fled to the forest with the drum.

The king lived for several years in the forest. He began to appreciate the beauty of the world around him. He learned to care for creatures smaller than himself, for all God's creatures, big or small. He grew strong and wise and selfless. His only companion was the tamarind drum; but now the drum too changed: when he beat it, it gave him all the advice and experience of the ancient tree. He learned to play it so beautifully that even the spirits of the trees were charmed. They went to the god who had given him the horns and pleaded with him.... The god revoked the punishment.

The king went back to his realm. He kept his tamarind drum beside him always and he ruled wisely. And yes, the barber kept his head, but lost his job.

Now Jane turned to the munshi. He smiled and together Jane and the old man and Miss Beston concluded the story:

'The story left for Kanchi and we for home.'

'What's the matter, Jane? Something's on your mind.'

'No, Thatha, the barber keeps his job, too.'

'How come?'

'The king has changed, hasn't he?'

∽

Once a month, Subbanna the barber visited the house; it was a discreet arrival, and a decorous departure. He came at dawn and crept into the backyard through the backdoor at dawn and slipped away quietly through the same door. But once inside, he was anything but quiet.

Even before his customer, Worker Aunt, arrived before him he took out the shaver from a tin box that was dented all over—it must have been as old as his career, but because he believed it was a good luck charm he refused to part with it, even when the ladies suggested it to him tactfully. In his days of glory, he had been a champion nadaswaram player, decorated copiously by the rajas of the region. He had played, on special invitation, at every important wedding—on all the five days of the ceremony—and thread ceremony. He was also the best masseur the region had produced; even rajas paid him a retainer because he alone came along with special herbal oils mentioned in books on Ayurveda. But now he was old, his breathing was not what it used to be, he kept away, or was being kept away, from such distractions. But his widow and Brahmin tonsures and cutting hair gave him as much aesthetic satisfaction and kept his zest alive. It was also an emotionally satisfying experience. The old ladies and the other widows of the town welcomed him because he respected them and valued their customs. The younger generation, developing a taste for Western hairdos, of course kept away, but the Vedic Brahmins requiring the cart-roof tonsure and a thick, long well-groomed tuft still sent for him.

He brought news and entertainment to the ladies, one reason why Appachchi too joined the party. The tonsuring, the gossip about the Boat Woman and the police officer who had never married because he would either marry the Boat Woman or never marry at all—this and more, all had to be completed before the men of the family stirred from their rooms.

Here, they heard more about the Boat Woman and her activities, all kinds, not just hunting and commercial. She was an old woman herself, and the proprietor of a big company. In keeping with the best norms of decency, Subbanna would lower his voice when he came to the juicy bits. And then the ladies would allow him to have his full say, but would appear to cut him short by saying, 'Why bother about her private life? And besides, she is a white woman. Our rules don't apply to the white people; they come from a cold country.'

It was through Subbanna that they came to know of the Boat

Woman's visit to the Guru of the Stream, how he had blessed her as he did every other visitor. He had only advised her to be cautious and prudent.

And that set off a debate: they agreed that the Guru had advised her to be cautious because she had made so many enemies.

'True, true,' Subbanna said, pleased and relieved that he had fulfilled his multifaceted mission.

∞

Law and order became a topic of discussion when Colonel Roberclaw, a gritty army officer, visited.

'In a typical Indian court,' said the Colonel, 'both sides lie, just lies and nothing but lies. Witnesses pack the court's quadrangle, sit under every tree in the vicinity during the hot day, and wait patiently, but all of them are practised, professional witnesses, coached easily by the vakils to lie convincingly.'

Roberclaw seemed to echo his bosses, every one of them. He was of the considered opinion that truth and Indian character didn't agree; the two were temperamentally incompatible.

'Mendacity is an old established institution in India.'

Roberclaw, at the same time, was equally struck by the contrast: 'When an Englishman is given a task, however difficult it may be, however remote its field, he could still put his mind to it and accomplish it. He is the acme of European civilization, the best human history and world geography have seen. He is Gulliver unchained. In Her Majesty's service, he will face and overcome any hurdles. His worst foe in India is not the people of India, but the climate. But even the most insidious climate in the world holds no terrors for him.... The state calls upon him, and he answers immediately.

'The saga of the British in India is unique,' he continued, 'an inspirational tale for the whole world, for all the races of mankind. Just a handful of them, in a manner of speaking, have for many years ruled wisely and beneficently a vast concourse of people quite alien to themselves in thought and habit. Ruled over a people who can't be more different from us. In a way, the natives have made it more difficult for us. They are the most slothful or enervated nation on the earth. For instance, whatever an Englishman will do standing, if needed for hours on end, a native will do the same job squatting and will take weeks.'

Many nodded their heads.

Mr Blotton countered with a quote from William Bentinck: '...nothing can exceed the popularity of a recent regulation by which, if a robbery has been committed, the police are prevented from making any enquiry into it, except upon the requisition of the persons robbed: that is to say, the shepherd is a more ravenous beast of prey than the wolf.'

And he quoted John Malcolm: 'I do not know the example of any great population, in similar circumstances preserving through such a period of change and tyrannical rule, so much virtue and so many qualities as are to be found in a great proportion of the inhabitants of this country: the absence of common vices of theft, drunkenness, and violence.'

Roberclaw had received tapal, the familiar red envelope, by 'express messenger. The police depot in the upcountry agency area had been in a state of siege...and the rioters had been having a high old time of it. Their ringleader was a cult figure of the hills, worshipped by the tribals of the vast tract stretching to Dandakaranya in the north-east. Money in treasure chests hidden in palanquins was on its way to Masula, with a postal peon to show the way through the Coromandel forest. The bandits attacked them, killed everyone of the party, including the postal peon, and carried away the treasure chests.'

David had ordered a platoon of his men to train for a day, loading their muskets with buckshot, and firing at straw targets until they could do it faster than any men in the Coromandel. His sepoys had been armed with flint-and-steel muskets until 1844. They had got percussion arms only in 1848.

They talked about the most exasperating feature of administration in India: communications. Adhering one lac seal to another en route was often the cause for letters being torn open before they reached their destination.

Miss Beston had thoughtfully arranged a fireworks show for her guests, on a high crag away from any possibility of a squib accidentally igniting a scrub fire.

∽

Whenever Nephew felt that Granny Appachchi was running out of chores, he would go to the market and buy and cart home a bag of Bengal gram or green gram. She would spend the free time cleaning the stuff, pouring out a few seers at a time into a bucket, and with the help of the winnowing basket, either along with Worker Aunt, or alone, all by herself, steadily weeded out the tiny stones mixed in with the gram—the merchants seemed to profit a lot from this unfair practice, she would grumble. She cleaned the gram, all off it, and stored it in tin canisters. Or she would herself get a banana doota, the core of the banana trunk, and prepare it for a curry. She'd spent the whole afternoon cleaning the doota, cutting it into fine round pieces. Picking a fibre thread and dipping her finger in sour buttermilk from time to time, she would unwind the thread from the doota slice; she knew the curry cooked, with the right spices, was a favourite with Nephew.

∽

Sir Arthur Blotton addressed a church missionary meeting. The retired architect of irrigation said: '…observing the progress of things among the native community, nothing can be more certain in my mind than that, through missionary operations and other means which have operated in God's gracious Providence, there has been a wonderful preparation for the spreading of the Knowledge of our Lord and Saviour, Jesus Christ, throughout India. The fields are ready to be harvested. First, the government has, in a great measure, withdrawn their opposition. Second, several of the local governors are most heartily supporting the missions, subscribing liberally to them, and presiding over the meetings.'

∽

A sanyasi from Kasi called on the family one day. Worker Aunt gave him the ceremonial alms. Nephew sat down for his meal with the sanyasin. The holy man lumped all items in his leaf plate with the rice and swallowed it in just a few morsels. That was his meal.

'I am returning to Kasi,' he told them. 'When you come to Kasi, come and see me.'

He would turn out to be a valuable contact for Worker Aunt in Kasi.

∽

Seshacharyulu garu expounded to Miss Beston.

Miss Beston nodded gratefully. She was listening to the munshi and looking out of the window at a gorgeous sunset.

'The time between the setting of the starlight and the sunrise is called Prathas sandhya by the sages.

'According to Daksha:, the last two nadis—twenty-four minutes equals one nadi—of the last three hours of the night is the beginning of the sandhya time. The sun's upward shooting rays signal the end of sandhya. The deity worshipped at this time is called Sandhya, hence this time is called sandhya time.'

'Samvartha says: "Prathassandhya should be worshipped when stars are still seen and Sandhya is worshipped in the evening, when the sun is half set."'

On the subject of Indian hospitality and mendicancy, the pundit reminded her of the ancient Greeks: no stranger at the door was asked who he was until he had been fed.

'Says Parashara: "A guest should be welcomed after Vaishvadeva. Give him a seat, wash his feet, serve meals with care, have pleasant conversation, and make him happy. When he leaves, go with him a short distance. Don't ask him about his education, family, and gothram. Treat him as a deva. Shastra calls a guest a personification of God."

'And Manu: "Even a poor man should take care of a guest. If there is no seat, he can spread darbha grass as a seat. If there is no bed, he can be asked to sleep on the ground. If there is no oil, water can be given. If there is no food, pleasant words can be spoken. A man should never disregard a guest."

'According to Haritha: "Do Vishnu puja with devotion, and give bhiksha to sanyasis. Sanyasis should be regarded as Vishnu. Shastra says that Vishnu Himself takes meals in that house. Where Vishnu takes meals, it is like feeding the three worlds."

'Says Vyasa: "That man, who gives the sanyasi a bowl full of food is freed from all his sins. He never becomes destitute."'

'That comes to the same thing as a dip in the holy Ganges, doesn't it?' said Miss Beston.

'It is not the body, it is the spirit that should undergo a cleansing.'

∾

'A little to eat and to live at Kasi' is the wish of every pious Hindu. Worker Aunt's wish had developed into an unshakeable resolve when she found that the way their home was being run was not at all to her liking. When Nephew briefed her about the goings on in the island, how a mere toddy tapper had affected the thinking and conduct of Granny Appachchi, she made up her mind; she couldn't live in a polluted home. When Granny Appachchi returned from the island village, Worker Aunt did not go and receive her. She avoided all points of contact with Appachchi; it wasn't difficult in a large home. Resentment, an uncharacteristic bitterness, got the better of old ties. The kitchen as well as the east room was out of bounds for Appachchi. Yet, Worker Aunt cooked the food as usual and left it in plates, one for Nephew in the east room and another for Appachchi in the veranda.

And Worker Aunt dunned Nephew to let her make the trip. The man of the family had to give in finally, make arrangements, give her enough cash, and send messages to his contacts in every town where pilgrims to Kasi normally halted for the night before resuming the journey of their life.

She went via Hyderabad and Central India and returned via Calcutta and Visakhapatnam.

Worker Aunt's return from Kasi was celebrated as a grand event in the village. Granny Appachchi led the reception and celebrations. The whole village turned up with drummers and pipers, welcoming her on the outskirts of the village. A great resounding reception. And with an unprecedented musical ensemble—a brainwave of Nephew's—a brass band from Rajahmundry. These stalwart men in colourful uniforms had even got a troupe of dancing girls from the town. 'I don't like the idea,' said Worker Aunt. But Nephew could see she was delighted all the same. So, he did not chide the band master for his expensive initiative. And it made him feel sentimental; it brought him memories of the Kshatriyas of Singapuram. As though in atonement, Nephew organized Narayana Seva—feeding of the poor.

The heart got the better of the head; Worker Aunt had shelved the past. On spotting Granny Appachchi next to Nephew, she opened her arms. The sisters-in-law hugged each other and wept.

Worker Aunt had given up bitter gourd at Kasi. 'Why not jalebi and ladoo, which you are so fond of?' asked Appachchi, her sense of mischief getting the better of her tact. She quickly added, 'Sweets are bad for your diabetes, bitter gourd is good for your general health.' Worker Aunt glared at her, and Appachchi slipped away to the backyard.

The Guru of the Stream said to Worker Aunt and Granny Appachchi:

> Service is an important ingredient in the nine-fold discipline of devotion.... If you do not feel the call at the sight of human distress, disease, or deviation from the right, how can you muster the determination and dedication necessary to serve the unseen, inscrutable, mysterious God?... The heart that does not melt at the sight of persons caught in the coils of ignorance, disease, or deprivation has to be labelled demonic; to call it bestial is an insult to the beasts.
>
> If you want to attain God, cultivate love; give up hatred, envy, anger, cynicism, and falsehood. Hurt never, Help ever! Hands that serve are holier than lips that pray!

Worker Aunt's buttermilk beneficiaries formed the core of a growing group of women and old men of piety. Worker Aunt, an heiress in her own right, delivered talks on her own experiences and other religious matters purely for their benefit. The villagers applauded Worker Aunt and kept applauding her. She had defied death, they said, citing the adage 'going to Kasi was going to your funeral'. She had opted for life and family. Her reputation was assiduously built by the buttermilk devotees.

On popular and insistent demand Worker Aunt narrated her story to her pupils of the club. Setting out for Kasi, she said, she had happened to visit relatives en route and found them caught in a famine, the worst famine the region had seen. With the money sent by Nephew for her expenses, she had opened free kitchens. Better to reach Kasi fasting.

The villagers responded to Worker Aunt's story of her Kasi pilgrimage with great wonder. Several of the party, affected by jungle air, Worker Aunt told them, contracted malarial fevers. They had to be carried on dholies. On the way Telugu pilgrims were getting sick for another reason—they could not find tamarind and red chillies. Affluent people wore saffron coloured clothes in the North. They all sported silver anklets; commoners covered themselves with thick blankets or barabandi. 'So that's where BA Garu's costume had come from!' the listeners whispered to each other. The pilgrim from Kasi had noticed a marked indifference to clothes in the North and to vessels in the South. Northerners were generous to pandas; unlike southerners. The pandas, devils in the guise of priests anyway, called pilgrims from South India demons. In Bengal, when greeting, people bowed their heads to the ground, both hands in closed fists, legs pushed into bellies in the traditional manner. The men were meek and mild.

There were these gangaputras, Brahmins from 1,200 families who were traditionally in charge of worship in Kasi. The gangaputra who sighted a pilgrim first acquired the right of serving him. Those who did not pay as demanded were harassed, insulted, or physically injured. They made the raja of Vizianagaram stay in his palace a whole year without his holy dip.

Shudras in the North were afraid they would catch a cold if they drank buttermilk at night. Things touched or smelt were not taken back by shopkeepers. In general, Brahmins shopped for food without water and without salt.

Granny Appachchi could not resist a crack. She said few widows and old women could afford this kind of public celebration, or demonstration of spiritual fulfilment—few widows even dared to leave for Kasi: they might be abandoned there.

Then Worker Aunt told them of the widows in Mathura and Kasi. She said the three great dangers at Kasi were the steps, the bulls, and the widows. Many had broken their necks while going down the slippery steps of the bathing ghats, or twisted their limbs badly. And you couldn't move around in the narrow gallis of Kasi without your path being blocked by bulls and other cattle. The barber who sighted a pilgrim first got shaving rights.

Appachchi noticed here a shift in her sister-in-law. Worker Aunt had toned down with exquisite delicacy two atrocities of Kasi: widows and ritual priests; both the evils had sobered somewhat her vadina's religious fervour.

At Worker Aunt's levees, the matins of the buttermilk bhaktas, she observed a special phenomenon she had come across in the North. 'The gopalakas, cowherds, are sachchudras, or virtuous Shudras: they don't eat meat, and Ganga water from them is accepted by everyone.'

'So, caste is not determined by birth, but by habits and purity of mind,' said a simple village woman.

Though the Guru of the Stream had been saying the same thing and had demonstrated the truth for decades, Worker Aunt resented the comment. She made a mental note to reduce the woman's ration of buttermilk. She shifted her talk on to more comfortable ground. 'We Brahmins purchased food without water and salt. The village Brahmins were orthodox; they observed all types of annual ceremony: anna, aama, hiranya. Consultation of the panchangam was widely prevalent; every vaidiki Brahmin carried one.'

Worker Aunt confessed to Nephew later that in the same village she had also learned that young girls were brought and sold at Jubbulpore. She was too ashamed about this to mention it to anyone else except Nephew. On her Silver Pilgrimage, she had picked up some sombre experiences.

Worker Aunt's extensive lectures continued with academic regularity. She even offered her services to the local school as a guest faculty. The kids welcomed a second teacher, but the add-on teacher, it turned out, had specialized in one area: Kasi.

'One day, on the way to Kasi, we passed through a village. A bhagavata kalakshepam (discourse on Bhagavata) was going on. Not even one person among the crowd turned to look at our palanquins—admirable concentration. That is the kind of focused attention you boys and girls must develop....

'In one village, we were put up in travellers' sheds: with cow-dung washed hearths, pegs for tying up cattle.'

'And then the bandits came!' said Gayathri, a neighbour's granddaughter.

'No, no, no bandits. Why should bandits come just like that? Not yet, I shall come to the bandits in a minute.'

'She is still on her way,' chipped in Granny Appachchi.

With the connivance of time and a complex well-manipulated code of rewards and penalties, gradually Worker Aunt grew more comfortable in her discourses. From time to time, she recalled how the Guru of the Stream had enjoined this duty on her. Enthused by the steady improvement in reception—or perception, one and the same—Worker Aunt discoursed on various spiritual matters to her captive audience. She concluded her discourses to these captive congregations with a prayer: 'God, give us peace and place.'

For the practical Sakhinetipalli women, who did not light the kitchen fire before calling on Worker Aunt—you never knew what the lady might gift them any one day—vegetables, fruit, or even clothes—a few holy words were hardly anything to pay for creamy buttermilk.

One day, a photographer from the Nizam's territory came to the region; all the landlords and their wives and families had their portraits done. Nephew brought the man along. The man with the magic box declared that saintly persons were rare, and that it was their duty to leave mementos for the edification of their families and society. Granny Appachchi turned down the idea, but she supported Nephew's proposal that Worker Aunt should sit for a portrait. She was reluctant initially but said later she would go in for one if Appachchi joined her. Appachchi refused to oblige; Worker Aunt relented finally and went in for a life-size portrait on one condition: the colour of her sari should be reproduced accurately, for Worker Aunt insisted on being photographed in her ochre costume. When the professional came back with a flattering result, she wasn't satisfied: the ochre wasn't bright enough, wasn't radiant enough. Appachchi agreed.

∞

Miss Beston had returned from Madras with—among many other things—a box full of books and a packet of question papers of Madras University. She enjoyed discussing the question papers with her munshi.

> Explain and illustrate the difference in the use of (1) that and which as relatives, and (2) each and every.
>
> What is tense? Construct short complex sentences, introducing correctly the forms: I was going, I went, I have gone, I had gone.
>
> Write down the past tense and past participle of sow, saw, smite, seethe, spoil; and the second person singular, past perfect, subjunctive, passive voice, of the verb 'call' expressed negatively.
>
> Remark in explanation of the italicized portions of the following words, and give another example illustrating each case explained:
>
> Kine, chicken, hillock, needs (adverb).
>
> (a) Tabulate, with care, the clauses in the following sentence and describe their character and relations:
>
> 'He who hath pleased himself with anticipated praises and expected that he should meet in every place with patronage or friendship, will soon remit his vigour, when he finds that from those who desire to be considered as his admirers nothing can be hoped but cold civility, and that many refuse to own his excellence, lest they should be too justly expected to reward it.'
>
> (b) (i) 'The King commanded his minister to see to the execution of the prisoner.' Recast this sentence, employing a clause in place of the infinitive phrase.

All the same, we should look at the grammar.

'He promised readily, but he is slow to perform.' Recast into (i) a simple, (ii) a complex sentence.

(a) Name the figures of speech in the following, giving the reasons for your identification, and give the meaning of (2) in figurative language.
> A grateful mind.
> By owing owes not but still pays,
> at once indebted and discharged.
> All Arabia breathes from
> Yonder box.

Expand into a fully expressed simile:
> Envy will merit, as its shade, pursue,
> But, like a shadow, proves the
> Substance true.

How are (i) advice—advise, (ii) quiet—quite, distinguished in sound and meaning?

Not for nothing the Vice Chancellor of Madras University, a Cantabrigian himself, had said that the Indian universities were as good, if not better than, the best anywhere in the West.

Her munshi added:

'The alumni are now among outstanding servants of Her Majesty's administration in India. Good old Thomas was not far off the mark.'

'Anyone you know, sir?'

'There was this anonymous Andhra boy, he said, born in a tiny hamlet in 1819.'

He told her another Coromandel tale.

His name was Kalamooru Veeravalli Ranganatham, son of a Sanskrit pundit. During the course of his life, he learned fourteen languages. By the age of eight, he was talking fluently in Sanskrit. By the age of ten, he could scale any wall, climb any tree. His father could not pay taxes; the East India Company put him in jail. As his mother cried because there was an obsequial ceremony to perform, the twelve-year old boy went to the district judge, a white man, who demanded surety. The boy offered to sit in jail in his father's place; the judge was impressed, and granted bail to the father. He also asked the boy to see him the following day. 'Will you learn English?' asked the white officer. 'I shall bear all the expenses.'

Ranganatham said, 'I must take permission from my elders.'

The officer talked to the boy's elders.

And he himself taught the alphabet to the boy the very next day. Ranga learned English in six months. Then, he took more English lessons from another white man, a missionary. Every day Ranganatham walked eight kilometres to his tutor. And the missionary's wife treated him kindly, gave him a half seer of milk for breakfast. Then he learned mathematics. There were no facilities for high school there, so the white judge decided to send him to Chennapatnam. The judge persuaded the parents to agree and sent him with a letter of recommendation to the head of the school. His master and Ranga together read English authors such as Adam Smith and John Locke. The boy was no way inferior to any European; on top of it, he had such integrity and gratitude. Later, Ranga tutored lower-class pupils. He returned home when his father was ill. He took up the head clerk job in a subordinate judge's court. He had plenty of time for leisure. He learned Hindustani, Persian, and Kannada. Later, he learned Latin and French, surprising his Supreme Court judge with proficiency in French. He became a friend of the judges. As chief interpreter, he made money on commission basis, earning 2,000 to 2,500 rupees, a colossal amount. He became a friend of Governor Sir Charles Trevelson, who made him judge in a small cause court in the face of stiff opposition. Then, Ranga learned Arabic, memorizing the poetry of Hafiz and Saudi. Several other honours. After retirement, he turned down the Salarjung family's offer to be a private secretary on a salary of

2,500 rupees. His routine: 4 a.m. to 5 a.m. exercise; 5 to 7, horse riding. Long walks in the evening. Riding for six hours. He died with a book in his hand. Among his favourite authors were Cicero, Plato, and Aristotle. He could recite Cicero's Latin speeches from memory. He read once, understood; read twice, memorized; read thrice, remembered forever. Could match any maulvi in Persian and Arabic. Just weeks before his death, he learned Hebrew. He spent vast amounts on books and palmyra texts. Loved teaching others. His motto was 'teach or learn'. He arranged symposia often. Gave gifts of up to 500 rupees to Sanskrit scholars. There were always five or six scholars studying at his expense; he provided them food and clothes. He was a social reformer. He was the first in Madras to wear boots and trousers. The natives mocked him. He believed in women's education, and taught Sanskrit, Telugu, and Tamil to his only daughter. He was a good Hindu who knew the Bible, the Koran, the Vedams. The caste system wasn't for him; he believed in karma theory. He'd been a reserved man.

'Ranganatham must have been just one Indian among many who adapted themselves to the new world order,' Miss Beston remarked.

Incidentally, the distinguished Indian had been one of her invitees at the inauguration of the Coromandel Railway.

∽

Sometime after Worker Aunt had returned from Kasi and established herself as a spiritual fulcrum of villagers thirsty for Vedanta and creamy buttermilk, Granny Appachchi gathered the local schoolboys and girls for yet another story.

The moment the children sat down in a semicircle in front of Appachchi, Gayathri made her regal entry. She went and plopped down on Appachchi's lap. Appachchi gave her a warm kiss. She was the granddaughter of the neighbour Seethamma. This little girl's mother had been the centre of a storm at one time until the her die-hard Brahmin father was beaten into submission by a band of wily women—and he did not know the full story until years later, when the girl child grew into a mature college teacher, and eventually principal, and married a colleague. Her first born was Gayathri was conscious and proud of her status as the firstborn of a college principal.

That evening, the protagonist of Granny Appachchi's tale was a mosquito.

'Suppose I tell you the story of a vegetarian mosquito, a sattvic creature full of thoughts of God, which keeps repeating His name all the time, a mosquito which sustains itself austerely on flowers and fruits, like a rishi or a muni in the forests?' she asked.

Worker Aunt seemed to know what was coming; she shouted from the kitchen, 'You are going to scare the children; they will end up screaming in their sleep.'

'I shall tell you the great story of a rare mosquito, a prince of a mosquito,' Appachchi announced.

'I don't like mosquitoes, princes, or paupers,' Gayathri declared with great conviction.

'Why not?' Appachchi asked to extend the interruption. 'What about you boys?' she asked the gathering.

They nodded in total agreement with little Gayathri. Now, what was happening to this generation, the hope of Bharat Mata? An antipathy towards maharajas and maharanis? All change is welcome. Oh—that was what BA Garu had said!

'Now I take it you also don't love mosquitoes because they bite you.'

'Yes,' they said. 'Look Potti Pantulu's face.' This little fellow was the second youngest of the group. He had made the mistake of wandering off into the veranda of his home and falling asleep on a wooden divan there. His mother had not noticed his absence until she had finished her chores. By then, he had been fairly covered with a blanket of mosquitoes. Now, his face resembled the red soil of the jungle track after the monsoon.'

Gayathri still looked sceptical.

Granny Appachchi tried to push her case. 'That's why I said she is a pious mosquito.'

'First you say boy and then you say girl. What is it? Boy or girl?'

'What would you prefer?'

'Girl, any day.'

'What do you boys say?'

'Boy,' muttered Worker Aunt in the East Room.

'Girl,' said two boys. The rest offered no opinion on the ticklish issue. They were playing it safe.

Appachchi paused, as though she was reading a book inside her mind, or reliving a memory. There was no point in telling this lot about pious creatures, they would rather go in for the exciting stuff like demons harassing whole communities of rishis and munis in the deep woods....

'It is a mosquito with memory, once it reads something or listens to something, it never forgets it. '

'Ekasanthagrahi,' one of the boys chipped in.

'Correct,' Appachchi patted his head. He had just been given a haircut by the village barber. The boy had been promised a Western-style 'crop', but thanks to a combination of factors, the village barber, a successor to the veteran Subbanna, had used his shaver to devastating effect, leaving the little fellow with a shiny, bumpy poll, which vied with Worker Aunt's.

'Are you interested in mosquito memories?' Appachchi asked him with a winsome smile which generally augured more goodies to come from her sideboard. 'A rare mosquito, with a long memory.'

Her campaign showed the first sign of success.

'Male or female?' Gayathri asked.

Appachchi paused for a few seconds, and said, 'Female.' She had made up her mind.

'How do you know?' Gayathri asked.

'Because only a female can take that kind of suffering and those kinds of beatings and still laugh.'

'Don't tell me about the beatings, tell us only about the fun, the games she played and the laughter,' Gayathri said.

The boys nodded in relief.

'How can I do that?' Appachchi said. 'But I shall try. Now, this mosquito was born on the shore of Kolleru. Do you know where Lake Kolleru is?

Late evening, one summer, Appachchi had roused visiting grandchildren and grandnephews and nieces quietly from their beds after they had turned in, and took them out. Appachchi asked them to climb the mound next to the house and look south. She had taught them the directions of the compass. And there, under the Southern Cross, it was a spectacular sight. The southern sky was aglow. Fire, Appachchi said. The reed mass of the lake was on fire. Worker Aunt was very annoyed in the morning that she had disturbed the children.

Going back to the mosquito by Kolleru Lake. 'Early in life, she had lost her father, and her mother had brought her up with great love and care.'

The audience had not noticed the gender shift. That is the juvenile species did not. Alertness sat up in the east room and twitched its ears.

'Very early, not just her mother, but everyone in the village was struck by the intellectual brilliance of the baby girl. Her mother taught her early the three Rs—reading, writing, and arithmetic—as they did in the local school. And she encouraged her to read books. Read them wherever they were available, whenever they were available. And another thing, this girl mosquito had an extraordinary memory, as I said, she didn't forget a thing. Believe me, she remembered things from day one of her life. How many of you remember the first day of your life?'

Gayathri's lips curled in contempt.

'How can anyone remember the first day of their life?' one of the boys said what Gayathri had left unsaid out of condescension. Worker Aunt admired the little girl.

'That's what makes this baby girl mosquito so very special, isn't it?' Appachchi had made her point.

'And that was a problem. The problem was the girl mosquito did not forget anything. Forgive and forget. I won't. Just forget. I won't.

'Her mother tried to convince her of the need to be selective, to erase some memories, the painful ones, such as the time the Brahmin of the Kali shrine tried to swat her and she had escaped certain death by a whisker. In retaliation, the girl mosquito gathered all her classmates, both boys and girls, vegetarian as well as non-vegetarian, and attacked the pujari; by the time the school of mosquitoes had finished, the Brahmin was a mass of pink.'

'Gory,' said Worker Aunt to herself, 'like the narrator.' She turned to her chores.

'Once, a teacher punished a pupil. The girl mosquito—'

'Doesn't the girl have a name?' The boy, Sambudu II, already looking so much like his father Podumburra, asked.

'Of course she does. Gnapakam.'

'What a name!'

'But all names are absurd in some context or place or other, like Thomas Babington!'

The children laughed. 'Bubbingto!'

'See! That's what I mean. Now imagine a teacher in England mentioning your names to her children. Those children will giggle.

'At any rate, I would like to remind you folks, the truth or falsehood of the story rests on the head of the narrator.'

'Never mind, don't you want to get on with the story?'

'When they were in school, Gnapakam and her friends set out for Kasi without informing their parents.'

'What ideas you are putting into their heads!' Worker Aunt exclaimed from the puja room. She was all ears once again. *This is too much! She wasn't there and she tells them what happened to me during the pilgrimage!*

'I am not telling them to do what the girl mosquito did,' Appachchi responded.

'Doing the japa in silence is considered the best way. Muttering the japa known as upamsu is regarded as mediocre and reciting it loudly is considered the worst.'

This was a direct hit. One of the great sources of dispute between the two sisters-in-law centred on the recitation of God's names and meditation. Granny Appachchi had suggested time and again to her vadina: 'Why waste your energy? God can hear you even when you speak to him through silence. In fact, the Guru of the Stream had suggested that it is better to pray to God in silence.' Guru or no guru, in this matter Worker Aunt's habit never wavered.

'The girl has a name,' reminded Gayathri.

'Yes, of course,' Appachchi said, and added, 'The story has a moral, vadina, you must have the patience to wait until the story reaches its end.'

Worker Aunt grunted in impatience.

'Who gave them the money?' one of the boys asked.

'Money? If you are a mosquito, you don't need much money to go to Kasi. You fly all the way. All that is needed is a sense of direction. As in life. If you are a mosquito, just set out and as you go people help, as they do any pilgrims to Kasi.

'Unwillingly,' said a boy. 'Who wishes to be bled by a mosquito?'

'What kind of things are you teaching the little kids?' Worker Aunt asked again.

'I am not suggesting they should do it.... But wait—' said Appachchi.

'Wait for the moral,' Gayathri advised sagely, 'the moral of a story comes at the very end.'

'Absolutely,' said Granny Appachchi.

'That's right,' said Gayathri, solemnly. 'The best part of a story comes at the end,' she added.

'So, with one wing fractured, Gnapakam was laid up for two weeks.'

Worker Aunt fumed, *This is too much! What is this woman! How has she come to know of my accident? Fortunately, I had only sprained my ankle.* Worker Aunt remembered the Guru of the Stream had confided to her the change to come in her vadina; be prepared for surprises, he had said.... *But how is one going to live under the same roof with this kind of woman! Fortunately, the story is a mix of fact and fiction.*

The storyteller marched ahead.

'When she regained the use of both wings, Gnapakam was a changed personality. She refused to touch meat and eggs, she didn't even drink milk. "All these," she said, "are non-vegetarian produce."

'"Then how will you sustain yourself? How will you eat enough to gain height and weight? Look at yourself," said her mother, "as it is you are skin and bones."

'"Fruits and flowers," Gnapakam said quietly.

'After that day, believe me, Gnapakam, true to her word, sustained herself only on fruits, flowers, leaves—and even honey which some of the bees in the neighbourhood sent her in admiration and moral support.

'Now, imagine a mosquito making that journey to Kasi; it is arduous even for tough people. You know the track goes through the north of our Telugu land and crosses so many princely states where they don't understand a word of our language.

'Now we must distinguish between robbers and bandits!' observed Granny Appachchi.

'Both are thieves,' said little Gayathri conclusively.

'True, but there are differences, minor or major. For one thing, robbers can be in your town. They can work individually. Waylay you in a narrow galli and rob you of your bundle. Bandits work in groups, like wolf packs. They like to accost travellers in the heart of a jungle, or on a deserted hill path.

'The villagers had no iron safes: they dug pits in their homes and hid their money underground.'

Worker Aunt sighed. It was as though Granny Appachchi was reading her experiences from a printed book.

'And then begin the Vindhya hills that divide the South from the North. You climb and climb and through thick forests, flame of the forests spreading cheer...where wild animals roam freely and wilder robbers live. On the way she starved, she went sleepless, they all grouped together, banded together, and all the women started singing aloud to scare off wildlife and wilder bandits. But the effect was quite the opposite.

'"What did Rama say?" The widows sang.'

Even Gayathri did not notice—or care for—the shift. The east room was all years.

'They got a response from a startling quarter. From the top branches of the thick forest cover.

'"You shaven widows! He asked us to fetch your bundles!"

'The bandits dropped like agile monkeys from the trees, and without even brandishing a knife, snatched their bundles, while all the widows and their escorts stood aside cowering. The bandits opened the bundles then and there, retrieved the gold, gobbled up the food, and left.

'Once again, the forest of the Vindhyas, dark-filled at high noon, death imminent. For a whole minute or two the light had gone out, even the sacred flame of the puja niche.'

Granny Appachchi quickly shifted tracks.

'Just at the moment a young prince happened to arrive looking for a good spot to hunt in the forest and she was rescued.'

Worker Aunt revived from her trance. 'The story, please?'

'The prince married her, and they lived happily ever after. Everyone knows.'

'Certainly not. The prince only chased the dacoits away and

helped Gnapakam and the band of pilgrims to resume their pilgrimage to Kasi,' said Worker Aunt.

'Pious mosquitoes don't make good queens,' said one of the boys.

'How wise you are,' Granny Appachchi said.

Gayathri opened her eyes a little wider and looked at the boy.

'But,' Granny continued quickly, 'everyone learns. This is a story of higher learning; and Gnapakam is a good learner.'

Silence followed. Appachchi allowed them to digest their experience, come to terms with it.

The boys looked more confident and interested in the story now.

This is the new generation, Appachchi repeated to herself, not a nation of slaves.

'Just a couple of days in Kasi, the sensitive girl Gnapakam was filled with disgust. The whole city of Kasi, the holiest city of the world, was filthy. And not just filthy, the people of Kasi were terrible, not at all religious or pious. There are always two ways for us: God's way and our way. The citizens of Kasi did not mind his way because it brought them pilgrims from all over the world and so much money for the residents of the city. The priests, the pandas, were the limit.'

'Are you turning them against their own religion?' She had secretly admired her sister-in-law for her Divine sight through which she filled up the blanks in her own account of the Silver Pilgrimage. But she also regretted bitterly having told Appachchi anything at all.

'No, they should know what true religion is.'

'And what is it, pray? Let me hear about it, please.'

'Love people, love all God's creatures. Love them for themselves. Is it not true religion, children?'

No legs to the tale, no ears to the pot, Worker Aunt thought.

The children nodded their heads vigorously; they didn't like any digressions; they wanted to hear more of the mosquito's adventures, and they didn't share Worker Aunt's concern for religion. The story and the story alone mattered.

Worker Aunt resolved to stoutly maintain her silence in hurt. She had been betrayed, her trust had been betrayed, and not for the first time.

Granny Appachchi resumed.

'Gnapakam was so filled with disgust she could not eat for two days; she had taken lots of stuff from home, parched gram and parched rice and jaggery, etc. All that had been consumed or lost on the way to the bandits. Now, her Kasi cousins welcomed her,'

Even in her most expressive moments she had kept this a secret. Those cousins in Kasi had fallen out bitterly from their family long ago over sharing of property, and Worker Aunt's father had snapped his ties with these greedy cognates. It was a desperate Worker Aunt, lost in the so-called holy city that resorted to search for the severed branch of the cognates.

Terror shook the old lady. She decided to talk to the Guru of the Fresh Stream.

Meanwhile, Granny Appachchi continued.

'And however they tried, and they tried hard, for in keeping with the spirit of the town they were non-vegetarians who looked to be doing pretty well, they went around and procured the best fruit and flowers for Gnapakam. But she kept throwing up for two days. Only after a visit to the sanctum sanctorum of the great God Viswanatha did she recover a bit, God alone, Lord of the Universe, restored her; she meditated long and deep. For the first time, not a sound escaped from her lips. She was totally silent, immersed in her meditation. And enlightenment came to her, impatient for course correction.'

'Like the Buddha,' chimed Gayathri.

'Absolutely,' said Granny Appachchi. 'You are such a bright girl.'

'All girls are bright,' said Gayathri.

'Is there a doubt about it!' said Granny Appachchi, glad to restore the morale. 'And that is the best I have heard in a long time.'

'And Gnapakam felt light. Suddenly, she realized that she felt light as a feather; the city no longer oppressed her. What had happened? The great God had blessed her. How? He cancelled her bad karma; God alone has the power to do such a thing; He revived her pleasant memories. When she left the ceiling of the sanctum sanctorum, she was a changed person. She danced in joy around the sacred lingam, taking care not to buzz. Her face radiated a glow; back at the sarai in the city, her cousins were impressed and wanted to know what the great God had conferred on her. She gave her first discourse from the top tendril of a watermelon vine on one of the mudflats in the river Ganga.

'Back home, devotees rushed to her, disciples flocked to her—each with a little empty pot.' Before they could ask, what for, Granny Appachchi added, 'To take wisdom back to their parched families, wisdom rich with the cream of experience, nourishing the mind and the spirit of everyone. But however she tried, she could not instil her own experience of wisdom into them. Wisdom is never taught, it is always learned, not from books, but from our own experience. See good, do good, Remember the good in life, rejoice in life, rejoice.'

The moral was met with deep silence. They heard a loud whisper from the puja room: 'That's what she has done all her life.'

※

Whether it was the Guru of the Stream working through the agency of Granny Appachchi or her own good karma unfolding, Worker Aunt graduated to the next stage: she set herself one goal—in the words of the Guru: 'Not words, but acts.'

Even before the Kasi episode, Worker Aunt had routinely fed the field hands, not just those who brought her produce from the fields. So, the field hands vied with each other to make this visit, until one man was chosen from among their numbers. Worker Aunt went about feeding them in a methodical, almost prayerful way. She asked the man to cut a leaf from the banana plant and clean it himself. When he brought it dripping with water, she took it and inspected it for any specks of dust or spider's webs or bird droppings. Then with a nod, she returned it. The man spread the leaf on a neat patch of the backyard close to the well. Worker Aunt brought out the goodies; every item on the menu of the day found a place on the leaf plate. The man generally preferred avakkai and dal. The amount of rice he ate was impressive. It was a small mound, and Appachchi watched from a distance in admiration; not just for the guest who consumed such quantities like Bhima, but in appreciation for her sister-in-law. Left to herself, she would have planted the man right in the east room dining hall. But then after her island jaunt, that sanctum of food and piety was out of bounds for her.

But Worker Aunt was of course different. She didn't like the idea of anyone watching the field hand eat for fear of the evil eye. When he left, Worker Aunt went into the kitchen and cooked rice again.

Worker Aunt began joining Granny Appachchi in meditation. And she too came to love the early outings, especially at the hour of dawn. She donated buttermilk and stopped diluting it with her own Kasi reminiscences. All the same, she did not know how time passed. Sometimes, she spent a while watching Appachchi contemplating of a peepul leaf. In the early morning, light yellow skein of veins covered by an almost transparent pattern of dewdrops. The sapling wet and cool. Down below, a scattering of slugs: inert, in various states of cosy sleep; she quickly restored the sheltering leaf. She watched the laboured flight of a crow. Or the masterly manoeuvre of a bat at dusk, or the impressive trajectory of the barn owl.

Both the grannies supervised the renovation of the fence. Reinforcing it with babul branches, they dug the water channels, taking water to the plants from the well. Granny Appachchi suggested to Worker Aunt that the water from the bathroom should not enter the garden. She got the helpers to dig a separate channel to take it away from the garden into a soil pit at the back. If the field hand was too busy, it was she and Worker Aunt who drew the water for the garden. The first light saw them touching a leaf of some plant or other, tenderly and very carefully to avoid hurting it at all. They observed both sides of the leaf, not to check for any evidence of a pest at work, but simply because they enjoyed the touch, the texture.

That was also the motto Worker Aunt now set for her post-Kasi audience. It was credible counsel. Worker Aunt had returned from Kasi with a destitute girl she had discovered on the way. The girl had been married early and when she came of age, she'd been sent to her husband. After living with her for a month, that rascal had sent her back to her parents. She lost her parents suddenly in a drowning accident, and was left an orphan. Worker Aunt invited her to come and eat with them every day. She advised her to go to school again, she herself taught her Telugu grammar. The girl completed her school and did well in her school final exams. Seethamma's daughter, now the newly-appointed principal of the town's women's college, invited her to teach in their elementary school; and there was no more need for her to eat with Worker Aunt's family. A month later, she returned to Worker Aunt for consultation; her husband had sent a message to her to go and rejoin him. They could set up home in her own village. Worker Aunt gave her considered opinion: 'A scoundrel, even if he is your husband, is a scoundrel. Just keep away from him; that dirty fellow is not interested in you, he is interested in your salary.'

And Worker Aunt went through her own bit of work. Though she did not need a cook, she engaged a woman because the poor lady had been widowed and she had no place to go. The cook was once a well-to-do woman, the daughter of a famous man. She had been married to a scoundrel. He had thrown her out after he had robbed her of her money and jewellery. She'd lived in penury for years. When he found out that Worker Aunt had taken her under her protective wing, the husband wished to send her a maintenance allowance. 'Nothing doing,' said Worker Aunt; 'Nothing doing,' said the young woman.

Granny Appachchi touched Worker Aunt's feet and did a formal obeisance. She said in wonder, 'Vadina, you are great.'

∽

Miss Beston overwhelmed Mr Blotton in two areas: Shakespeare and the Bible.

Both quoted from the Bible. She welcomed any discussion on the Gospels—or what she called Bible-ography—especially the contradictions among the four authorized Gospels. Her interest developed over the decades into an intellectual passion, quoting, among others, from Irenaeus.

She now quoted from a German professor who had recently discovered the gospel according to Mary. She was thrilled by the document, and she started a running commentary on the career of this unorthodox, non-canonical gospel: it was stolen, it was lost, and it was traced back to the United States! Where else! She was excited: they had also traced an old parchment which could be the long-lost gospel according to Judas. She urged her lawyers in London to go and take a look at both. Present themselves as prospective bidders and take a look, she instructed them. Take along Professor Aitkins of Oxford University, who knew Coptic and Aramaic. They did. Miss Beston quoted from her the Bible at her gatherings, almost tingling with the excitement of an archaeologist presenting new findings. 'He who has ears to hear, let him hear.' 'He who has a mind to understand, let him understand.' And she even greeted her visitors, with 'Peace be with you,' or 'Receive my peace unto yourselves.'

'For the son of man is within you' appealed to Seshacharyulu. He said, 'This sounds so much like our philosophy!'

'Those who seek him will find him.'

And Seshacharyulu responded: 'Yes, all seekers will succeed. No seeker will ever fail. It could be in this birth, or it could be in the next, or a thousand births later.'

'Isn't Christ undermined by his Church establishment? Look at this: he told his apostles, "Do not lay down any rules beyond what I appointed you."'

Mr Blotton shook his head.

It seemed to Mr Blotton that Miss Beston and her comrades discussed the Bible with more interest than knowledge. He said: 'Rules regulate practice. They are demanded by the developing situation, by the post-Christ context. Without rules and regulations how can the common man pursue his spiritual life? They are not rules but guidelines.'

Seshacharyulu concurred.

'Rules are rules,' said Miss Beston. 'Rules promote the establishment, every self-serving oligarchy. And then the establishment grows too large and moves away from its original goals. And you have only greedy pardoners, amorous friars, and fornicating bishops.'

She quoted often from her unique 'gospel': 'Do not weep, nor grieve nor be irresolute, for His grace will be entirely with you and will protect you.'

Miss Beston pointed out that Jesus had said to Mary: '"Blessed are you that you did not waver at the sight of Me." Of all the chosen group, she alone did not waver. When Peter wavered, he alone didn't, all the apostles did, or would, otherwise Jesus would not have made the point. Peter's momentary loss of faith was exemplary.'

Miss Beston found it especially amusing that Peter worried about a woman being chosen by the Master for a unique vision.

'What would have I done in Mary's place?' mused aloud Miss Beston. 'I most certainly wouldn't have wept. But she did. I don't despise her for it. It was the society. Today, she would most probably tick them off.... Levi did what Mary didn't, refrained from. Levi told Peter in no unmistakable terms to back off: "Peter, you have always been hot-tempered. But if the Saviour made her worthy, who are you indeed to reject her? Surely the saviour knows her very well." The Mary episode foreshadows the male dominance of the Church, and for that matter, of any religion.'

Added Seshacharyulu: 'Matthew shows that without Jesus's leadership the group of disciples would have been lost.'

'Judas and Mary: they are the fringewala and fringewali,' said Miss Beston. 'I'm especially interested in the attempts made by some of the male apostles to bench her. Not all, some did appreciate her sincerity and Jesus testified to her character. God ordains, Church decrees. And so has it been down the centuries: decrees have stopped the Christian spirit.'

'That is true of every religion,' said Seshacharyulu.

He had a query: 'How come Christ the Avatar was in such a hurry to conclude his mission?'

Miss Beston looked at Mr Blotton, who said, 'The Mission was carried on by Paul.'

Miss Beston said, 'How are you sure he has done a good job of it?'

'I have no doubt.' A stout Anglican, he added, 'It was only the later popes who brought a bad name to the Church.'

'Even Paul,' said Miss Beston. 'Wasn't it under him that they established the canon of Gospels?'

'But they are the best of the available ones,' Mr Blotton said.

'What about the gospel according to Mary Magdalene?'

'Nothing of importance; it is not there in the canon.'

'A woman's point of view is bound to be of interest in any age.'

'True…'

'And wasn't it under him the Church became anti-feminist?'

Seshacharyulu garu had listened with interest. Now he added, 'Our own Adi Sankara concluded his mission in his thirties.'

Another day, Miss Beston responded to the theological activities of some civilians in India. 'People think of nothing,' she said, 'but converting the Hindus. Religion is often used as a cloak by the greatest schemers.'

She was of the view that there was in all theological methods little or no difference, whatever be the religion.

'For countless generations, the European has been taught to look down upon the poor heathen of the East. But the very same heathen has survived the climate, survived the hordes of invaders, and still preserve something of his culture and civilization. They ask, how can the sun be a god, and the god of effulgent intellectual illumination? For the sun is just a star, we have known that for four centuries now! But surely, it is the prayer and the spirit of surrender to a higher entity what matters; if it makes the devotee a better human being, a better mind, better human, that's all that matters. Any one of these Indian employees of the British administration is superior to our white trash back home, idling away on some garbage dump. There is far greater spiritual urge in the rudimentary worship of the common people here than in much of the hollow ecclesiastical pomp of the West.'

'As for me,' she continued, 'I have no other design in view than the glory of my queen and country.'

Mr Blotton asked the munshi about Granny Appachchi. 'Is it true?'

When Seshacharyulu confirmed the story of Granny's powers, both requested him to arrange for an interview with the Guru of the Stream and his disciple, Granny Appachchi.

⚭

A childhood pal of Appachchi's was an early visitor to the house. Fortunately, Nephew was away; he had left the day before for Rajahmundry to consult his doctor, and wouldn't return for three days. You don't often take the trouble of making that journey by boat, bullock cart, and on foot to return without settling all outstanding matters in the town.

'She is already drunk,' whispered Worker Aunt to Appachchi. The woman was drunk so early in the day, and it was not the first time. Worker Aunt's disgust was evident.

'Papam, poor woman,' whispered Appachchi. She greeted her friend. 'How are you, Jayalakshmi? Happy? Doing well?'

Jayalakshmi tottered a few steps, almost tripped over the doorstep, and drawled, 'Getting on, somehow.'

Even Worker Aunt could appreciate the experience behind those words.

Jayalakshmi had been married into the most orthodox of Brahmin families of the district. Her husband was a great Sanskrit scholar and a loving husband. They lost child after child, but he did not marry again, did not send his wife back to her parents' home. He was the man who introduced certain ancient Indian texts in Sanskrit and Pali to the white scholar-administrators of the Coromandel coast. One of the white scholars, who made quite a name for himself as an Indologist, introduced him to scotch; scotch soon degenerated into country liquor, and finally, hooch. His wife discovered the great potency of the liquid in these bottles as an anodyne. A few drops of it, a glass of it, and now, the poor scholar had passed away, but the habit did not. She was drunk by morning.

Exercising the greatest forbearance and self-restraint, and congratulating herself on her own success, Worker Aunt withdrew into the kitchen. Appachchi led her friend into the paved open quadrangle of the backyard. She set her down, and asked her if she would have something to eat.

'I haven't…haven't brushed…my teeth.'

'It is all right, if you can drink that dreadful liquid, you can eat something good to keep the damage down.'

She brought a banana, peeled it, and gave it to her. The woman took a bite, just a nip, chewed it, and put the rest of it down by her side. She put her hand into her sari folds and fished around. Appachchi anticipated her: the moment the little quarter bottle peeped out like a shy bird, Appachchi grabbed it by the neck and confiscated it.

'You can drink it later, when you return home. Don't drink here. If Nephew sees you doing it, we will have big trouble.'

The woman protested feebly, but Appachchi was firm.

Worker Aunt appeared from behind the door and gestured to Appachchi to send Jayalakshmi home.

Appachchi nodded back reassuringly.

This was the only Brahmin home still open to Jayalakshmi. Both Appachchi and Worker Aunt sympathized with her. She had been such a dutiful wife; had done everything and anything her orthodox husband had wanted. And after his death, she discovered that her husband had, in collusion with a vakil, left all the property to his children, making no provision for her. She was dependant on her own children. Still she taught the grandchildren, raised them, until they too left. At the end she was alone, all by herself. After the eldest son had died in an accident, she was reduced to beggary. No one, not sons, nor daughters, nor *their* sons and daughters thought of her; didn't have the time, probably.

Some days later, when Appachchi casually dropped in to see Jayalakshmi, she found her friend lying in a sagging string cot. She had fractured her ankle two days earlier and no one had attended to her. The whole place stank. Appachchi rushed to the village doctor. He put Appachchi in his own jutka and arrived promptly. He gave Jayalakshmi medicine and bandaged her; he said to Appachchi and Worker Aunt that it was a wonder how gangrene had not set in. The fracture healed somehow, God only knew how.

After that Worker Aunt made arrangements for Jayalakshmi's subsistence on condition that she gave up drinking. She agreed; but promptly went back on her promise. She had no money to buy rice and vegetables, but they realized that she had been bartering things—the furniture, the clock, the kitchen utensils—for cheap hooch. Not much later, she passed away.

Entry into the dining sanctum and the kitchen had to wait, however, until the rite of final purification—death.

'Appachchi is going crazy,' Worker Aunt said to Podumburra when he next met her.

Podumburra looked up.

'The last few months I have been observing her. First, she was talking to crows and kites; I thought it was a pretty way of keeping them away. "Watch a bird, watch a child," she said. She played on the fiddle to the cows, said it would improve the milk yield. She played to the brinjal plants, says the plants will give you larger brinjals and more brinjals. A plant grows best around the full moon, she says, every day it goes through two cycles and both are influenced by the moon. It is the movement of the moon and the planets and the constellations which influence strange animal behaviour. Is this true?'

Podumburra nodded his head—neither yes, nor no. His mind was not on the details, he was worried about the extraordinary woman. No one extraordinary has a chance in this world, still less an extraordinary woman.

'Then, she is talking to caterpillars—earlier she was, if you remember, ruthlessly squashing them between two pot shards. Now, she talks to them with some placatory words and carries them carefully on a twig and reaches them to a more luscious plant—as if they can't find their way. And today, she was talking to flowers and plants, to jasmine, champak, and the pagoda tree.'

'What do you want me to do?' Podumburra asked her. 'Shall I talk to her?'

'No,' said Worker Aunt.

'Shall I talk to the doctor in Rajahmundry?'

'No, don't,' she said. 'I shall observe her for some more time.'

'The Guru of the Stream had predicted this, hadn't he? There are so many things I never could imagine to exist, now they do, now I know they do,' he said philosophically. He closed his eyes, waved his hand to sweep the entire world, and recited: 'There are more things in heaven and earth than are dreamt of in your philosophy, Horatio!'

When he opened his eyes, Worker Aunt had disappeared.

⁂

Granny Appachchi gathered the children around her as she went about attending to the plants. She talked to the plants, joking with them as though they were human.

'Granny Appachchi, we can hear you talking to them. Can they also hear when you speak to us?'

'Why not? And not just these. Those too!' she pointed at the cattle in the byre.

When Worker Aunt connived with Granny Appachchi to help Podumburra realize a dharmic dream, she had either forgiven or forgotten the family humiliation, or she had overcome the tapper trauma. And of course, the two old ladies had to carry out the Guru's command. Podumburra had gone to the Guru of the Stream, and carried his message to Worker Aunt. The two grannies helped him perform, in defiance of the orthodox, the first widow remarriage in the Coromandel. Without their support, Podumburra confessed later, he wouldn't have been able to fight back the tidal wave of reactionary resistance.

The Guru of the Stream asked Worker Aunt not to worry: as much as Appachchi enjoyed talking to the peasants and the villagers, she rejoiced in the company of God's other creatures. And what was more remarkable to Podumburra was that the animals, birds, even plants responded to her; if she was pleased and said some praise, they all perked up; if, on the other hand, she upbraided them, they looked crestfallen until she patted them and made some consoling sounds. Soon, the cattle would take slops and straw only from the hands of Appachchi. Even if the others gave water to the flowerbeds, they drooped by afternoon. Granny Appachchi noticed their plight and added just a spoonful of water with some endearing words, and within a short time, the plants glowed with green health and stood erect like sepoys at a parade. Podumburra could not believe what he saw.

∞

Now the same houseboat, retired but re-employed on sentimental grounds, climbed the bank on the far side and served Miss Beston as a camp office. Perched on solid stilts, visitors climbed a short ladder of neatly painted steps to enter her reception room. The view from the windows was hindered no more: it was a clear open field right up to the Grand Trunk Road.

'Watch that road now, Mary,' Miss Beston told her granddaughter. It was the same window, but it was no longer lined with a money plant. The foliage had been trimmed out and cleaned up: the mosquitoes hiving there might poison her little girl.

Mary came running. As they both looked out through the famous window, a peasant woman came into view, with a gongali over her shoulders. She held the hand of a little boy, who was respectably dressed in a single clout piece. He was of Mary's age. 'He's a fatherless boy supported at school by a mother pounding paddy for a wage. Later, she admitted him in a town school for English education. Mr Black has now invited that boy to join his school.'

When Mary returned a decade later, she learned from her grandma that the boy had been sent by the local raja for higher studies to England, and had just returned a barrister. He had joined the non-Brahmin party of South India with the help of John Pathappan, a professor from Madras University.

Her Majesty wrote to Miss Beston:

> I hope very soon to send you Photographs & also new Lithographs of some of our Children. Winterhalter has just painted a beautiful Picture; it is wonderfully like & a beautiful

work of art.

The distance & the length of time between the Mails is very trying & must be harrowing to those who have (& who has not amongst the gentry & middle classes in England—Great Britain I should say?) relations in uncertain & dangerous places.

…I cannot say how sad I am to think of all this bloodshed in a country which seemed so prosperous—so improving *&* for which, as well as for its inhabitants, I felt so great an interest.

But I did not at all object to leaving my monotonous London life, & I took great delight in all the novelty of impressions on coming to a new country. Of late, it has been painful, & anxious, & terrible; might see India again prosperous, & on the way to good order, though fifty years will not put it back into the same state in which it was… so far as attempting to civilize & give liberty, & our English ideas of blessings to the country.

∽

The two sisters-in-law, widowed for decades now—or more, perhaps a century or so, it seemed to the little scholars of the various schools of the village—went into a mango orchard and meditated under the very tree that had escaped capital punishment thanks to Granny Appachchi's intervention. After a while, Worker Aunt found it difficult to continue; the mosquitoes wouldn't just let her meditate, they buzzed all around and attacked her greedily. She threw up her hands and moved away. She brushed away patch after patch of the pest. When she looked at Appachchi, she was surprised; covered thick with mosquitoes, the woman was in deep samadhi.

The Guru happened to be passing by. 'Do not disturb her,' he said to her. 'She will come out in another hour.'

And she did.

'Appachchi, you are great, you are blessed. But I have a long way to go,' Worker Aunt said.

A century and half later, memories of Appachchi and Worker Aunt still were welcomed in the village of Sakhinetipalli.

When Worker Aunt passed away, Appachchi directed the two women whom Worker Aunt had sheltered to perform the last rites. As Worker Aunt had taken sanyasa—though in a huff—her body was buried. While the villagers wept and mourned, they said no villager noticed even a single tear roll down Granny Appachchi's face, which was now ridged with wrinkles, baulks, and embankments like a paddy field.

Part VI

Podumburra

He had been ceremonially named Samba Murthy by his parents. Few remembered his real name, however. Some called him Sambhudu for short, but every villager knew him as 'Podumburra', or snuffbox head. The villagers had nicknamed him very early in his life, not just because his head looked like a podumburra, a snuffbox. It was also for his capacious head, his devotion to studies.

He always gave the credit for his success to his mother. The diligent woman woke him up in the early hours. Brahma Kalam is the best time for studies, she told him—and this was confirmed by two neighbour grannies as well as by his banyan tree schoolteacher. His mother woke him up before daybreak, if not earlier, and lit the earthen lamp or the bottle-wick lamp on the arugu, his study; if there was a breeze, his mother lit the more expensive hurricane lamp. When he came out on the arugu of their home, few other villagers had risen from their slumbers, and the village was, as all other villages are, an early-rising community. He scanned the sky, brilliant with the familiar constellations, all of them like a god's muggulu, especially the Southern Cross, which a god must have drawn at the very end, a conclusive configuration. He liked the way Scorpio leaned to one side now, as though relaxing after a night's rigorous duty. Podumburra cleaned his teeth with cow-dung cake ash drawn from the milk-boiling hearth of the bustling buttermilk-dispensing grannies. He splashed some water on his face, allowing it to run down his body. Still in his clout, fed on taruvanee rice, he sat near the bottle-wick lamp or the hurricane lantern and revised the previous day's lessons and prepared for the day ahead.

He reached the banyan school before anyone and started reading aloud from some class book or the other. The housewives and others, when they came out to clean the front yard, would say, 'There is our Sambhudu.'

Like the other pupils, Podumburra too attended the banyan school with a gantam, or iron stile, a square matting of palmyra, an inkpot, and a pen. He learned alphabets on palmyra leaves only. He practised good handwriting in sand spread before him; later, coarse paper, slate, and slate pencil came into use. He learned the vowels and consonants, and practised them on a slate. He learned multiplication tables in Telugu and Hindustani.

He always scored Sri at the school, never a dot, and thus there was no question of a spanking. The first among the class was rewarded with a 'Sri' in his palm; the next child got just a dot in his or her palm, and anyone and everyone after that received a stroke of the cane from the ancient asthmatic teacher practising under the large banyan tree next to the last house of the village. The full moon and the new moon were holidays, and on those days, each of the pupils gave the teacher their offering to the guru, a humble dakshina, one dabbu. The homework on those two days of the month was memorizing a verse from an epic. From the first day, Podumburra was assigned the duty to coach his classmates. As he moved up, he continued to tutor the pupils in the lower classes, and he enjoyed it. Every evening, one of the senior pupils would recite aloud from the *Pedda Bala Siksha* and the younger pupils all repeated it aloud after him. The session concluded with the prayer 'deepamjyoti parabrahmam'.

Miss Beston had been shunned in the early years by the top officials and visiting Europeans. 'Unlike in England,' Miss Beston observed, recalling her early life in India, 'a successful speculator in India inevitably remained forever outside the sacred barrier: a private person could never move into the high society of the services.' This determined entrepreneur now got the European elite crowding her railway inauguration, and class natives as well—a sprinkling of maharajas. At a time fixed to the minute by her munshi, she waved the green flag and formally dispatched her first consignments by rail to Madras.

Everyone went up and complimented her also on her marvellous recuperation. Incredibly, out of what was still left standing of the Coromandel forest, mostly babul and keekar, a leopard had sneaked out on her. And when it did, unbelievably, the celebrated hunter had left her rifle standing against the bole of a kachnar stump. Amazingly, her faithful poligar dogs too had been left chained in their kennels. If a boneyard coolie had not advanced menacingly with the thigh bone of a tiger, interposing himself between Miss Beston and the beast, more damage would have been done. She was rushed to the military hospital at Rajahmundry; they managed to save her, though not her right leg. From the knee down it had to be amputated and an artificial leg fitted. And one matching glass eye.

They had all thought that the gory leopard attack would compel her to put off the big occasion. But she was back at her post. She had worked from her hospital bed: she sent a thank you note to the Guru of the Stream and regretted she had not taken his warning seriously enough.

She had acquired enough influence in Fort St. George: while still in the hospital, special container wagons were manufactured for her special goods train. And enough again, to suppress news of the new century, she received by express telegram the news of the death of the Empress. The past is significant only as long as it shapes the present.

Now, she stood there on her legs, the most successful exporter and importer of South India, supervising the first dispatch by rail of merchandise from the Coromandel. Her products included everything and anything under the sun. Mr Blotton remarked: 'The Kumpini in comparison projected a moderate ambition: "a million pounds of pepper".' The Kumpini's gifts had been cheap: beads and mirrors; so modest had been the beginnings of Indo–British commerce. Miss Beston's gifts to natives on the occasion included toys, sugar candy, and parrots.

∽

When little Podumburra developed redness of the eyes, his mother tried blowing into a handkerchief and pressing his eyes with it. But the redness continued even the following day. Then, she sent him to Seethamma for a home remedy.

Seethamma enjoyed a reputation for yielding milk years after childbirth. How her body managed it, God only knows, said Granny Appachchi and Worker Aunt to each other.

'You also come,' said little Podumburra to his mother. He felt too shy. He had heard that his cousin had received the therapy and was rid of the redness.

Podumburra was curious. But he did not know how to convey his problem to the dispensary aunt. So, he put a finger in his mouth, brushed the dust on the floor with a big toe, and did not move.

'I am busy,' said his mother. 'I cannot leave the kitchen and come now.'

So Podumburra went. His own mother had had little milk to nourish him, and the buffalo milk had not agreed with his constitution. He was perpetually malnourished, and though many did not know about it, at the peak of his career he would suffer from night blindness.

But when Seethamma welcomed him and seated him, he was tongue-tied. Especially with his clever cousin, the future principal, hovering behind her mother. Then, Podumburra's mother, Lakshmamma, came out and shouted the message: the boy's eyes were red. Most damaging publicity. The girl giggled, the boy winced.

'Come into the inner room,' the aunt said. She understood the boy's need for privacy. So, she sent away her daughter, 'You go and play with Kalyani and come back to eat.'

The girl looked roguishly at her shy cousin and flitted out like a giggly butterfly. She couldn't resist one last dig though. 'Booms,' she whispered to him, and ran like the wind. He cringed. In one of his moods of affection for her, he had pronounced 'bums' by exaggerating the 'u', and the silly girl had been tickled to death. Whenever their paths crossed, she teased him about it.

The smiling aunt put the small-limbed big-headed boy in her lap and pulled aside her blouse and squirted milk into his eyes. The milk ran down his thin cheeks and entered his mouth. He put out his little pale tongue and quietly licked his cheek. When she took her sari hem and wanted to wipe the overflow, he pushed her hand away.... So this is mother's milk, he realized with wonder.

What was more, Seethamma allowed the boy to touch the wondrous appendage and cup its curve in his hand.

Seethamma was amused. Little Podumburra had endeared himself to everyone in the village with his studious habits; he had actually singed his forelocks by reading too close to the chimney of the hurricane lantern. She gently fondled his crown of hair and then playfully squirted a bonus into his mouth. Scholarship, the boy realized, had its rewards.

Twice a day.

Podumburra looked forward to it, though his cousin had gathered a couple of equally nasty girls outside the house, and they all sniggered the moment he came out a dreamy, contented boy. He visited the lady eagerly for the next three days. He loved it.

In just two days the redness of his eyes disappeared. He wanted to continue the milch routine, but his mother ended his trips. He no longer needed the Seethamma therapy.

※

The two grannies found themselves in battle mode again. Only this time, they were not the foot soldiers, though they had enjoyed that role every time. This time, they were field marshals, no less. They were the invisible leaders in a secret mountain hideout, moving whole brigades and armed corps across the field maps. This time, their quarry was a Brahmin neighbour with a well-nourished male ego.

Seethamma came for a consultation: her husband was opposing her idea of sending their daughter to high school. Education was only for boys, a daughter's intelligence is in no way helpful to the father of the girl,' Podumburra's uncle had said. 'I speak for those who have daughters, and let those who have sons listen.'

So, no high school for Podumburra's cousin Sumati. He had already given that girl more education than was good for her, her father had declared, the girl must now turn to domestic duties, so no high school for her. The mother pleaded on her knees. She used the banyan teacher's testimonial: the girl is extraordinarily intelligent, the teacher had told Seethamma. 'Don't I know,' the husband heckled. 'Who will help you with the chores at home, and who will take care of the orchards? The byre?' And he had turned away. The man of the family had decided, and that was that. But Sumati's mother pursued the matter at every meal.

'I am there to help you, am I not taking care?'

He didn't allow her to continue, 'How can one woman deal with these illiterate field hands and coolies?'

'Is not Kamakshi amma managing her lands and orchards?' She was referring to Worker Aunt, her friend and patron.

'She is different. She is not a woman!' the husband tried to laugh it away.

'It was her husband himself who educated Granny Appachchi.'

'Very good,' said the father. 'But BA Garu ended up the way he did.'

It was a dig that brought tears to Seethamma's eyes.

Lakshmamma accompanied her sister to Worker Aunt and Appachchi for advice. Sumati's mother broke down.

If grass does not grow upon rocks, what fault is it of the rain?

The two ladies were moved by the plight of their young friend.

They knew Sumati like their own granddaughter. They put their heads together and counselled patience. *She who has not patience possesses not philosophy.*

'What shall we do to convince the man?'

'You cannot convince him; he is not of this modern age.'

'I have decided.'

'What?'

'I am not eating until he agrees to send Sumati to high school in the town.'

The grannies were shocked. Seethamma turned down the tiffin at their place; she accepted only water with a sprig of tulsi thrown into it. She had already started her passive protest campaign.

Her husband was not impressed.

Seethamma still cooked for her husband and family, and as ever, she did a good job of it. In fact, the brinjal curry with green chillies and ginger was better than what she had ever given him before.

Within three days, however, she grew feeble. She could not cook after a week, and could not rise from her bed after ten days. *Whether the banana leaf falls on the thorn or the thorn on the banana leaf, it is the banana leaf that suffers.* Sumati, the centre of the storm, attended to her mother's chores, and attended on her as well without tears. She said to Podumburra, 'Even if my father relents, I shall not continue my studies.'

'Don't be silly,' said Podumburra, 'I am sure your father will change his mind. And you must go back to your studies.' It was she who had introduced him to algebra, which neither John nor BA Garu had.

'Booms,' he said.

And she burst out laughing.

On Seethamma's request, Worker Aunt and Lakshmamma had been sending food to the husband and the children. The husband joked, 'Worker Aunt cooks better than you.'

But the food no longer tasted good in his mouth. And as the

list of donors grew—more families were ready to send food to him—he was alarmed. As he walked down the hamlet, women peeped at him from behind doors, sourly, he felt. A few of the men themselves didn't seem to approve his obstinacy.

Sumati wept in the inner room, but came out clear-eyed. She loved her books, she loved clearing examinations, she loved teaching. She had already decided she was going to be a teacher, and she had Podumburra's tacit support. The children did not leave her mother's bedside. Podumburra, a favourite with Sumati's father, grew sullen.

Passive resistance hadn't worked. The grannies went over to Seethamma, persuaded her to break her fast, and helped her sip a glass of water with a sprig of tulsi and a dash of lemon juice.

The following day, Sumati's mother came again to the grannies.

All three women huddled in the paved quadrangle of the backyard for a couple of hours and hit upon a stratagy. The revised scheme evolved by the women was two-pronged: the man would be punished in his stomach, where it hurts.

'If you cannot convince him, there is only one other way,' said Worker Aunt. 'Cut him off from your food and bed.'

Granny Appachchi was delighted. 'Wonderful suggestion, vadina.'

'Ideally,' continued Worker Aunt, 'do both at the same time.'

They looked at each other.

'Disappear for a few days.'

Seethamma, true to her name, was a husband devotee. The step proposed was too extreme.

So, it took Granny Appachchi and Worker Aunt much patience and energy to convince the wife to hoodwink her husband.

The women held a review session and redrew their strategy.

'Now, just disappear from the village,' Worker Aunt suggested.

She has specialized in this tactic, Appachchi muttered to herself.

When her husband was away, Seethamma packed a bundle and, in the dark of the night, stole into Worker Aunt's veranda room at the back of the house.

The following day news spread in the village that Seethamma had left home. No one knew where she had gone. The husband confessed to Nephew, who was laid up in bed, that they had had a quarrel; when elders pressed for the cause of the quarrel, he revealed that he was opposed to Western education. He wanted some education for his boys, but girls should not be spoiled with education; that went against the grain of our culture, and even the boys should be sent to a Sanskrit pathasala and not English schools.

With six little kids, how was he going to run the house? The housewife had left home for a good cause. It was clear to the whole village that the man had his work cut out. And he deserved it. The village missed Seethamma.

The grannies consoled the husband and offered to send food to him and the children twice a day. The die-hard Brahmin was comforted somewhat. But unfortunately, after the first couple of meals, he did not enjoy the food. For Worker Aunt had let loose another trump card: she put Granny Appachchi to cooking for the man in distress. Appachchi generally hated the idea of cooking, and when she cooked, she got carried away with her adventurous recipes. The husband rapidly lost his appetite; he no longer looked forward to his meals as he had done when his wife was slaving for him in the kitchen. Worse, he actually dreaded the idea of sitting for his meal. The food also gave him embarrassing flatulence.

And then the rajasic Brahmin began to miss his bed mate.

He still refused to surrender. He held on mulishly, filling his belly with dried gram and puffed rice. The supplementary food worsened his indigestion.

No white flag, no surrender.

Worker Aunt was puzzled.

'I can understand him subsisting on gram and puffed rice. But what about his mattress's well-being?'

Seethamma pointed out the lacuna in their calculations.

'You are forgetting his keep, Rajyam.'

'That's true! How could I have forgotten!' Worker Aunt said.

Among the landlords of river districts, all upper-caste machos, you were not a man if you didn't keep a mistress. And, of course, the mistress's caste did not matter. The bed recognizes no caste.

Rajyam was an outcaste woman. Seethamma's husband visited her every evening, but even under the strain and pressure of hunger, he refused to eat at her place; he did not even drink a drop of water at her house. Bed was not board.

Worker Aunt came up with a shocker. She shared her plan with Granny Appachchi, who nodded solemnly, amazed. They decided to open a third front.

Unknown to anyone, in the early hours, after Podumburra's father had left for the island fields, and all the children had gone to bed, without anyone noticing them, the women assembled and sent for Rajyam. They conferred in the byre, out of view of the street. Rajyam almost shrieked on spotting Seethamma there; she too had believed that the poor lady had really gone away somewhere—inquiries had revealed she had not reached her mother's place.

It was a brief discussion.

Rajyam was sent away regally like a muttaidu—a woman whose husband was alive—with gifts of bananas, coconut, betel leaves, and areca nut; on her forehead shone the bottu, larger than ever.

From that day, even the concubine's company lost its taste for the recalcitrant Brahmin. Three battle fronts were too many for the man. He surrendered.

Seethamma came calling again and again to thank Worker Aunt and Appachchi. The three women celebrated quietly behind the house with corn on the cob roasted on the coal brazier. Rajyam duly and quietly received her share.

Podumburra's cousin was set on track again. When Sumati graduated, the first woman graduate in the district, her picture appeared in the *Prabhudda Bharata* of Madras. Another feather in the cap for the village of Sakhinetipalli, after BA Garu. Everyone congratulated the father for his progressive attitude. The young lady went on to found the first women's college in the Coromandel.

'Her mother, Seethamma, turned the course of the family from agriculture to English jobs,' said Podumburra, introducing the guest speaker, Principal Sumati, at one of his weekly meetings in Rajahmundry.

Seethamma survived her husband by three decades. In coordination with her friends, she engaged in charity work. After Worker Aunt's death, she realized that she too had to go and so had a big choultry built on the bank of the irrigation canal. She founded an English-medium school, personally heading the committee to recruit teachers; she gave clear instructions to her children on its management, and with her children and grandchildren around her, she passed away.

The topic was water; with Mr Blotton around, it was impossible to avoid it.

Mr Blotton had just returned from one of his rare visits to his home in Scotland. He had had a great time on board, voyaging by steam ship. Earlier, just a decade ago, the voyage to England would have taken four months, during which time smallpox routinely broke out on board. And his services would have been needed as self-taught medic and self-envisioned evangelist. For while carrying out his official duties scrupulously as the Chief Engineer of the greatest irrigation system in South India, he had still found time in the early mornings and evenings to help in mission work. He also regularly attended the service on Sunday in the little local church.

Today, however, the debate on Miss Beston's houseboat had developed into a curious construction.

'The chemistry of water is endlessly fascinating,' Mr Blotton began.

'Of the four elements, there is no other that interests him,' Miss

Beston joked. 'He should be conveyed to a water-logged planet. Is there one?'

'None, as far as we know…and can you imagine a world without water? Water is integral to life, like air. But let me continue. Here are other virtues of water. One, water remains water over as much as 212 degrees Fahrenheit and beyond; it is like saying, a friend is a friend who is with you through thick and thin. And two, water can dissolve, can absorb, many things; it is what the chemist calls a "universal solvent"—'

'Egoless—like the British race,' Miss Beston chipped in. 'Like the British genius for adhesion and cohesion, under the most trying situations and circumstances.'

'The high heat capacity of water—'

'Like that of the British—'

Mr Blotton nodded '—makes it an excellent globetrotter to transport large quantities of heat on the earth—'

'—The British spreading warmth over the best part of the globe, bringing civilization, culture, and values, personal and societal, to vast continents of the earth.'

'And then the density of water: unlike other elements, it becomes lighter when it solidifies. Ice is lighter than water!'

'In a crisis,' chipped in David, 'the Englishwoman doesn't lose her head, she keeps her cool, she is unaffected, she ever rises above the situation.'

'You are too kind. David…I don't mind if you include all English people, the English race.'

'Perfectly illuminating, sir,' Seshacharyulu got into the spirit and said, 'and thank you very much. In our own culture, water is a symbol of purity; the lotus in our scriptures is a symbol of the atma.'

'That explains why there are so many mouldings of the lotus in your temples,' said Miss Beston.

'It may not be a mere myth,' added Mr Blotton sagely. 'Scientific observation holds up the best of literary and cultural symbols. When water falls on a lotus leaf, it acts as a cleanser more than on any other surface; water packs up the dust on a lotus leaf and puts it on its shoulder and carries it away.'

'Standing neck deep in water and slush all its life,' added the pundit, 'the lotus is like a rishi engaged in tapas.'

'Summing up,' Mr Blotton said, 'water is as important as the air to us humans. In the ultimate analysis, nothing else is important. And water is scarce, only a fraction of all water is fit for drinking.'

'Just a tiny fraction of humanity, a few million, have come to impose law and order over the best part of the globe. I am not wasting water, Mr Blotton,' said Miss Beston.

She paused for a second or two, as though giving time for her denser pupils to digest another image. 'I am a raindrop on a lotus leaf.'

'Let us offer up thanks to the Almighty for providing us with water,' said Mr Blotton. 'As the Hindu might put it, water is God's gift of grace, Divine prasadam.'

The pundit concurred. 'I cannot agree with you more. It is so precious that we offer it as a gift to God every time we perform sandhya.'

'No need for the British to emulate the element,' responded Miss Beston, reflectively. 'We British are an inclusive race. Like water.'

⁂

After the victory of light over darkness, Granny Appachchi gathered Podumburra and his friends, boys and girls, Brahmin and non-Brahmin, and told them the story of maredu, the bael tree, in her veranda school.

The story was called 'Why Brahmins Remain Poor'.

The bael tree is supposed to be the abode of Lakshmi, consort of Vishnu and the goddess of fortune. In fact, Bilvapatrika, she who lives in the leaves of the bilva tree, is another name for Lakshmi.

Lakshmi enters mortal homes and those whom she blesses prosper and are happy. But Lakshmi is supposed never to have entered a Brahmin's house.

'Why?' asked Vishnu of his consort. 'Brahmins keep the temples, they are holy and pious and worship all of us. Why are you so adamant about not blessing them with your luck?'

Lakshmi answered petulantly, 'All Brahmins are my natural enemies. I cannot even rest peacefully in my house, the bael tree. For every day they pluck its leaves and offer them to Shiva. If they destroy my house, why should I enter theirs?'

The tale has left for Kanchi and we for home.

⁂

Podumburra was admitted to an English-medium school in a nearby town. Having mastered Telugu earlier, Podumburra completed the English readers in just a few months. The boy was sent home on the complaint that he respected only one teacher, and worse, made his contempt obvious for the others. That mutinous streak surfaced early.

There was no high school in his maternal grandfather's village. So, along with a few other students, Podumburra went and joined another high school in a town around fifteen kilometres away; every day, they walked down to the canal, swam across, their books tied on their heads, attended the school, swam back, and walked home.

Talking of the rebel in the boy, Podumburra led an agitation against a particularly bad teacher who was also the headmaster. This gentleman lacked confidence in himself in spite of the position he occupied, and couldn't raise his eyes to the class before him. He looked away, at the ceiling, or through the window, not to observe the peaceful scene outside where in the grassy fields cattle grazed, but nervously with unseeing eyes. Each period with the class was a torture session for him. Podumburra drew up a petition to the inspector of schools and got the signatures of his fellow students. But then the teacher got wind of it, and he bribed a student to get the paper for him. The headmaster destroyed the damaging document, and flogged almost everyone who had signed it, except Podumburra. He only warned him of dire consequences if he persisted with his ill-conceived move. The boy did not give up. He got another petition ready and sent it. The inspector of schools came down and opened an inquiry. The headmaster was transferred. That was the first trial and victory. A series of such victories followed. His classmates adored him. They felt safe with him. And he could help them with any of their lessons—English, Mathematics, or Telugu.

Podumburra challenged his classmates to spend a night in the cremation ground. A couple of them agreed to accompany him. They did not let a word reach their parents or elders at home. Podumburra was especially considerate to his mother; she had been widowed at the age of twenty, and she had taken such trouble with raising her sickly child and sending him to school.

His companions got scared soon after the taluk office gong had struck nine and quit; but Podumburra stayed for the whole night. He only caught a bad cold. Being asthmatic, he gave an anxious time to his mother.

Soon, he challenged far more formidable adversaries. While still in middle school, Podumburra challenged his friends to prove the existence of ghosts and spirits. Each of his friends had a female relative at home, a widow, or just a middle-aged or old woman, a champion of numerous deliveries and miscarriages and abortions. And these women, each one of them, had been possessed by a ghost at one point or the other. Or, so they said! Exorcists were very busy; almost every street had one of these working from morning till night, especially at midnight.

These exorcists also doubled as medics—they dispensed basmalu, soorkalu, thailalu; all kinds of dishes: lehya, bhakshya, bhojya, and chyoshyams. And the one principle which they followed, and which killed more people than any disease was langhanama paramaushadam—fasting is the best medicine.

Podumburra troubled the local exorcist. 'Penki balaka,' the spirit-handler called Podumburra. The obstreperous boy.

'What do you know of the world of spirits? You haven't even finished school. I have studied the esoteric shastras in Orissa and Assam. I have sat at the feet of the great mantrika, Marthandeswara guru, in Bhubaneswar. What do you think of yourself?' the exorcist scolded him.

It developed into a fight.

'All right, let's see how competent you are,' said the mantrika.

The exorcist realized the boy was a tough nut; there was grudging respect, his tone was conciliatory as he asked, 'Can you spend a night on the banyan in the southern cremation ground?'

For a modest populace, the town had more than one cremation ground; the morbidity of the place warranted several. Of all the funeral grounds, the southern slot was the most forbidding; it was surrounded by a thick wood of black babul. The jackals of the place were particularly vocal, day and night. Even during the day, few residents of the locality went that way; during the night, none did. The only one who had frequented it, the keeper of the cremation ground, had caught a mysterious illness and passed away. He had been buried in his former territory. The exorcists said he had offended the spirits and paid a price for it. It was this notorious patch of ash and dust and bits of bone and broken pots that the exorcist threw at Podumburra.

Agreed, said Podumburra.

His friends shook with terror; his mother started weeping. With great difficulty, he and his dear friends, just two of them out of a lot of ten or twelve, managed to convince her that her son would have company, and so he would be safe. And the two hardy souls stuck to his side when he went to the cremation ground and took a look at it. The remains of a recent cremation greeted them. The ashes had not been collected yet, which meant the dead man's spirit must be somewhere very close. When they approached the banyan—people had nicknamed it the mantrala marri for its association with sorcerers—it appeared more fearful than they had expected, dishevelled like a demoness. It was an ancient banyan, with burrows in its bole where wild animals could easily dwell in comfort. Its roots gave an impression of thickly knotted hair on the head of a sorcerer who had not allowed a barber to come anywhere near him for a hundred years. By the time Podumburra's friends dutifully climbed the tree at sunset, the crickets were already hoarse chirping. The jackals emerged from their hideouts and started nosing around, driving away a couple of pariah dogs, looking for an easy meal. They went to a pit and pulled out what looked like a human leg. A harsh fight broke out among the beasts. A hyena or two sauntered out, took a good look at the banyan until the boys froze further and merged completely with the thick leaf cover. Podumburra tried to encourage his pals, but they were shivering. No doubt it was turning cold, a chill had set in, but he knew it was fright that was unnerving them.

'All right,' he told them. 'There is still time, you can go back.'

They remonstrated weakly, allowing themselves to be persuaded a little more before climbing down and running towards the village, scattering the jackals and the hyenas.

The exorcist, hiding behind a clump of trees, had been watching; he didn't like the idea of being beaten by a mere schoolboy. He waited an hour longer, then two hours, and around midnight, emerged out of his hiding place among the babuls, covered in a white bed sheet and howling like the devil. Podumburra took out the cat-o'-nine-tails he had brought for such an eventuality; he had practised at home until he could hit a banana at fifteen paces. He had also carried a mysterious jute bag with him, and kept its contents a secret. He had thoughtfully put in a copper bottle of water, a book, a pencil, and a notebook to take down his experiences. The whip he had borrowed from a friend's uncle, a retired police officer. It had a silver handle, multiple leather thongs, and a history of reforming the most recalcitrant of history-sheeters. Now, Podumburra let it go. He lashed so accurately, that the thongs shot out like a multi-headed king cobra. Professional pride kept the exorcist from crying out in pain, not a sound beyond a muted 'ayyo' emerged from him. He attempted to snatch the lash away from the thin, undernourished schoolboy. But Podumburra's practice had not gone in vain; he deftly pulled the thongs away from the mantrika's hands. The exorcist howled in pain and opened his palms and licked them. The exorcist howled and howled, and begged for mercy, but Podumburra did not stop until the victim fled.

The man did not give up. He exhibited the welts as trophies from a mortal combat with a particularly vicious ghost on a client's behalf. He sent more warnings to Podumburra, his disciples threatened him with dire consequences. After all, their guru was the unquestioned master of all the spirits of the district and beyond. Podumburra dared them to go ahead and do their worst.

In a week, the exorcist fell ill. He told everyone that Podumburra had let loose a particularly vicious spirit on him. The man who had thrived on spirits in the neighbourhood—he was even sent for from long distances—a spirit-handler of formidable repute—lost his appetite within a matter of months. His food tasted bitter, and he lost weight rapidly and became a ghost of a man. He left the town quietly one night. In the end, it was the exorcist who succumbed.

After that, the population of exorcists in the town came down; only a few knew why.

Podumburra had taken a law degree from Madras University, which had been a dream of his since he'd been introduced to BA Garu's library. During the two years at Madras, he called often on John, who was a celebrity by then, spear-heading a movement to wrest power from the upper castes. John was deeply impressed by

Podumburra's earnestness. He explained the ideology of his political group to him, and also advised him on various academic matters.

Podumburra returned home and took up legal practice in the district headquarters. He made a name for himself; the judges admired his work, his grasp of subtle legal points, his knowledge of the judgements delivered by the courts in Madras as well as in London. And they were certain he always took up the brief of the wronged. Soon, he was practising in the High Court at Madras.

He was thin, hardly fifty kilos, subsisting for decades on rice, buttermilk, an occasional curry, and dal. It was not that he could not afford to eat better. Once he established himself, the money came, and he was fussy about his mother's food, urging her to eat well, bringing for her the best fruit and vegetables, especially ladies' fingers, her favourite vegetable, from the weekly shandy. He was frugal with himself. He kept the better part of his earnings for his service activities.

Sometime after Mahatma Gandhi's first visit to Madras province, Podumburra delivered a talk at the Madras University Historical Society.

The topic: Miss Beston.

Miss Beston was born in a family of sailors in Southampton in 1831: 'the year the queen came to the throne,' she said—'the year of Nandana, the Great Famine,' wrote Mr Blotton in his diary.

She sailed to Madras along with her father in an Indiaman in 1843, at the age of twelve. She loved the place, and extended her holiday indefinitely. With the support of her father, she started her own export–import business at fourteen, becoming the youngest businessperson in the subcontinent. She discovered the canal system of the Godavari delta and moved to the Coromandel. After compounding her success in commercial enterprises, she married in 1861, at the age of thirty. Her daughter Jane came into the world a year later, in 1862. Roberclaw was the same age as Miss Beston. He arrived in India in 1853, aspired for her hand. She refused; she preferred a member of the titled gentry.

Queen Victoria took considerable interest in her English subjects serving their Queen and their country in hostile environments, especially in India. She wrote to Miss Beston regularly. The Queen had discovered a typical representative of her loyal subjects in Miss Beston. The correspondence between the Queen and Miss Beston confirmed the entrepreneur's houseboat as a tourist stopover for Europeans in India.

Miss Beston ended up a dame and a fulfilled grandmother. Her artificial leg did not stop her, nor the glass eye, from being good company to little children. During the great durbar, on public demand, they proclaimed her the Star of the Empire; the government officially notified the change in the name of her 'native' village: no longer Sakhinetipalli but Bestonpalli.

She died at the beginning of the Great War. She died in her own four-poster bed, like Shakespeare, in peace that climaxed a lifetime of professionalism. Her grave in her native town is worth a visit.

Miss Beston had the distinction—fortune favours the brave—of becoming the recipient of the last letter written by the Queen. The letter reached Kristos at the height of World War II, in the early 1940s. Kristos were very concerned for its safety and security; Hitler had been sending over those unmanned bombs. So, his Financial Director hired a cottage in the Highlands and kept the document with him, under lock and key in an old pirate's chest in a cellar concealed under his bed. This piece of paper was considered so valuable they never put it up even after the war; and they bought from her heirs all the other letters. On public demand, the British Government requisitioned the last letter—and to celebrate the historic event, *The Times* wrote a long, emotional editorial on the unique relationship between India and Britain. There followed a great legal battle between Kristos and Her Majesty's government. Finally, the Lords decided that as Miss Beston had run her business in challenging circumstances and made a great success of it and brought laurels—and considerable wealth—to the United Kingdom, her papers could go wherever they wished. Or something to that effect.

By now, Miss Beston herself, dead for years, had become a national icon, like Shakespeare; fan clubs celebrated her exploits once a year on her birthday, 8 January, at the Indian Boar in Miss Beston's birthplace. A portrait of Miss Beston in sepia holding a rifle welcomed the guests to the inn.

After the Second World War, Kristos hired a special vault in the Bank of England and preserved Miss Beston's letters in it, next to the gold reserves.

☙

Podumburra's slender frame—all of fifty-five kilos now—burned with rage. He knew he must hurry; for he was developing night blindness. He wrote fiction and street plays in Telugu to spread his message of social reform, especially widow remarriage. He conducted public disputations in English through the columns of the Madras newspapers, as well as the local tabloid. And he delivered talks on Indian history and culture.

He wished BA Garu had been there. He had of course been in touch with John; a regular flow of letters strengthened Podumburra in his mission. And John's name was respected at every level of the administration. In his weekly colloquiums, Podumburra put the British rulers in perspective:

'Let's come to terms with our history. Don't blame history, try to understand it. Your understanding need not be mine. But we can try and see things together.'

Podumburra had dug out some details.

'A petition addressed to King Henry VIII in 1511 reads: "The Indies are discovered and vast treasures brought from thence everyday. Let us therefore bend our endeavours thitherwards." For the same reason the Spaniards had gone to the Americas. And to Africa. Clive's famous reply to his detractors after the sack of

Murshidabad in 1757 sums it up: "I stand astonished at my own moderation." In a word, an accident, a sordid motive, brought the British to India.

'The Company was granted its first charter by Queen Elizabeth I on the last day of the last month of the last year of the sixteenth century—31 December 1599—as if to usher in a new era in the East–West relationship at the dawn of the new century.

'The British had a powerful ally on their side: history. For the British came at a critical juncture in our history.

'And let us take a different view: reviewing the course of British commercial intercourse with India through its different phases.'

Podumburra added insights into human nature and polity: 'Where there can be no great men by their own exertion, there must be great men by birth, to leave to a conquered people some greatness of their own.'

'What does it mean?'

'You find out, you work it out,' he said, with some of his famous impatience. 'If you divide the revenue of a country between two governments, you are sure to cripple the resources of the one and the administration of both.'

And corruption. The East India Company powered its way to success with 'gifts'—in hard cash—to men who mattered.

The fight for sharing the spoils, 'the wonderful treasures', is imagined to have been won by the Kumpini's conquests in India.

Would any journal of the day in London print Marx's exposition? Why not *The Times*! It had been left to the *New York Tribune*.

Marx's analysis of history was unmatched: 'the events of seven-years-war transformed the East India Company from a commercial into a military and territorial power'. The time, Marx noted, was opportune: lose North America, gain India. How hollow democracy was—going to be later, is, will be—politicians would shoot down any move to bring succour to the poor. 'The Oligarchy absorbed all of its power which it could assume without incurring responsibility…'

'Look around, how many democracies are democracies? Oligarchies, not democracies.'

During all this time, all parties in England had connived in silence, even those which resolved to become the loudest with their peace can't....

A different view! Marx was a master of a different view!

Marx's 'different' vision changed the course of a century and more of mankind.

How ruthless he was, and how incisive: 'The Indian monopolists were the first preachers of free trade in England.'

Has that changed?

Of course not, no nation compromises on commercial gains. The West has only fitfully championed humanism, gold they worshipped—Mammon of the puritan Milton. India, Marx put it lucidly, was a true mine of gold.

What was India to Marx?

And Marx to India?

Who can match Marx's heart?

How different India had been at the dawn of the eighteenth century.

'Bear in mind that the commerce of India is the commerce of the world and...he who can exclusively command it is dictator of Europe.'

None other than Peter the Great of Russia.

'The discovery of America and the cape route to India were the two greatest and most important events recorded in the history of mankind.'

That was the Adam of economists!

And then it happened.

Enter East India Company (EICO)! Goodbye India!

In 1687, the Directors of EICO advised their Governor in Madras: 'Establish such a policy of civil and military power, and create and secure such a large revenue, as may be the foundation of a large, well-grounded, secure English dominion in India for all time to come.'

Not much later, in 1689, the golden goal was set: 'the increase of our revenue is the subject of our care as much as our trade; 'tis that must maintain our force when twenty accidents may interrupt our trade; 'tis that must make us a nation in India.'

Make us a nation in India!

'I shall only say that such a scene of anarchy, confusion, bribery, corruption, and extortion was never seen or heard of in any country but Bengal; nor such and so many fortunes acquired in so unjust and rapacious manner.'

Who said that?

An Englishman of course. Robert Clive!

'...and they have, both civil and military, exacted and levied contributions from every man of power and consequence, from the nawab down to the lowest zamindar.'

Robert Clive was not just a pernicious intriguer among Indian rulers, gaining most of his victories through the treachery of important players. He was also an astute manipulator of East India Company stock....

'It was...the subjugation of India that allowed Britain to emerge as the most powerful and modern nation state of the new nineteenth-century world order.'

Yet, historiographers have not recorded the link between the imperial power and the rise of Britain.

Opportunities for seizing territorial control came up first in South India.

Josiah Child obtained royal patronage for the (mis)deeds of the Kumpini by sending a gift of 10,000 pounds to the Stuart King James II, and backed the Catholic king against his enemies.... Child's son-in-law, who had succeeded Child as Governor of the Kumpini, obtained a reprieve by bribing everybody, including the King....

Daniel Defoe understood the close relation between war and

the prosperity of London:....

....How the imperatives of revenue collection and tribute remittance could override all considerations for justice or loss of human lives! The fact that the first era of globalization in India and the world (1870–1914) was also the era of some of the worst famines in global history can be obliterated from widely used textbooks of Indian and global economic history.

Among ironies germane to this history: in 1765, Clive banned private trade among EICO staff.

Didn't democracy promote and support an empire? The British parliament was fascinated by India; British rulers worshipped Jeremy Bentham, and the administration of India in nineteenth century followed suit.

How thinkers and intellectuals singe innocent lives in all kinds of places! In all kinds of ways! Sear to cinders. What was Bentham to a Vetapalem weaver? In fact, to all the 1,000 weavers of red muslin and other material of Vetapalem, who have vanished?

After some initial hiccups, the brouhaha about Hastings, and his 'trial', the democratic, humanistic spirit of Britain danced a jig with the imperialists. Think of a Kipling or a Churchill. The imperatives of revenue collection and tribute remittance could override all considerations for justice or loss of human lives…all at the cost of the peasants and artisans of India. The British Empire was a huge system of outdoor relief for the British aristocracy and the upper classes.

In the hunter's language, India was shot out. Denuded of wildlife; drained of resources, natural and moral. Postcolonial societies are shot-out societies.

Insult to injury: Charles Grant, Chairman of the Court of Directors, condemned the people of India as 'a race of men lamentably degenerate and base; retaining but a feeble sense of moral obligation…and sunk in misery by their vices.' The 'Indian' seizures pay. In this land, 'a vile country', for some at least, 'one and one make eleven.' We must remember, as one of them wrote, 'heat and flies are an excuse for writing anything'.

The white women in India represented the imperial attitudes more naturally, without any tantrums of the conscience. They lived in a difficult country, whether with bravery and competence or not will depend on which corner of the boxing ring you are speaking from…all the same, think of it, they did so before antibiotics and modern communications. Give it to them.

British India drifted from one famine to the next—two centuries of famines.

The quantity of gold which reached the mints must have been only a fraction of what was sold by the natives to the dealers; in the years of the great famine in Madras and Bombay, a large amount of gold was sent from India to England. All this came from the better-off people, drawn from them by the high price of food.

Meanwhile, the debate, not the famine, preoccupied the colonial government: the great debate of pros and cons: how much food to give: one pound or one and a half?

Sir Arthur Blotton, the famous engineer of the anicuts on Godavari and Krishna, responded to his bosses:

'Unhappily, a feeling prevails, particularly in official circles, that famine in India is to be accepted as an inevitable evil. Famines, it seems to be argued, will come, are coming nowadays with a frequency before unknown. It is all very dreadful. But they are the act of God. All we can do, when they come, is to mitigate their consequences as far as may be.'

If it were an act of God, His creatures, even though they be rulers of India, ought not to be found fighting against His decrees. 'What can I do?' the gentle Scotsman lamented, 'Instead of water the British rulers have given to the people of India iron.'

When a great famine occurred in South India in 1876–77, and the House of Commons debated measures to mitigate the dangers of such calamities, references were made to the extension of irrigation and the role of Arthur Blotton in the Cauvery and Godavari deltas.

Owing to the difference of opinion over the advisability of spending on irrigation in preference to railways, the subject was referred to a Select Committee with Lord George Hamilton, the Parliament Undersecretary, as its chairman.

In 1878, Arthur Blotton had to appear before the Select Committee of the House of Commons on India Affairs, consisting of eighteen members—not one of them an engineer—to justify and vindicate his stand that irrigation expansion any day deserves a better investment than railways: '...the railways cannot carry either the quantities, or at the price, that is essential in India...or nothing can be more certain than that in the present case the future of India's millions depends greatly upon whether money is still expended upon Railways, to cost 9,000 pounds a mile and carry 30,000 tons at one penny, or upon canals to cost from 2,000 to 8,000 pounds and carry two or three million tons at one-twentieth of a penny, and whether districts are to be put into the state of Tanjore, Kistna, and Godavari, or left in the state of the rest of the Carnatic last year and of Orissa, Bihar, and Central India a few years ago...'

When Arthur Blotton read criticism by Lord George Hamilton in the House of Commons on 22 January 1878, he prepared a fitting reply and sent it to the Secretary of State for India, appealing for justice and due publicity of his defence. The appeal was in vain. Detailing in several pages all the statistics he could gather in defence of the utility of irrigation in a country like India, Arthur Blotton concluded: 'My Lord, one day's flow in the Godavari River during high floods is equal to one whole year's flow in the Thames of London.'

Arthur Blotton's explanation of the benefits that accrued from the construction of a barrage justifying the investment was not only commended, but he was knighted, and Major Arthur Blotton became Sir Arthur Blotton. Even today, you can see the portraits or photographs of Sir Arthur Blotton in almost all government offices in the East and West Godavari districts.

Marx too commiserates with the people of India, 'a people living on rice'. But his contempt for India's so-called royalty is patent: 'royalty in its lowest stage of degradation and ridicule.... Royal idiotic race, left to itself, propagates as freely as rabbits.'

What was India to Marx?

And Marx to India?

Who can match Marx's heart!

Marx is forever.

The devastation caused by Western trading companies in Africa, South-East Asia, and Latin America!

Out of the ashes of India emerged a new Britain. Out of the turd world rose the industrial West.

'The appeal of history is intellectual; not sentimental': true, though!

By 1800, a new attitude to India prevailed: sharply critical of all things Indian. The radical transformation in imperial attitude went beyond and sought to help India progress (through James Mill, and William Bentinck, the governor general in 1829). Some of the officials who came to India then and subsequently were deeply influenced by the 'radical' outlook. Another factor: the reforming Whigs were in power after 1830. For the vast majority, the laudable objective was imperialist exploitation of India. Self-serving paternalism dictated their India policies.

There is certainly an original sin operating in history, not just European. Whichever country you look at, what is there in it to feel proud about? Human history, 'civilization'! An embarrassment to the Creator, if there is one....

In the long course of her history, India had passed through many dark ages; of all of them, the latter half of the eighteenth century was perhaps the darkest. In the political chaos, in the atmosphere of fear and insecurity, our culture barely survived in a 'vast and weedy desert'. The foreigners were received as saviours. Even the priests of the Temple of Jagannatha in Puri welcomed the victorious British general in sycophantic Sanskrit, because the 200 years under the rule of the Mughals, the Pathans, and the Marathas had created completely anarchical conditions in the country.

Podumburra read to them from a recently published account of a pilgrimage to Kasi by an educated Andhra of Madras: 'It is evident that restrictions or customs of various kinds are only creations of the mind, obstacles to right thinking.'

⁂

Podumburra now had the means and the prestige to support his social reform movement. He made it a point to publicly felicitate select citizens in recognition of their social service. He lauded Nagaraja kavi, a poet famous in the village of Veeravasaram—his prabandham had been published by the local raja. This poet had used his influence with the raja and helped dig a tank in the village. Podumburra's felicitation of the poet was well publicized; he honoured the poet with ear pendants and a shawl.

And he took up the ugliest social practice of the time. Girl children married early, almost in their swaddling clothes, and were widowed early, and widowed for life. These little women led lives of model misery. Some of them entered brothels.

'A house of girls is like a fire of little twigs. Little girls are married off to old grooms, the belief rampant that a girl is saved from early death by marriage. At the age of three! For God's sake! Then imminence of puberty is the sword of Damocles: if the girl is not married before puberty, the parents will have to drown themselves. Why shouldn't they? Let them! Good riddance it will be,' Podumburra thundered.

There is another side to this evil.

A middle-aged man had sought the assistant collector, Mr Black's aid to marry such a girl.

'The more daughters a man has, the better off he is; as there is always a rapid demand for them; but to get a son married is difficult and costs a large sum. A widower finds the difficulty still greater. Earn merit by establishing an orphan as householder,' the middle-aged man said.

Mr Black sought Podumburra's advice. He responded: 'We Hindus are limited to two aspirations: construct a house of our own and perform a marriage.'

But in this case, said Podumburra, 'Nothing doing.'

'Thank God we are not in the North,' said Podumburra later to his friends. 'Just the one city of Mathura, the city of Lord Krishna, is enough to make you hang your head in shame.'

He said he would not look beyond the Telugus. And among them, mostly, the Brahmins.

Podumburra debated the evil with the fellows in his social reform circle, which met every weekend under the mature mango tree in his backyard. 'Life in a society like ours,' he reminded them, 'is a continual fulfilling of obligations, acquitting of debts to society.'

Podumburra called a meeting of the town's elders in the town hall. Sumati, the principal, presided. The town was split in two: the orthodox opposed him bitterly and sought scriptural support for their stand; equally competently, the firebrands, under the leadership of Podumburra, condemned the evil practice. If the almanacks are lost, will the stars and planets disappear? they asked. The orthodox walked out. The house passed a resolution in support of widow remarriage.

Podumburra delivered a series of public lectures on the duties of man. The meetings were well attended; even white officers set aside other engagements to listen to him expound the perennial philosophy.

Quoting from the scriptures of several religions, Podumburra said:

'The Gita recommends—prescribes—the full active life of man in the world with the inner world anchored in the Eternal Spirit. The Gita is therefore a mandate for action. The Gita asks us to live in the world and save it. We become masters of karma by developing detachment and faith in God. And engaging in service to fellow men.

'The Mahabharata speaks of four classes of devotees of whom

three are phalakama, or desirous of rewards, while the best are single-minded worshippers. Others ask for favours, but the sage asks for nothing and refuses nothing. He yields himself completely to the Divine, accepting whatever is given to him. His attitude is one of self-oblivious non-utilitarian worship of God for His own sake. Here, service to humanity is declared to be an essential part of the discipline. The Mahabharata has the following prayer: "O, who would tell me of the sacred way by which I might enter into all the suffering hearts and take all their suffering on myself for now and forever." Jesus did just that.

'Combine bhakti with seva; devotion and service should go together. The sight of a poor man is a request personified. The sight of a man in distress is a request personified. He who lends to the poor gets his interest from God.

The Gita offers practical guidance; it does not lead you to a mysticism that focuses entirely on man's inner being. It does not turn you away from your societal and moral duties; far from it, it accepts duties as so many opportunities for achieving spiritual freedom, the happy freedom of the human spirit. It offers a way, a method to live your life to the full, and at the same time, rise above it and beyond it. It tells you that God is not remote, God is within each and every human being. Human life is a joint enterprise between God and man.

'Why only humans, God is there in every animate and inanimate creature and thing.

'The distress of Arjuna is archetypal: it is a dramatization of a perpetually recurring predicament.... The only option for us as soldiers of the spirit is to prepare ourselves, equip ourselves properly for this battle of the spirit. Let us conquer the six foes within, the arishadvargas, and the mighty mother of evil: our ego—the most advanced human mind can suffer from this formidable handicap, so crippling spiritually. Man is basically spiritual. The Gita portrays the evolution of the human soul. The fight is universal, not an Indian monopoly. And there is no need to worry about the time limit. There is no limit: it can be one life, this life; or it can be ten thousand.

'The only goal deserving of our attention and struggle is harmony: of head, heart, and hand.

'Ostentatious and selfish renunciation is not advised by the Gita. Better the inward withdrawal. You don't have to shun the senses; the senses are the horses—how can the chariot of man progress without the horses? Don't unyoke the horses, but guide them, govern them, through the reins of the buddhi, the intellect. Renunciation need not be robed in ochre; it is best experienced within each of us. Renounce selfish desire, work for your fellow man. Christ gave excellent examples of service to humanity: for example, in the Samaritan.

'A reading of the Gita convinces anyone of the absurd misinterpretation of the Hindu calm as the killer! The Gita enjoins on us a life of work, work, and more work. And God only knows how much work awaits us in this benighted India of ours!

'The sthithaprajna—the man of steady wisdom—lives a life of disinterested service. And service to all God's creatures. He works as God works; he is not involved.... He is not involved because he works for no reward, no expectation; he is governed by his immortal self....' Podumburra reminded his audience, 'Even the shunning of action by fools amounts to action!'

Spiritual values must control social ethics. He quoted Boethius: '"He will never go to heaven who is content to go alone." Come, let us fight this great battle against imperfection and sorrow and work for world solidarity.'

On the four-fold caste system, the chaturvarnyam, he said: 'In the four-fold order, the emphasis is on guna (aptitude) and karma (function), and not on jati (birth). Quality of mind and work determines your caste. Not birth. Classes and castes are not determined by birth or colour but by psychological characteristics which fit us for definite functions in society. The Guru of the Stream has discoursed on the Purusha Suktam: the pundits had totally misread the great poem.

Podumburra now narrated a story he had heard from Granny Appachchi: the story of a ber, or jujube, tree.

> Anaga anaga, anaga, once upon a time there was a ber (jujube) tree.
>
> Sita had disappeared from the forest. Rama and Lakshmana hunted anxiously for her, but they did not know which direction to take. As they searched, they heard a small unkempt ber tree call out to them.
>
> 'Rama, my Lord, I saw Sita being carried away. She passed by me, and I caught her garment with all my strength to stop her. But my branches are weak. See, I only succeeded in tearing her garment and a scrap of her dress is still clinging to my thorns.'
>
> The tree drooped in shame.
>
> But Rama was pleased and blessed the tree for its courage.
>
> 'Ber tree, for this act, you will achieve immortality. Even when you are hacked down to your roots by men, a single root of yours remaining in the ground will bring you back to life again.'

Granny Appachchi also narrated the story of Sabari and the half-eaten fruit:

> While the Lord Rama ate happily the ber fruit the tribal woman gave him after tasting it to test it, Lakshmana received his share but quietly threw it away; sanjivini grew out of the fruit which Lakshmana would not eat.
>
> Over there in the North they call this fruit the Sorrow Remover.
>
> The tale has left for Kanchi and we for home.

Samadarsinah: see with an equal eye. The Eternal is the same in all, in animals as in men, in learned Brahmins as in despised outcastes. He narrated an episode from Adi Sankaracharya's life to illustrate the point. 'An untouchable asked the acharya a pertinent question: "Do you want the eternal atma in me to get away from you?" When we realize that it is the same Divinity which dwells in every creature, we "see with an equal eye".' Samadarsinah. "He who sees me everywhere and see all in me; I am not lost to him nor is he lost to me."

'True Liberation can be attained here on earth. In the midst of human life, in the marketplace, in the workplace, anywhere, everywhere, peace within is possible.

'Once we come to believe that all work is for the sake of the Supreme, we are on our way. Man has not only to ascend to the world of spirit but also to descend to the world of creatures.'

'God is our true friend, philosopher, guide. The Bhagavata says: "Of whom I am the beloved, the self, the son, the friend, the teacher, the relative and the desired deity."'

Podumburra talked of 'the glad freedom of spirit': 'The Gita says we must get out of the bondage to petty worldly things to gain the happy freedom of spirit. When we are one with the Divine in us, we become one with the whole stream of life. We have had wonderful examples of this in our tradition of gurus. Be free, be divine.

'There is no question of defeat in our spiritual striving; it is just a matter of attitude, approach, and time. All are pilgrims on the way to our Divine Destination. No effort is wasted. Death is not the end of life. Our goal should be perfection here and now, through a combination of knowledge, devotion, and work. With the characteristics of freedom, love, and equality, man becomes God: "He attains unto my state." The Gita is the great poem of hope: "Be free, be divine."

'And give. Give to the needy, give to the lowly, help the least of the society. The giver enriches himself within. He who gives receives. Blend bhakti with seva; devotion and service to humanity go together.

'The Gita sets us the goal: the conversion of all works into nishkamakarma, or desireless action. The Gitacharya prescribes the practice of karmayoga to begin with: move next to bhakti, devotion, and then to gnyana, knowledge. Salvation is the attainment of an impersonal outlook, and that is possible only with the renunciation of our ego. Evil activities are ruled out in a state of inner renunciation.

'Happiness is a variable goal. It is directly linked to our guna. Tamas is linked to violence and inertia, blindness and error; rajas to wealth and power, pride and glory. Ananda of the spirit is possible when we become one with all beings. The Guru of the Stream is a living example for us. His outward life expresses his inward being. Divinity is integral humanity.'

∽

Gradually, a whole cross-section of people came to support Podumburra in his campaign for widow remarriage. Widows had a right to marry; in fact, they must marry again, his supporters said. And everyone, English educated or not, must support the idea. Towards the end of the century, Podumburra joined the Congress.

The spirit spread.

Podumburra had built up a reputation as a rare lawyer; 'he is truly Sathya Harischandra', they said. Now, almost every home had youngsters fighting Podumburra's battles. Not one remarriage had taken place though, but the orthodox were outraged. Podumburra was the ringleader, destroying peace in every home in the Hindu community. Yadardavaadee lokavirodhi—a speaker of truth is the world's enemy.

The orthodox were powerful, they had large resources, they used the priests in the temples in and around the town as well as the Brahmins who presided over rites and rituals at Hindu homes to show their displeasure.

The influence of the orthodox, however, was neutralized by Podumburra's reputation and prestige in the province, the power of the white officers quietly standing behind his efforts to cleanse his community of evil practices, and the influence of John in distant Madras.

The official support from the British officers tilted the balance. 'Fortunately,' the officers told Podumburra, 'these people had no access to firearms.' Podumburra and friends could be attacked with staves, that possibility was real, and according to well-wishers, imminent and certain, someone could throw a rock from side lane, but they could never be ambushed with firearms.

The first widow marriage was quite an adventure. His uncle, who had been a big support to his mother and who was his own father-in-law, was dispatched by the orthodox to persuade his mother and wife to restrain him; if not, he would face dire consequences. The old man barged into Podumburra's home with others while he was away in Madras. Srilakshmi, Podumburra's wife, didn't budge. She told them that she herself supported the idea and she would never join those who were opposing and harassing her husband at every turn.

The mob left.

Podumburra called for the final campaign meeting.

Government spies filed reports. The meeting was well attended. A number of Brahmins who supported the cause attended the meeting. Women came in large numbers. Some zamindars sent their blessings, and a few yogis their tacit support. Europeans, including the District Collector and his wife, sent messages of support. A small number of people swore to stand against the reforms.

Podumburra addressed the spirited gathering. They listened with rapt attention.

'The most disturbing aspect of human history is the inevitable callusing caused by institutionalized religions, and by the self-appointed agents of the Supreme Spirit. This society had collected much filth.

'Let us go back to essential religion. Essential religion is love. Essential religion is service. Essential religion is harmony. No religion advocates hatred. It is only the selfish priests and caste leaders who bring down essential religion to their own narrow, limited levels, and interpret and misinterpret to suit their evil ends. As you could see from the town hall debate, no Shastra, no Purana advises this kind of cruelty to our daughters. This is a malignant ulcer, let's cut it off. What is needed today is some kind of surgical operation; let us put this society of ours on the table, and cleanse it of its accumulated toxic wastes. Let us make a beginning. Clean up the filth of generations.'

Exhorting his friends towards right action, here and now, Podumburra quoted extensively from the Bible.

> Because sentence against an evil work is not executed speedily, therefore the heart of the sons of men is fully set in them to do evil.
>
> To every thing there is a season, and a time to every purpose under the heaven: a time to love, and a time to hate; a time of war, and a time of peace.
>
> Wherefore I perceive that there is nothing better, than that a man should rejoice in his own works; for that is his portion: for who shall bring him to see what shall be after him?

Now, he laid down a few rules of conduct for his followers. He quoted Jesus:

> Be not rash with thy mouth, and let not thine heart be hasty to utter any thing before God: for God is in heaven, and thou upon earth: therefore let thy words be few.
>
> If thou seest the oppression of the poor, and violent perverting of judgment and justice in a province, marvel not at the matter: for he that is higher than the highest regardeth; and there be higher than they.

> ... wisdom giveth life to them that have it.
>
> Imbibe the common sense.... For there is not a just man upon earth, that doeth good, and sinneth not.
>
> Also take no heed unto all words that are spoken; lest thou hear thy servant curse thee: for oftentimes also thine own heart knoweth that thou thyself likewise hast cursed others.

Jesus knew the character and meaning and potential of humanity better than most of his contemporaries.

> All this have I proved by wisdom: I said, I will be wise; but it was far from me.
>
> Dead flies cause the ointment of the apothecary to send forth a stinking savour: so doth a little folly him that is in reputation for wisdom and honour.

Don't give up:

> If the spirit of the ruler rise up against thee, leave not thy place; for yielding pacifieth great offences.

Podumburra concluded: 'Be free, be Divine,'

He ended the meeting with 'one of the greatest prayers ever':

Asathoma sadgamaya
Thamaso ma jyothirgamaya
Mruthyorma amrutamgamaya.

And Smastha lokah sukhino bhavantu repeated three times. There was no need to convince his soldiers to action. They were all determined that the only way for Bharat to attain its freedom again was through self-reform; inner freedom first, liberation from the foreign yoke next. That's one reason the sepoys had failed in their uprising.

'Now, let me make one thing clear. This kind of thing is not for the feeble-hearted. If any of you would like to back out, please do so now. I assure you I shall remain a friend, well-wisher, and legal counsel. But think of your own community, think of those girls, quietly putting up with this kind of hellish ostracism. Now tell me, how many of you believe we shall go ahead and perform the first widow remarriage?'

'We will go ahead,' they said, 'and we shall do it in this very town, and not surreptitiously in some out-of-the-way village.'

'Easier said than done!' smiled Podumburra.

'Remember, the orthodox gentlemen will not like it.'

Yes, they knew the adversary will do anything to stop it.

'Remember, the orthodox are not confined to just one caste or two.'

Yes, they knew that too.

'This will be the first ceremony of its kind, as far as I know.'

The most difficult enterprise for them.

'One widow marriage, and the others will follow; it will demoralize the orthodox, break the encrustation of centuries of filth! Encourage fathers of widowed daughters to come forward and join our campaign.'

They sat late into the early hours. They decided to scout around and identify the best possible case to take up. To each taluk, two members of the group would go. They would have to go on their own, at their own expense, and go quietly. No one should get wind of what they were planning.

They met again the following Sunday. They shortlisted the suitable candidates; the parents of the girl and the girl herself had to agree. Then, they looked around quietly for possible grooms; they shortlisted a few—on the top of the list was a young man Podumburra had coached for his matric exam.

But the immediate problem: it wouldn't do to let the young widow travel from her village during the day. The young bride-to-be would need an escort, a cover. Podumburra sat with his cousin, Sumati, to figure this out.

'I know one,' said Podumburra.

'The same as I know. And the one I am sure you have thought of.'

'Granny Appachchi?'

'Who else?'

Podumburra and his cousin went to the village, and sought the blessing of the Guru of the Stream. 'Appachchi,' said the Guru. Just one word. As though it was a mantra of initiation. He raised his hands and blessed them both.

They went and canvassed the two ladies, Worker Aunt and Granny Appachchi. They put before them their whole plan. The opposition was sure to kidnap the bride. The girl had been married at the age of four; her groom had been nine. By the time she was nine, he had died of smallpox. Now, the parents of the girl were willing to defy the head of their math and get her married again. Though Worker Aunt was opposed to the whole idea because her own math head had issued a fiat against this outrageous assault on Hindu society, after Podumburra, who was like her own son, and Appachchi talked to her at length about what was happening, she opted for constructive neutrality. Her role was limited to dharmic silence; if anyone were to ask about Granny Appachchi, she was to tell them she did not know where her hare-brained vadina had gone. Fortunately, unlike Yudhishthira on the battlefield of Kurukshetra, her unblemished record of truth-telling wasn't tested. The opposition camp's intelligence and organizational resources were crude and limited.

Worker Aunt delayed Appachchi's departure; she had to wait for the right omen. A tiny bell was heard, someone had risen early, and was performing puja in Brahma Kalam. 'Go safely, and come back gainfully,' Worker Aunt sent her off with a blessing.

Strictly following the plan devised by Podumburra and friends in consultation with well-wishers in the administration, the family of the girl 'went on a pilgrimage to Tirupati'. The timing was perfect: Granny Appachchi reached the village just as Udaya Bhanu, the bride-to-be, and her parents and her younger brothers were entering it.

Granny Appachchi charmed everyone with a toothless smile, and Udaya Bhanu bowed low and touched her feet, Granny Appachchi sensed how nervous the girl was. 'What a pretty girl!' Appachchi said and enclosed her in her arms; she could hear the little heart thumping furiously.

'God has sent me to see that you become a householder. I am here,' Appachchi comforted the girl.

The first thing Granny Appachchi did was to get Udaya's mother to give her ritual bath, with oil massage and nalugupindi and turmeric. Then, she asked the parents to dress her in the most colourful pattu sari in their wardrobe. Granny Appachchi herself combed Udaya's long tresses, as thick as peepul foliage in June. She collected all the malli buds available in the back garden and overwhelmed the girl's head with fragrant garlands.

And after a quick meal, Granny Appachchi told the family one of her stories, 'The Tale of Fragrant Hands'. The girl relaxed.

'Once the sage Narada called on Sri Mahavishnu. The sage was about to go around the worlds on one of his periodic recce-cum-educational trips and he very much wanted to do so with the benedictions of God of Gods. When he bowed reverentially to Mahavishnu—'

'Narayana, Narayana,' Udaya said, and her brothers joined her, 'Narayana, Narayana,'

'That's right,' said Appachchi.

'Then what happened?'

Resumed Appachchi: 'What did Vishnu tell him?'

'What is your mission this time, sage?' Bhanu said. She had regained her natural poise already. Her brothers hardly opened their mouths; Granny Appachchi had to make a special effort to draw them out.

'"I want to educate myself, Lord,"' Appachchi continued.

'"I know," said God, with a smile, pleased with the sage. Why is God pleased with the sage?'

'Because he is always educating himself.'

'Because sage Narada is a learner all his life. Now, I need no more teach these little ones,' said Granny Appachchi, silently addressing the east room in Sakhinetipalli.

'God said, "Narada, during your pleasure-cum-research trip, please look for a human being with fragrant hands."

'"Fragrant hands, Lord?" the sage was surprised.'

'I would love to, myself!' Udaya Bhanu wanted to chip in. But she looked around at her brothers and parents and realized her feeling was shared by everyone.

'"Yes. Fragrant hands," said Vishnu. "Just go near every human creature and with or without their knowledge smell their hands."

'You know, children, that's a funny business. Many will not allow you even to approach them. And when you tell them what you intend to do—though it is for a research project commissioned, blessed, and supported by the Great God Himself—they will not allow you to get anywhere near them. And then, how can human creatures tackle the problem of logistics? From the palaces of kings and emperors to the hutments of servants and the cottages of artisans, all in one day. For this sage, however, to wish is to act, nothing is impossible. "My job is easily done; it is always good to do the Lord's bidding first, before I turn to my own humble duties and interests," he said to himself. How many people are so fortunate, engaged in carrying out God's wishes? And such a simple thing, and so predictable in its results! From his own experience with God, though, Narada worried: God's designs are unfathomable. What appears simple is never so.

'Suddenly he felt energy filling him up, and he felt younger than ever. Now, he could carry out the most arduous task with the greatest ease. Engage in a Divine Mission and He gives you the necessary energy.

'Narada first called on the greatest emperor of the earth. The sage arrived at the inner palace purposely at midnight, when the king and his consorts were fast asleep in their royal quarters. Even the carpet had been sprinkled with perfume—'

'Imported from England, granny?' asked Sattibabu, the littlest kid.

'That's a legitimate doubt,' said Granny Appachchi, brought up short again. 'Everything is imported from England these days, isn't it? So, we have a bright boy, here, and don't frown on him for asking. When in doubt, ask, never go to bed with a doubt in your little belly. I must check on that, Satti. Can I continue?'

'Please do,' said the chorus.

'The walls of the royal palace were hung with perfumed tapestry, the agarbattis and incense sticks burned sweetly. The scene was promising; the whole place smelled fragrant.

'Narada approached the king who was fast asleep—and the sage made a discovery: even His Majesty snored. But he reminded himself he was on a Divine Mission! It was not for him to be diverted by trivial things, no distractions while on a job! Single-minded devotion, right?

'Now the sage was in for a real shock: the king's hands smelled foul. He dropped the bejewelled, ringed royal hand rather too abruptly. Fortunately, the king had had a hectic day suppressing an uprising, and he was sound asleep. The sage put up his hand to his delicate nostrils, and smelled the king's hand again. He rushed out, and took a deep breath. The fading marigolds exuded a subdued fragrance. He gulped the scent greedily.

'The sage couldn't describe it: it was a royal stench, but a kind he had not experienced before. It must be the worst stink anywhere.

'"Thank you, Great God, I have already got the drift of your design. You certainly have something for me!" he prayed in gratitude.

'Recovering from the shock, he looked at the principal queen now. His heart told him there was no point in going back to her. But she was such a beauty; so delicate and fine-limbed, sculpted hands with tapering fingers'—at this everyone looked at their own hands—'though even she seemed to be no different from other women in her careless posture.'

'That's not fair,' protested Udaya Bhanu. 'You don't need to be decorous in your bedroom. Otherwise, when will you relax, and where can you ease up if not in your own bedroom, in your own home?'

There was a chorus of approval and support.

'Don't mistake me,' said Granny Appachchi hastily. 'It is the sage, not me. As far as I am concerned, you know my feelings…'

'The story,' several voices reminded her.

'Now, where was I?…ah, the queen's hands, Her hands were especially well-shaped; and they smelled. Not of any fragrance, they smelled of something rotting. The sage held a hand over his nostrils most delicately, and rushed out again for a breath of fresh air. This was more shocking to the sage than the experience with the king.

'However, scientific research demands selfless labour. He tried every queen and consort in numerous harems all over the world. And then, every nobleman and minister. Not one passed the test. Holding his nostrils, the sage thought to himself, so after all, the God of Gods is living up to his reputation. Why would he ever send his devotee on a simple errand?

'These are all earthly creatures, of the world of courtly luxury. That is the lesson, I am sure, he told himself.

'So, the sage did not waste any time, he straight flew down—thinking was flying, remember?—to the hermitage of the most renowned rishi on the earth. It was the world of the Spirit, austere, serene, peaceful. The opposite of royal ambience. What a relief! The great soul did not snore; he lay in total calm, his breathing, even, and long and soft. But then, shock of shocks: it was the same stench!

'Narada did not waste any time. He went around the whole world, trying dignitary after nobleman and thinker and educator in every kingdom of the world.

'He was possessed now, like a scientist who senses that he is on the trail of a new virus. He forgot all about his own private business, and hunger and thirst; he whizzed around in a frenzy of intellectual investigation and inquiry. It was going to be dawn, and he had not got any positive news to take back to God. Don't worry, that's the message Vishnu wanted to convey, he told himself. His hypothesis was ready. Now he could go back and report to Him honestly: after hectic investigation and exploration, it is discovered that there is no such thing as a fragrant hand in the mortal world.

'The sage was exhausted by now. The discovery had drained his spiritual energies. He looked around for a place to relax and recover his spirits before flying back to God's Abode.

'He spotted a wick lamp in a small hut on the banks of a river. And he heard the whirring of a wheel. He went closer. There, he found a potter at work, shaping a pot out of a lump of clay freshly dug out of the riverbank. The man was covered in mud. The sage almost closed his nostrils in anticipation of the stench, now very familiar; but was he glad he had not done that, for a wonderful fragrance wafted towards him, like the scent of spring blossoms. Almost bursting with curiosity, he rushed and, as the potter raised his right hand to push his hair away from his face, already knotted in mud, he smelled the potter's hand.

'"Got it!" he shouted.

'But, of course, the potter neither heard nor saw the sage; Narada had the magical powers of all such sages. "I have found the man with the fragrant hands!"'

'Just a second, Granny,' chirped the youngest. 'Wasn't it possible it was the mud that Narada muni smelled?'

'This is the new generation,' Granny Appachchi proclaimed. 'The latest generation of Podumburras. Now no one can stop this country.'

'Once again,' she turned to the boy, 'we shouldn't forget he had those spiritual powers. He could filter the mud and reach the hand.'

Little Sattibabu scratched his head. His body language said: I wouldn't accept it unless I experience it myself.

Granny Appachchi went back to Narada.

'Narada rushed back, and avoiding the upper classes and the nobles, he did a thorough investigation of the labouring class. It was the same perfume. He felt rejuvenated.

"I must report back to God, and at once, he told himself.

"'No need, Narada, I am here," said the Great God, standing next to him. "I was there too when you met the potter, but you did not spot me. I am there wherever people labour honestly and earn their living."'

Udaya Bhanu put her head in Granny Appachchi's lap; she looked at the old woman with dreamy eyes. Granny Appachchi gently held the young woman's locks in her own callused hands and gently set them in place. Then, Granny Appachchi sang a hymn.

Udaya hugged Granny. The kids followed. Everyone around smiled. 'Careful, you will suffocate Granny,' they warned.

Leaving behind the bride's family—they were to follow by another route, as roundabout as Granny Appachchi's—Granny Appachchi and her charge set out after 9 p.m. in a closed bandy. They travelled all night. The girl put her head in Granny Appachchi's lap and slept. Anger rose in Appachchi at the injustice done to this simple soul. 'Don't let anger cloud your mind,' the Guru of the Stream had told her. He had blessed her before she left, and the visit had calmed Worker Aunt. 'Be free, be Divine.'

Granny Appachchi and Udaya Bhanu first went north towards the hills, then forded the river in a freight boat, not the regular passenger vessel.

By dawn, Udaya and Granny Appachchi got off the boat at a pre-arranged spot, not a regular jetty, but a landing next to some paddy fields. A man recognized the girl, and wanted to know where she was going.

'None of your business!' snarled the wizened woman of uncertain age.

The man was taken aback at the truculent response.

'Where is she going? She is my niece, and I am taking her to my village!' she snarled. She lowered her voice conspiratorially, 'Worry about your own wife.'

The man was shaken.

'What's happened to my wife?'

'That man over there will tell you.'

A man was running along the bund to catch up with them. He panted down the embankment and shouted, 'Yerraiah, your wife has eloped with your nephew.'

The man fell on his knees before Granny Appachchi.

'Please forgive me, Amma. Tell me, what shall I do now?'

'"Whoever hath given his heart to a beloved object hath put his beard in the hands of another".... I will tell you if you promise to take back your wife. God is with you, your wife has already regretted her decision. Go north and take the Trunk Toad. You will find her sitting under a banyan at Kothapalem. And remember, if you break your promise.... Ha, one more thing: some things must be hidden even from the mother that bore you.'

The bride-to-be was amazed.

As the man rushed off, Granny Appachchi recited from the *Svetasvatara Upanishad*:

'Thou art the woman, thou art the man, thou art the youth and maiden too. Thou art the old man who totters along, leaning on the staff. Thou art born with faces turned in all directions.'

Their contact came down and quietly received them. He was a Velama, all his womenfolk observed strict purdah. He took the travellers to his own home and introduced them to the women in the zenana. They spent a day there and enjoyed the Velama hospitality. The womenfolk heaped gifts on the bride-to-be. In the early hours, at Brahma Kalam, they resumed their journey.

The Velama landlord waved aside the field hand and got into the driver's seat.

In his family carriage, with curtains tightly drawn, they set out on their last lap. The passengers within could see the passers-by and enjoy the passing scene, but no one outside could make out who was within the bandy.

Granny Appachchi went on merrily with her work. She told Udaya Bhanu the story of Rain Murthy, which she'd told to many children before, and which all of them loved.

∞

As Podumburra had anticipated, they were stopped by orthodox goondas with staves and faces muffled in soiled cloths. It was still dark. The passengers weren't worried: the goondas didn't know Granny Appachchi, and they were in a cart driven by a short-tempered Velama. The Velama routinely carried a stave and a spear with which he kept wild boar away from his crops, but Podumburra had instructed him to restrain himself even in the most trying circumstances, and he did.

The goonda leader waved them on.

'Pindari ruffians,' said Granny Appachchi.

'My grandmother told me about pindaris!' said the girl. 'The great thing the white rulers have done is destroy the vermin.'

'Vermin, that's right,' said Granny Appachchi. 'Happily, they are behind us, a fading memory even for me. Shall I tell you a story of that experience?'

The girl was delighted.

This is about a brass alms pot. There was a village in Guntur called Gannaram. Word reached the villagers that they would be the next target of the pindaris. They were terrified. They took out all their valuables and hid them in their haystacks.

Jambulingam, a simpleton, used to subsist on alms he collected every morning from the village households. The most valuable possession for him was a brass alms pot. When he saw everyone hiding their precious jewellery and gold in the haystacks, he too tucked his brass pot in a haystack.

The savage pindaris swooped down. They were accomplished in scenting and digging out hidden cash and valuables in the Coromandel villages. But though they dug up the whole place they drew a blank. Then, they tortured the villagers to reveal where they had hidden the valuables.

'Ours is a poor village, where can we get valuables?' the victims lamented unanimously.

For a change, the pindaris turned back.

On their way out they found Jambulingam sitting sedately outside his cottage, one leg on the other.

One of the pindaris recognized him as the village simpleton and remembered that he had only one brass pot to hide.

'Hullo, Jambu, where have you hidden your brass pot?'

'Where else?' replied Jambu. 'Everyone was tucking their gold and jewellery and cash into the haystacks, and I too have done so.'

The girl laughed. The solemn Velama guffawed. Granny Appachchi joined them.

Granny Appachchi offered silent thanks to Podumburra: 'to a childless woman, a woman who never knew what motherhood is, you have conferred by God's grace, the joy of grandparenthood. Denied motherhood by fate, I have received through you a granddaughter.'

Granny Appachchi, out of gratitude, told her another story.

And then, for the first time, Granny Appachchi recounted that extraordinary experience she had gone through with the Guru on her fateful visit.

She had just bitten into that piece of coconut prasadam the Guru of the Stream had put in her hands, when he put his hand on her head by way of benediction: energy radiated through her head down to her toes; then she went blank. She experienced a vision.

The Guru had held her hand gently and they both rose into the sky. She could see and hear the feeder stream gurgling; she could see the houses distinctly, her own home down below, with Worker Aunt in the backyard issuing some instructions to a field hand who turned and went to a banana plant and cut a long leaf. They rose higher, high above Sakhinetipalli. She worried for a moment that if the guru were to let her go, she would fall. She looked at him; he smiled and let go. She flew on, with him by her side. And they went so close to the hills that she could spot tussocks of grass on the slopes. Then, they both returned to the ashram and landed by the granite boulder. He said, 'I have found the Ancient One.' When she reopened her eyes, she was standing in the midst of devotees; the Guru had gone back to his loom. In her ears, she heard his voice again: 'I have found the Ancient One.'

When Granny Appachchi finished, the young woman felt she could roll up the sky like a prayer mat.

An hour before dawn, the Velama stopped at a friend's farmhouse. A quick wash, a light meal of curd rice and lime pickle, and back in the bandy. By daybreak, they came within a half-kos of the town.

In the light of dawn, Granny noticed the granite boulders jutting out here and there. The hills sported a new look, a thriving green. The texture thrilled her, recalled to her a memory: the charcoal trace on an adolescent boy's upper lip.

Nestling close to Granny Appachchi, Udaya watched the passing scene. From a stroke of watercolours, the hills slowly grew into a canvas in oils. It was communion time; the world was more than a puja vessel; it was Divinity itself.

Suddenly, a fanfare of crows. The track dipped into a stream. The bullock splashed up a shower on the bridal party.

Something happened. For the bride-to-be, the everyday world threw off its veil and revealed a presence—fresh, vibrant, absorbing. Her whole being reset in repose. What was commonplace mesmerized her.

They passed through an avenue of rain trees. A blend of fresh rain tree blossoms and bird droppings.

A granite trough lay on its side in a field, exposing its bran-stained interior.

How many kinds of cacti!

The summit of a hill peered over the shoulder of a range. From its height, the village would look like a high-rimmed eating bowl.

A double bullock cart carried a load of empty gunnysacks.

Village girls came out, in blouse and langa, and with faded cotton towels for upper cloths in honour of the passers-by. The mongrel dogs were as excited as the village boys. A mentally handicapped girl, podgy, hair thick as tamarind foliage, came close to the bandy and, ignoring the forbidding driver, took a good look at the bullock, and though she could not see them through the slats, she grinned happily.

Granny Appachchi shared some of her wisdom with the girl. For in the years following BA Garu's death, Granny discovered that the monsoon added ostentatiously to the repertoire of scents. Even trees past the season made their presence felt, like the sour tamarind. Following the first rains everything lay soaked—the thick green on the branches; the dead leaves on the ground had their own message: dead green. It's easy to distinguish between the wet green and the dead green; the wet green scent was vibrant; the dead green more shy, waiting to be noticed, honoured, so it demanded a higher level of olfactory sophistication to notice it, even a philosophic vision. And Granny made further distinctions: smells and scents to her were like birdcalls to BA Garu; she would suddenly stop in her track and look around for a wet green neem tree, wet green babul, etc. Appachchi stood by the eastern window in the morning and the western window in the evening, taking deep breaths of the fresh flower-fragrant air; the soil-tempered breeze after a late monsoon shower sent her into ecstasy.

Appachchi was inebriated on airy nothings, mere olfactory notations, the girl realized.

'Would you like to eat a few of the tender Bengal gram on the stalk?'

The girl's eyes sparkled.

'How do you know I love the tender pods?'

'All girls do and all boys. I do.'

'Be free, be Divine,' said the girl with a twinkle in her eyes.

Granny Appachchi laughed loudly. She patted the girl's head.

The Velama escort said, 'Be quick!'

Udaya helped Granny Appachchi climb out of the cart; they entered the field like a cow and calf. Granny Appachchi asked the girl to wait, and called out to the farmer squatting on the manch, who came running in a couple of minutes. Granny Appachchi put a silver coin in his hands; the man was overwhelmed. She asked the girl to go and pick. 'Not too tender, then you hardly get anything to bite on; and not too ripe, then there will be no fun. Come, I'll show you.'

She gathered a few, more tender green than hard, with bloom on them, and showed her. The farmer got the hint; he himself plucked enough and put them in the cart. The women resumed the journey.

Udaya dilated her nostrils, and looked around. It was a mango tree. In bloom.

On the bank of a pond filled to the brim with rainwater-tinted deep turmeric stood country date palms closely pared for tapping.

On the roadside, frozen in meditation, almost blocking passage, was a granite boulder. Behind a light veil of mist, backing the village, stood hills.

A little boy stared, in an old peasant blouse-shirt two sizes too large with a pink upper cloth, which he obviously prized. A little girl, a toddler, was 'chased' by a butterfly.

Udaya smiled. She sang with Granny Appachchi:

Watch a bird, watch a child.
Be free, be Divine.
Watch a bird, watch a child.
Be free, be Divine.

Both women fell silent. All talk ceased. For it was communion time, when the everyday experience stood out in a glow, the commonplace revealed its halo.

A flock of sheep and goats passed, reasonably caked with dust—they were washed only once a year before the farmers sent them off to the fair. Their stench was unmistakable.

A couple of village donkeys stood around hobbled, in contemplation of the human condition.

A few stray fruit, a fading grey, were on the tamarind tree: they had escaped the harvest hook the previous season.

On a hilltop, a lone tree, an acacia, with a tabletop crown. A granite boulder on the hill over there, perched in precarious poise, 'like a muni in tapas balanced on one leg,' said Granny Appachchi. The girl looked for a full minute, and said, 'How can anyone think of God while worrying all the time about loss of balance!'

Appachchi laughed.

A whoop, a series of four whoops, from the foliage of the tree above.

The girl opened her eyes wide. 'Monkey?' she whispered.

'Crow pheasant,' said Granny Appachchi.

She signed to the girl: wait a second.

The answering whoops came back from a distance.

'Look over there!' Granny Appachchi pointed out to the girl. The bird hopped from a lower to a higher bough. 'A male crow pheasant. A duet,' smiled Granny Appachchi. 'They will soon establish a home and raise a family.'

'What dress sense,' said the girl. Granny nodded.

'He wants to get a better view of us, of you.' She added, 'Now, watch.'

She whooped, exactly like the bird. And almost immediately came the response. Both birds sang back. The girl was thrilled.

'I am sorry, I have only confused them. If I do it again, I will completely disorient them. And I will be guilty of a sin.'

Udaya said, 'I cannot associate you with sin.'

Granny Appachchi smiled.

Over the shoulder of a wooded hill, the luminous rim came up briskly, like a butterfly releasing itself from its chrysalis: come on, shake your wings and take flight, be free and take off.

In a farmer's compound, the harvest stack lay like a termite queen near her term.

On the hedges, a malathi creeper in fragrant bloom.

A brightly white-washed wall on a hillock, marking a Muslim prayer precinct. Not far off, a fatheree school; it had a modest, practical granite slab fence all around.

A wedding was in progress, the whole village had turned up. It was the marriage of a neem with a peepul.

From time to time, a woman stood up in the field, straightened her back, and looked at the proceedings.

A mound of cattle dung next to a cattle shed. And tens of cow-dung cakes drying in the sun. A coconut tree wiggled its fingers. A male koel in absurd fright flew right over them, scattering liquid notes all around.

Two rock pigeons on a newly laid telegraph wire. On the hillside, grazing sheep, still as rocks.

Green paddy seedlings—the rich seedbed green.

The sun in a puddle cradle, rocking meditatively, effulgent, shooting a blinding shimmer. With a peepul and neem for company, the village pond, still as a slab of polished turquoise, holding the hills around. At its centre, a white lotus, perfectly solitary.

Acknowledgements

Though last in the list of publications, Ranga Rao's *Those Women of the Coromandel* has been long in the making.... Well over three decades.... Its highly experiential essence can be traced to his strong roots in the Coromandel where he spent his childhood and, later, his annual summer vacations with family, sometimes almost two months long. The compelling characters bear resemblance to the people he met and interacted with there and this book is also a celebration and idolization of these resolute women. The dolls on the back flap (designed by Dr Prashant Luthra in consultation with Ranga Rao) come from these experiences. They represent authentic Andhra culture in the geographical context and setting of the novel. The dramatic fusion of three dolls looking in different directions reflects the three key characters who, despite their differences, stay deeply connected through the narrative. (Kondapalli is a town near Vijayawada in the Krishna district of Andhra Pradesh. The dancing maiden remains one of the most popular Kondapalli toys.)

What is also noteworthy and conspicuous in the novel is the indelible impact of the spiritual retreat of Sri Satya Sai Institute of Higher Learning, Puttaparthy, Andhra Pradesh, where Ranga Rao served for nearly two decades after he retired from Delhi University.

An indulgent friend, Ranga Rao believed in actively cultivating friendships, many of which lasted a lifetime. Often starting as professional engagements, they metamorphosed into vibrant personal bonds. Some litterateurs mentioned here contributed immensely to the creation of this book with their incisive critique which Ranga Rao often readily incorporated. Says a grateful Ranga Rao in his email to Dr D. S. Rao, 'It held your interest, a mind like yours, a reader like you, that's more than enough for me. Remember I have been working on it for how many years now? About two decades, am I glad it has some shape now. It will be a better book because of Dr D. S. Rao.' Thanks to Dr Laxmi Reddy, Dr Amarendra, Dr Prashant Luthra, Dr Subramani for their invaluable contributions. We are sure Ranga Rao would have added to this list.

Such a monumental project could not have come to fruition without the diligence of Team Aleph: the patience and assiduousness of Pujitha, the sagacity of Rosemary, and the methodical Aleph team. It is providential that Ranga Rao's last book is being published by Aleph, which is headed by David Davidar who was the chief editor of Ranga Rao's first novel: *The Fowl-Filcher* (1987). '[I] Trust your instincts', says Ranga Rao in an email addressed to David in 2012. Thanks, David; we are eternally indebted. It stands to reason that a posthumous publication of a manuscript long in the making was propelled in no small way by the inspiration and conviction of Mrs Vadrewu Vijayalakshmi (wife of Ranga Rao). She was a trustworthy and candid critic of his creative work, a contribution he admired greatly. On behalf of Ranga Rao, we (Suguna Gurazada and Shiv Vadrewu) have found this journey from manuscript to print an extremely gratifying and spiritually rewarding exercise.